The Gael Gates

The Gael Gates

Galactic Adventures Book 2

Scott Michael Decker

Many Thanks to the beta readers
Anne Potter
Kelly Erickson
Sutton Carter
Elise Abram

Titles by the Author

If you like this novel, please post a review on the website where you purchased it, and consider other novels from among these titles by Scott Michael Decker:

Science Fiction:
Cube Rube
Doorport
Drink the Water
Edifice Abandoned
Glad You're Born
Half-Breed
Inoculated
Legends of Lemuria
Organo-Topia
The Gael Gates
War Child

Fantasy:
Bandit and Heir (Series)
Gemstone Wyverns
Sword Scroll Stone

Look for these titles at your favorite e-book retailer.

Reader Comments on The Gael Gates:

"Wow! That was intense!" — http://www.wattpad.com/user/jeshi99

Contents

People, Places, and Spirits

People in alphabetical order

Amyntas, Ancient King of Galatia

Armel Gallou, Golaseccan Druid (red-robe) on Tucana Prime

Arturo Lubri, Chief Druid at Las Cogotas

Bébinn Nankivell, "Bébe," Captain, pilot to Druidess Sionann Lìosach

Belenos Ontonio, villager at Las Cogotas

Blodeuwedd Chynoweth, Doctor on Tucana Prime

Breno Feijóo, go-between with Los Caciques/El Caciquismo, father of Gobán

Brígida Mosquera, "Gida," apprentice Druid at Stonehenge

Caoimh Baragwanath, Chief Druid at Puppis

Cathasach Bolloré, "Satch," Engineer, Nerolead Interstellar, Clio's sister, Culann's ex-wife

Celtalpines, the Celts collectively (Senones, Golaseccans, Cisalpines) on Tucana Prime

Ceridwen Gwilym, "Ceri," Ceannaire, President of the Gael Federation

Cisalpines, a Celtic tribe in the mountains on Tucana Prime

Clíodhna Ròsach, "Clio," Professor of Particle Physics, University of Cardiff, Satch's sister

Culann Penrose, "Cull," Investigator, Professor of Astral Physics, University of Cardiff

Dylan MacAskill, Potentate of Alrakis

El Caciquismo, Galician for "the chieftancy" (group)

Fáelán Trevelyan, "Lane," Chief Druid in the Ophiuchus Constellation

Finnán Cadeyrn, "Finn," Chief Druid at Göbekli Tepe

Gobán Feijóo, thesis student, University of Cardiff, son of Breno
Golaseccans, a Celtic tribe in the mountains, on Tucana Prime
Gwrtheyrn Jézéquel, Procter on Tucana Prime
Jamie, forensic videographer for Investigator Culann Penrose
Llewellyn Gutraidh, "Lew," apprentice Druid at Stonehenge
Los Caciques, Galician for "the chiefs" (plural)
Méabh Abgrall, Chief Druidess for the Southern Triangle
Medraut Bhodhsa, "Mede," Chief Druid and Proctor at Stonehenge
Niamh Lozac'h, Captain of the battleship Tylwyth Teg, of Alrakis
Noba Pacem, villager at Las Cogotas
Óengus Tàillear, Cisalpine Druid (white-robe) on Tucana Prime
Phelan Brogimāros, Cadet on Alrakis
Piritta Quemener, Cadet on Alrakis
Ríoghan Tanguy, Archeologist at Las Cogotas, Professor
Scathach Ogham, "Scathe," Druidess of the Exalted Martyrology on Tucana
Prime
Senones, a Celtic tribe in the mountains on Tucana Prime
Sionann Lìosach, "Nann," Chief Druidess, Minister of the Druidry
Tristão Andrade, Druid from a village near Las Cogotas
Yezekael Seznec, Senone Druid (brown-robe) and Proctor on Tucana Prime

Places (henges, cities, planets, stars, constellations)

Alcyone, capital planet of the Gael Federation
Alpha Tucanae, binary star
Alrakis, planet in the Galatia/Anatolia constellation, location of Göbekli Tepe
Ancyra, Capital of Galatia on Alrakis
Appenines (mountains) on Tucana Prime
Draco, a constellation in the Gael Federation
Durouĺ¯ernon (Canterbury), Capital City of Alcyone
Fanum, "sanctuary" or temple on Tucana Prime
Gael Federation, the six Celtic constellations
Galicia, planet orbiting Gamma Doradis
Gamma Doradus, a constellation in the Gael Federation
Gamma Draconis, star in the Galatia/Anatolia constellation
Göbekli Tepe, henge on Alrakis

Las Cogotas obeliscos, the henge on Galicia
Las Cogotas, village on Galicia
Montefortino de Arcevia, henge on Tucana Prime
Nemetobriga, planet in the Southern Triangle
Nevalı Çori, henge on Alrakis
Ophiuchus, a constellation in the Gael Federation
Pleiades, a constellation in the Gael Federation
Puppis, a constellation in the Gael Federation
Tucana Prime, planet orbiting Alpha Tucanae
Tucana, a constellation in the Gael Federation

Spirits (and otherworldly places)

Annwvyn, a Gaelic afterlife, also an underworld, otherworld
Arawn, a Psychopomp, one who escorts souls to the underworld
Balor, King of the Elemental Ether
Djinn, King of the Salamanders, the Elemental of Fire
Ghob, King of the Gnomes, the Elemental of Earth
Gwitihn, demon
Idris, demon, god
L'annawnshee, Proto-Gaelic for Underworld Fairy
Niksa, Queen of the Undines, the Elemental of Water
Paralda, Queen of the Sylphs, the Elemental of Air
Tír na nÓg, a Gaelic afterlife

Chapter 1

Yawning, apprentice Llewellyn Gutraidh peered toward the hilltop, the night sky brilliant beyond the Henge, the lack of moon leaving the stars all the brighter. Crickets chirped at regular rhythm, and night birds called out for mates. A chill wind blew him the scents of grass, flowers, and trees.

Five large trilithons surrounded by thirty smaller trilithons made up the inner circle of Stonehenge on Alcyone, all the thirty-five post-and-lintel structures built with the native sarsen stone. Four stones stood at the edge of the ring, marking the monument boundaries, a station stone to each the east and west, a slaughter stone to the south, and a heel stone to the north.

Gnomes supposedly ruled these domains, Stonehenge their home. Llewellyn had never seen them and didn't expect to. A disciple of the Elemental Air, he studied the sylphs, his skill at summoning them meager as yet.

Not the most exciting of duties, the vigil at Stonehenge was taken by turns one night out of every fortnight, the apprentices disliking the duty almost as much as serving the slop. Standing beside the slaughter stone, Llewellyn pulled his cape tighter, trying to keep his senses alert, these night vigils especially difficult in the cold, when all a body wanted to do was sleep. He jerked his head back to attention, his eyelids desperately wanting to close.

Atop the hill, Stonehenge was outlined by the blue brilliance of several sisters, the Pleiades Constellation all young stars, none more than two hundred million years old, their multiple suns giving mutual light to their siblings' planets at all hours, the surface of Alcyone bathed in blue. Perched atop the largest trilithon, the main gate lintel easily twelve feet long, was sister Pleione, the pulsating star like a beacon marking the gate.

Llewellyn pinched his eyes shut as though to squeeze the sleep from them, then stifled another yawn.

A wraith slipped from the main gate and then was gone.

Startled, Llewellyn blinked up at the Henge, poised to run up the hill. A gnome? he wondered.

Nothing else moved.

Had he actually seen something, or was it an afterimage? An Elemental, perhaps?

"Proctor, you awake?" he asked on his com.

"What is it, Lew?" Medraut's voice was groggy with sleep.

"Thought I saw something come out of the main gate, but then it was gone."

"Wasn't a ghost on the inside of your eyelids, was it, Lad?"

"Don't think so, Sir." He might have taken umbrage at Proctor Medraut for implying he'd been asleep. Llewellyn continued to scan the area, seeing nothing untoward. The crickets chirped, the night birds called, and the wind blew.

A few minutes later, Proctor Medraut joined Llewellyn, still shrugging on his tunic. "Pleione throbs brightly tonight, I see. Shall we?" He gestured Llewellyn to take the lead.

The apprentice stepped over the invisible barrier they all knew as the Ring. Stonehenge was sacred ground, never to be entered unless necessary, and never alone. The grass inside the Ring was even-cut, remaining green throughout the year, always standing three inches exactly, maintained it was said by an invocation to the mythical Gwitihn.

The Henge stood atop a knoll that was so even, round, and symmetrical, that geologic forces couldn't have formed it. Llewellyn led the way up, keeping a sharp gaze on the main gate, the dewy grass soon dampening his sodhoppers.

The circular stand of trilithons comprising Stonehenge seemed menacing tonight, where during the day it stood sentinel over their domains like some ancient guardian god.

Nothing looked out of place as they approached the main gate, the south one. Three other slightly narrower gates at east, west, and north also looked empty. Intermediate gates in between, varying in height all the way down to half that of the main gate, stood quiescent as well, no sign to Llewellyn that any had been used in the last few minutes.

"Do you see that?" Proctor Medraut asked, his stare fixed to the main gate's lintel, a foot-thick slab ten feet long and two feet deep. How the ancients had lifted it eighteen feet above the ground was an enigma.

"See what, Proctor?" Llewellyn extended his senses as he'd been taught, seeing with not just his eyes, but with his entire being. There, a spark. At head height, in the center of the gate, a dim aura, a slight warming, as though someone's passage had left a wraith of the person's presence.

"A spark," Medraut said.

"Yes, faint, but there."

"It's nothing," the Proctor suddenly said, shaking his head. "You were sleeping again, Lew."

This time he did take umbrage. "I wasn't, I swear!"

"You were, and you know it, and you're to serve the slop until your next turn at vigil."

"But that's two weeks," he protested.

"Would you like it a month?" Medraut turned and descended the hill.

Leaving Llewellyn gasping in his wake like a fish out of water.

Serving slop in the kitchen for two weeks would subject him to the calumny of his peers. They'd all excoriate him. Further, it'd be the last time anyone would wake the Proctor. Fat lot of good vigil at the Henge would do their enclave if none of the sentinels raised the alarm. It wasn't how Llewellyn would run things.

His back to the main gate, he watched contemptuously as Medraut made his way down the hill and across the Ring, leaving Llewellyn inside the ring, alone.

A surreal force seized Llewellyn's shoulders and yanked him backward into the gate.

#

Captain Niamh Lozac'h of Alrakis stared up at the hill toward Göbekli Tepe, one of two guards patrolling the stand of stele, the capped stones like a small forest of nearly two hundred pillars. In the night sky above her, Gamma Draconis blazed, her orange light bathing the dry, rocky hilltop.

A veteran warrior and pilot, Niamh didn't mind the occasional nighttime duty. In her thirties, she had long ago lost the impatience of youth, which her younger companion guard still possessed in blunderous abundance. Also unlike her, he was not Galatian, his home world a temperate planet farther along the Orion Spur.

"It's cold out here, by Idris," Phelan said through chattering teeth, huddling in the lee of the guard kiosk.

"It won't be Idris who keeps you safe." Niamh swept the stele with her gaze, ever vigilant. The last war with the Eltanin tribes had started with their pouring through the Göbekli gates. It wasn't going to happen on her shift, she vowed, having lost her sister and brother in the intense fighting that'd followed. Alrakis ships eventually had pulverized the Eltanin Navy, but the first attack had come not by ship, but by warrior pouring through the Gael Gates of Göbekli Tepe. Any lapse in vigilance was an invitation for another attack.

Water was this monument's patron Elemental, and undines purportedly called it home. Captain Lozac'h had never seen an undine. Not a Druid, uninitiated into the Druidic Mysteries, she didn't expect to. She thought it odd that water was the patron Elemental on a desert planet. Undines seemed no help in making the planet more habitable.

"I'm going to walk the perimeter," she told Phelan. "You go the other direction, meet me on the other side."

He snorted dismissively. "And freeze my cherries? No thanks, Captain."

"It's clear they've already shriveled," Niamh replied. "Suit yourself." And she strode into the darkness to the east, her gaze sweeping the forest of perpendicular stones again. Pulling her jacket tight, she commed base command to alert them she was walking the perimeter.

Many of the stele capped, the twenty circles of stones had stood sentinel on Alrakis for nearly a thousand years, serving as gates between worlds since ancient times. How they worked was a technology long lost to the Federation, but that hadn't kept the Gaels from using the gates. Only the Druids knew how to use them, pilots like Niamh flying between worlds by conventional A-warp starship.

On her last command of the battleship Tylwyth Teg, Captain Niamh Lozac'h had led the attack on Eltanin itself, just after learning of her brother's death. Her grief had fueled a ferocious attack, the assault considered the decisive battle credited with bringing the war to an early end.

Niamh glanced back once at the guard kiosk, seeing Phelan only by the misting of his breath. The quality of soldier these days, she thought, disgusted. She knew she was rare among her colleagues to take duties such as this, most of them simply paying a midshipman or cadet to do their patrol for them.

While never one to shirk a duty, Niamh was here for another reason. The stele had always fascinated her, the Henge like its counterparts along the Orion Spur drawing her since childhood. A precocious child, she'd grown up just north of Göbekli Tepe and had considered a Druid apprenticeship. There were no female Druids on Alrakis, her father had pointed out, and so Niamh had pursued her second choice.

She stopped at the eastern terminus of Göbekli Tepe and looked up at the stars, trying to pick out the other Henge systems—Pleiades, Ophiuchus, Puppis, Gamma Doradus, and Tucana.

Movement among the stele caught her eye. An undine? she wondered, scanning.

Nothing there.

Senses tuned, Niamh slowly widened her scan of the circles, only the westernmost stele occluded by the hill. No movement, nothing untoward.

Still, the sense of a presence wouldn't leave her. I couldn't have seen an undine, she thought, not Druid initiate, nor even a believer. "Phelan," she commed, "I thought I saw something up here. You see anything down there?"

"All clear, Captain."

"Time to walk the perimeter, Cadet, whether you have the cherries for it or not."

"Yes, Sir," he replied.

At least he didn't resist, she thought, eyes quartering the stand of stele. The gates only opened between two stele with capstones, which about half the stele had. Although varied in height, all the stele were nearly identical in width and depth, one foot by two feet. A divine dimension, according to Druid Finnán Cadeyrn, Counselor to the Potentate of Alrakis, Dylan MacAskill, and Chief of the Gates at Göbekli Tepe.

After a few minutes, seeing nothing, Niamh continued around the perimeter toward the northern terminus, where a pair of stele without capstones stood sentinel, soaring to sixteen feet. She sighted along them to Gamma Draconis, the orange pinprick bright enough to tint the rocky ground at her feet, but not enough to wash away the night.

She brought her gaze down to the central ring of stones capping the hilltop, where all the stele had capstones. Also of varying height, these stele stood between ten and twenty-five feet, their capstones of proportionate length and balanced precariously. Comprised of ten stones each, the twenty rings varied in size, one large ring at the center, five medium rings surrounding it, and fourteen small rings encircling them all.

A wraith appeared between two stele and was gone.

Startled, Niamh half-crouched, ready to pursue at the first sign of motion, despite the ancient admonition never to enter Göbekli Tepe alone. The Tepe was sacred ground, never to be entered unless necessary, and never alone. She hadn't seen enough of the wraith to describe it. Besides, what did an undine even look like? she wondered. "Phelan, I saw something again, center ring, between the northernmost pair."

"I'll be right there."

He too knew the admonition, inculcated at an early age wherever a Henge did stand.

She'd always wondered if the admonition weren't the Druids' way of keeping their nocturnal travels clandestine. Fairies and Goblins were rumored to snatch people too foolish to ignore the taboo.

Silence seemed to have settled upon the monument, the megaliths as lifeless as death. Where before cold gusts had blown, now the air was completely still. Not a cricket dared to chirp nor bird to trill.

The crunch of Phelan's boots on ground approached.

Niamh kept her gaze on the two stele where she'd seen the wraith.

"Between those two?" He pointed.

"Aye," she said, slipping back into her childhood dialect. "Keep a watch while I check my arms. Have you ever seen an undine?"

"Never have. Druid Cadeyrn says they're a mischievous bunch."

Phelan's gaze on the stele, Niamh checked her blaster charge, beside it her sword. A large, heavy, two-handed bludgeon, the sword had been her father's, and his father's, and his father's before then, she the first female in six generations to wear it. Blaster in hand, she signaled that he check his own while she kept her gaze on the stele.

With a nod between them, they crept into Göbekli Tepe, backs to each other in a half-crouch, blasters held ready at shoulder. They circled one small outer ring, neither wanting to pass through it. They skirted a medium ring and approached the northernmost stele of the large inner ring.

They stopped just a foot away from the gate, the capstones nearly meeting in the middle twenty feet above them atop the stele on either side.

"This is ridiculous," Phelan said, snorting in contempt, holstering his weapon. "Eh? Have you lost your mind?"

"No, in fact, it's clear you've lost yours. There's nothing here." Abruptly, he turned and went the way they'd come.

Stunned, disbelieving, Niamh stared after him, her back to the gate, her mouth working, her brain stumbling in its attempt to formulate words.

Suction grabbed her at nape and waistband and yanked her backward into the gate.

#

Professor Ríoghan Tanguy frowned at the stand of obeliscos dominating the skyline at Las Cogotas, on Galicia in the Southern Triangle. Under a cloudy sky, smoke billowed from between the obeliscos, the natives preparing for another transit. Or another travesty, she thought.

Although Celtiberian in extraction, she scorned the beliefs of these superstitious provincials. Give me an angstroscope and microcalipers any day! she thought. She and the local Druid, Arturo Lubri, had clashed publicly over their differences, Professor Tanguy excavating an ancient tor over the ridge, the local Druid claiming it was a sacred site abandoned by the proto-Celtiberians and therefore inviolate. Sylphs of the patron Elemental Air made their home at these sites, according to the Druid. Professor Tanguy had never seen one and scoffed at the Druid's assertions.

Clad in her digs, dun-gray and drab, garb meant for the dirty work of excavation, Ríoghan grimaced and made her way uphill toward the obeliscos. A straggler or two also made their way toward the hilltop, the plumes of smoke like a beacon, most the villagers having already assembled.

Druid Lubri is probably exhorting them all to dance and writhe! Ríoghan thought, greeting those who strode uphill beside her. Their lively dress, frilled cotton cloth embroidered with multicolor thread, made her look positively dumpy. She'd get no work today from the local laborers she'd hired, all of them attending the ceremony, Lubri herding his flock like an assiduous sheep dog.

The straight streets on Galicia were somewhat at odds to the winding, narrow labyrinths common to other planets in the Southern Triangle, the constellation occupied mostly by settlers of Celtiberian extraction.

The mechanism of transport through the Gael Gates was thought to derive from the principles of Alcubierre warp drive, and yet the Druids continued to mythologize their gate use with elaborate ritual and prestidigitation. Such sordid sortilege did little to advance a scientific understanding of the Gael Gates, hypotheses which still eluded astral and particle physicists, who posited that they operated on A-warp, in which time and distance were fundamentally the same properties, differing only in their articulation.

An archeologist, Ríoghan cared less about the theory and more about the ignorance being perpetuated by the Druids. She'd arrived at Las Cogotas through the gates two years ago to study the ancient sites on the planet. Gamma Doradus, the double-star system of her home planet, Nemetobriga, contained very minor proto-Celtiberian sites, all of them catalogued and excavated long before.

Each obelisco in the Henge on Galicia was etched in Celtiberian runes all the way to the top, the script still indecipherable to modern linguists, their study forbidden by both local superstition and the imperious Druid, Arturo Lubri.

Ríoghan reached the edge of the obeliscos, an area bordered by a low rock wall, the rocks fitted by hand without mortar, encircling the hilltop and the obeliscos within, nine pillars of stone poking into the sky, two smaller sets of three pillars standing twenty-seven feet on either side of a third, larger set soaring eighty-one feet. Each set known individually as a tribelisco represented one of the three Gates sacred to Neo-Pagan Druidry—the Well, the Fire, and the Tree.

Balderdash! Ríoghan thought.

Druid Lubri stood in a wide stance before the largest tribelisco, waving his heavily-embroidered and -sequined cape with an elaborate flourish as he intoned in ancient Galician the incantation needed to open the gate. Villagers encircled the tribelisco, hands held as though in vigil, repeating the Druid's utterances. New arrivals were incorporated into the ring, the archeologist along with them.

Arturo spun, flaunting his cape as though taunting a bull, his eyes glazed in ecstasy, a fine froth of spittle collecting at the corners of his mouth.

He looks possessed! she thought, as if he had rabies. Hydrophobia occasionally cropping up in isolated places such as this, she wondered what he'd do if she threatened to throw a pail of water on him. A giggle escaped her, and the woman beside her, Doña Noba Pacem, shrank in disgust.

Druid Arturo Lubri froze, his gaze fixed to Ríoghan. "We have an infidel in our midst! She who mocks the sylphs and desecrates our sacred sites!" His arm leapt at her, finger stabbing toward her. "Seize her!"

Multiple villagers converged on her before she could react.

"Bring her here," the Druid commanded. "A rope!"

They easily overcame her struggles and dragged her into place between two of the eighty-one foot obeliscos. They tied each limb with rope, her legs three feet apart, her arms suspended at forty-five degrees overhead.

Lubri stuck his face into hers. His breath stank of queimada. "You'll desecrate no more, Infidel! You'll meet the sylphs face to face and then you'll believe!"

"What are you doing, Cabrón?!" she spat, seeing he was drunk.

He backhanded her, and her head flew to the side. "Perra pequeña! Cona! Back in position, everyone! Let's send this succubus to moura encantada!" As he backed away and resumed his chants and gyrations, the villagers joined hands again.

Her lip and cheek stung, and she tasted blood. She strained against the ropes, but none of them gave, her stretched-out arms giving her no leverage. "Dom Ontonio, help me!" she called to her lead laborer, who'd helped her recruit her dig crew.

Belenos Ontonio kept his place in the circle, sweat on his brow and fear in his eyes.

Lubri whipped his cape back and forth, grasped it with both hands and thrust it to the ground, kneeling at Ríoghan's feet and ululating stridently. Then he abruptly straightened and flung the cape back over his head.

Professor Ríoghan Tanguy heard a thunderclap, and she was sucked into the gate, rope and all.

#

The white-robed Cisalpine Druid, Óengus Tàillear, was nearly invisible against the scree of storm, helped by a spell to obscure his presence. Fuaranders played merrily at his feet, the six-inch Elementals each creating their own mini-snowstorms. The skies of Tucana Prime perpetually clouded, the planet was beset with unforgiving cold, hypothermia claiming thousands of lives every winter.

But the storm suited the Druid's purpose. He and his two companions stood at the rim of Montefortino, a henge of nine megaliths, whose divine placement created twelve Gael Gates, three megaliths in each triangle, the three triangles placed at the vertices of a larger triangle. Each smaller triangle of megaliths called a trigalith, the area around the megaliths was tessellated with tile, which was oddly free of snow. A knee-high, foot-wide stone ring encircled the henge. Beyond the henge, a thin forest encroached, the trees so thick with snow that branches couldn't be seen. The landscape was hilly and rocky, huge boulders jumbled upon each other in chaotic profusion. And all of it glaciated with perpetual snow.

Behind the three Druids stood the Monastery and Scriptorium, their lights barely penetrating the thick snowfall. Three Druid orders occupied one Monastery—Cisalpine, Golaseccan, and Senone. Cisalpine Druids were adherents of the fuarander, the Ice Elemental, while the Golaseccan Druids maintained fealty to the salamander, the Fire Elemental. So contentious was their rivalry that the Senone Druids constantly had to mediate. The two Elementals, Ice and Fire, were antithetical, always at odds with each other.

"Tis a good, thick night to cover our tracks, Brother Gus," said the red-robed Druid beside him. Golaseccan Armel Gallou was one such salamander adherent.

"So good and thick we'll be buried in snow if we don't get on with it," croaked the ancient crone beside them. Procter Gwrtheyrn Jézéquel, a Senone Druidess, stood barely five feet in her perpetual stoop. Gnarled hands held fast to a wormwood staff, snowflakes already accumulating on the bluing fingers. A skein of web-like hair hung over her face, so tousled no spider would deign to live there.

"Gwerth, you summon Air; Mel, you'll invoke Fire, and I'll conjure Earth." Despite their professed fidelities, Gwrtheyrn and Óengus prepared to beckon other Elementals in violation of their oaths. This alone was enough to incur the Ministry's castigation, hence the invisibility spell that Óengus had cast. "Are you sure you want to try the final step alone, Gwerth?"

"Aye, Laddie, better that a senescent fool like me risk censure than either of you." The old proctor was known to wander through the woods, even during blizzards, as though she were the embodiment of inclement weather. "Our success may bring the wrath of the Druidry upon us, perhaps even the attention of the Minister herself, Druidess Lìosach."

"What could that fickle wench do to us?" Armel asked with a sneer.

"Blast you into the next universe, if she's a mind to," Gwrtheyrn replied. "Let's get on, then."

All three stepped into the ring, the tessellated ground no warmer than the thick drift they'd stepped from, but somehow, snow didn't stick to the tiles.

"Mel, remember to modulate the stability. You know what happened last time we brought Fire and Air together."

Armel threw a glance her direction, scowling. "Yes, Gwerth," he said.

As if Armel doesn't already know Fire's affinity for Air, Óengus thought. The one Elemental had nearly consumed the other.

Gwrtheyrn moved to the northern-most trigalith, while Óengus took the southeastern triangle and Armel the southwest. "I'll go last," Armel said, Fire the most difficult to maintain in such frigid environs.

"Air, Earth, and Fire," Gwrtheyrn began, "hear our plea." She raised her staff above her head. "Paralda, Queen of Sylphs, bring me your life-giving breezes."

A sylph coalesced inside the three stones, taller than Gwrtheyrn but slim as a willow, a storm swirling above her head, her eyes made of storm and her hair made of wind. "Gwerth of the Senones, I am yours to command." She wore only a swirl of leaves.

Óengus at the southeastern corner turned to face the trigalith. Each stone soared to twenty-seven feet, a divine height. "Ghob, King of Gnomes, show me your fertile Earth!" he said, casting his arms over his head.

Inside the trigalith, a gnome sprouted from the ground, as gnarled as Gwrtheyrn but taller, its face a worm-rich loam, its hair a bright green cap made from grass, its build squat and thick like rock. The Elemental King could have crushed Óengus flat with a nasty glance. "Gus of the Cisalpines, I heed your call."

To the southwest, Armel turned toward his trigalith, and his red robes ballooned outward as he raised his arms. "Djinn, King of Salamanders, bring forth your life-warming Fire."

A fiery lizard as tall as the Druid flared to life inside the trigalith, flames licking around its head in halo. "Master Mel, my friend indeed, how may I serve thee?"

"Paralda, Ghob, and Djinn," intoned Gwrtheyrn, gesturing with her staff, "follow me hence and draw together." She hobbled into the center, around her the hexagram made by the six stone pillars. "Come to me from your trigaliths, and blend your energies in divine concatenation."

They all three resisted. "Do this not, Druidess Gwerth!" hissed Paralda, her edges spinning into a dust devil, her middle a swirling maelstrom, turbid with debris.

Fire leered at Air, and Earth spread above Fire. Outside the henge, the wind picked up, whirling around the perimeter like a snake coiling around its victim.

Óengus restrained Earth by drawing his fist closed, and Armel dampened Fire by pushing both hands down.

The three Elementals reined, Gwrtheyrn swirled her staff in a circle as though mixing, and wisps were sucked off their bodies. Air howled, Fire writhed, and Earth roiled, all their faces in rictuses of pain.

Above Gwrtheyrn gathered their entrails, a whirling mix of tailings. As the mass grew turgid above her, the Elementals each grew smaller, their incarnations leaking slowly into the abomination taking shape in the center. Streaks of red, orange, white, and brown mixed into a gray muddy mess. The storm around the henge intensified, the blizzard so thick that it obscured the surrounding forest behind a solid white wall of sleet.

Óengus held Earth's integrity close, Ghob as likely to disintegrate into its composite elements as to slide into a thick slurry. He could feel Armel's exertions with Fire, the edges of their essences intermingling in the rich soup above Gwrtheyrn.

The mass began to form into a creature thrice the Elementals' sizes, its skin striated, its hair streaked and spiky, its limbs grotesque. As the last of each Elemental leaked into the monstrosity, a roar shook the stones. Eyes formed on a bulging, primordial face. Protuberant lips peeled back from a prognathous jaw, and a guttural voice thick with glottal stops snarled, "Who dares to wake me?"

"Druidess Gwerth, demon!" she snarled right back, undaunted. "Bow before me and prepare to do my bidding!"

"Miscreant Druidess! So *you* think!" And a mighty fist with Fire for bone, Water for blood, and Earth for flesh, swept around and snatched her from her feet.

Óengus put his hands out, summoning his power from deep inside his soul, and hurled fuaranders at the beast.

The demon vanished and along with it, Gwrtheyrn's scream.

A curtain of vapor was all that remained, and that too dispersed as the storm that had swirled around the henge descended upon the pair of Druids.

Óengus found Armel somehow in the blistering blizzard. "What happened?" He had to scream to be heard above the storm, his mouth near his fellow Druid's ear.

"We couldn't control it! Arawn blast, what do we do?"

Óengus pulled Armel in the direction of the Scriptorium, that part of the monastery closest to the henge. "We have to get out of this storm!" He wasn't sure his companion even heard him.

Together, they fought their way toward the Scriptorium door, spikes of cold driving nails into his ankles through his feet, his hands like lumps of ice at the ends of arms that wouldn't obey him. He attempted to summon a warming salamander, but his magic failed him.

Or maybe I've failed my magic, Óengus thought grimly.

They found the door somehow, and as it shut behind them, so too, it shut out the storm. Armel held a cyanotic finger to his lips for silence.

Óengus heard nothing but the faint scream of the storm just outside the door. And the echo of Gwrtheyrn's scream in his mind. "What do we do?!" he asked in a harsh whisper, barely able to keep from screaming himself.

Gwrtheyrn taken by a demon after they'd violated their vows and fused the Elementals! They were sure to be prosecuted for murder, or worse, stripped of their titles! Óengus could hardly think. His heart hammered in his ears, and sweat trickled down his back.

"First," Armel whispered, grabbing Óengus' parka hood on either side of his face, "first and foremost, we tell no one. No one! Do you hear?"

Óengus nodded in time with Armel's shaking him. "No one!" he whispered back, the Scriptorium likely empty at this time of night, but taking no chances.

"Swear it," Armel whispered.

"I swear to tell no one. Now you."

"Of course I swear, idiot. You think I want to lose my standing?"

"What about Gwrtheyrn?" He loosened his parka somewhat, not knowing whether he was shaking from cold or shaking from fear.

"What about her? She knew the risks. She's nowhere near as daft as everyone thinks. Besides, they'll assume she wandered off and fell into a snow bank, won't expect to find her frozen body until spring."

"But …but …"

"But nothing!" Armel's whisper was harsh, his tone cutting. "We'll look for her soon, but for now, we just wait and regroup."

"How ..." Óengus was so terrified, he could barely speak. "How long?"

"Four days," Armel said, shrugging off his red parka and shaking the snow off it. "We give it four days, and then we'll look for her. All right, Gus? All right?"

Óengus saw that Armel was as frightened as he was, sweat soaking his Druid robes with darker patches of crimson. "All right, Mel. Four days," he repeated, unable to stop shaking. They threaded a path through towering shelves of parchment toward the main monastery, Óengus wondering how he was going to keep his composure for the next hour.

Let alone four days.

Chapter 2

Culann Penrose, forensic physicist, frowned at the obeliscos standing in trinity before him, soaring to eighty-one feet, their sides inscribed with the ancient indecipherable script of his forebears. None of the Henges were so intimidating as these obeliscos on Galicia in the Southern Triangle, the tallest among the monuments. It wasn't any wonder that the patron Elemental was Air. Sylphs flew in between and around the obeliscos like wraiths.

"Druid Arturo Lubri wouldn't ever send anyone into oblivion like that," said the meek little man beside Culann. Druid Tristão Andrade had come over from the neighboring village after Druid Lubri's arrest.

Three peoples' disappearance in one day into Gael Gates along the Orion Spur had alarmed the Druidic Ministry. The Ceannaire herself, her Lady Ceridwen Gwilym, President of the Gaels, had ordered the appointment of a special investigator. Unfortunately, the Ceannaire had also ordered the Gael Gates shut down until the disappearances were investigated, forcing Professor Penrose to arrive by conventional means, rather than by gate.

Professor of Astral Physics at the University of Cardiff, Culann Penrose had been chosen specifically for his expertise in the confluence of Druidic Mysticism and Alcubierre Warp Theory, his previous work at the Ministry of Investigation well known.

Culann looked at the obeliscos on either side of the gate, sylphs scattering from his line of vision as if trying to evade his gaze. He'd come to Galicia first, the local Druid charged with involuntary manslaughter, the whole village of Las Cogotas having witnessed the disappearance of the archeologist, Professor Ríoghan Tanguy. "Druid Andrade, when did you arrive?"

"El Señor Investigador asks whether I witnessed these events, no? I did not, Señor."

Culann nodded. "An upstanding man, Druid Lubri?"

"Sí, Señor, a kind and gentle soul, perhaps upset at the excavation of our sacred sites, but well-meaning."

Culann looked among the villagers who'd gathered at the Ring wall, a low rock barrier of fitted stone. "Who among you was here yesterday?" he called.

All the hands went up.

He pointed to a gentleman. "Señor, how close were you to Druid Lubri?"

"I was as close to him as El Druido Andrade is to you, Señor."

Culann waved him over. "Señora," he said, pointing to a woman, "how close were you?"

"I was holding hands with la perra pequeña, Señor."

He sensed she had no sympathy for the outlander archeologist, the epithet spoken with the sneer of a pejorative. But she'd been close enough to see what happened. "This way, Señora. What are your names?"

"Belenos Ontonio," said the man, approaching.

"Noba Pacem," said the woman, soon joining him. The two of them stood apart, as though they weren't fellow villagers.

"Dom Ontonio, Doña Pacem, grazas, benvidos." Culann knew a few words of the local dialect. "Doña Pacem, tell me what you saw."

Her gaze narrowed, her brow already wrinkled with scorn. "El Druido Lubri summoned us for an invocation, and Señorita Tanguy joined us well into the ceremony, inserting herself in the ring beside me. She was wearing her ugly clothes, the ones she always wore. She looked like El Home, a man. A minute or two after she arrived, she laughed aloud. Very disrespectful of Señorita Tanguy, no respeto, that perra. That was when El Druido Lubri called her to her fate."

"Dom Ontonio, what did you see?"

"As Doña Pacem said, Señorita Profesora Tanguy arrived late and seemed amused with El Druido Lubri's behavior. He'd had several cups of queimada, a local bebida."

Culann had heard something about it. "Queimada? What's that?"

"A punch made from wine and flavored with lemon peel, sugar, herbs, and cinnamon. He prepared it with an incantation to summon special powers, and then he set it alight. After each cup, his gyrations grew wilder. He has a liking for queimada, too great a liking, in my opinion. When Señorita Profesora giggled, he turned on her, ordered us to grab her and tie her to los obeliscos." Dom Ontonio dropped his gaze and bit his lip. "She called for my help." He swallowed heavily and blinked rapidly. "Then El Druido Lubri banished her to moura encantada with a thunderclap."

Culann had briefed himself on the local legends, some still practicing the old rituals. Mouras encantadas were young, beautiful maidens considered dangerously seductive, shape shifters and guardians of ancient megaliths like these obeliscos and the barrow that Professor Tanguy had been excavating. They were believed to live in such megaliths still. How and why the sylphs had come to occupy the obeliscos and made them their home was unknown. He wondered when the Elemental Air had become their patrón. "A moura encantada is believed to have built the obeliscos."

"Sí, Señor."

"You seem upset that you didn't help."

Ontonio's voice caught, and he gave Noba Pacem a quick glance. "I supervised her crew at the barrow, Señor. Of all the villagers, I knew her best. She was kind and considerate, but she was contemptuous of ignorance, a condition that plagues isolated villages such as ours."

A major Gael Gate, and yet the surrounding denizens ignorant out of isolation. "Graza, Dom Ontonio, Doña Pacem. You've been very helpful." He bowed to them both, and then turned to the obeliscos, where sylphs continued to frolic, some having lost their timidity.

He looked at the left obelisco, seeing the aura eight feet up where a rope had held the archeologist's arm, the right obelisco having similar traces. At the base, each exhibited signatures of aura corresponding to the legs. At each place, the force necessary to break the ropes had left traces of rope fiber clinging to stone. "Jamie, you imaged this?"

The young videographer nodded, his insect-eyed camera coming down from its perch on his shoulder. "Even the fibers, Sir."

Culann grimaced, wondering if Professor Tanguy had been hurt, such force easily enough to break a limb. "Good work today, Jamie. I'll need you at the jail in about an hour."

"Yes, Sir." Jamie headed for the ring, where most of his equipment was.

Not that Culann blamed the boy for wanting out of the ring quickly. Half Culann's age at twenty-four, Jamie had been with Culann on other investigations, but he still couldn't think of the young man as anything but a boy.

Culann knelt three feet away from the threshold between the two obeliscos, two sylphs fleeing.

Boot prints three feet apart made straight lines right up to the threshold, but not beyond.

And beyond? Culann wondered. Where might that be?

Alcubierre Warp Theory posited that compressing space in front of an object and attenuating space behind it would cause an object to arrive at its destination faster than light. Culann had arrived in his A-warp yacht, and not by Gate, because the Ceannaire had ordered the Gates shut down until the disappearances had been investigated and their use deemed safe. Arrival by Gate was instantaneous and much preferred. The Gael Gates were thought to operate by similar mechanisms as his ship, but the ancients hadn't left a single schematic to that effect, just the gates themselves all along the Orion Spur.

He concentrated, sometimes able to sense information from a gate's aura, that invisible manifestation of its essence. The Gael Gate between the two eighty-one foot obeliscos surrendered nothing to his probe.

Culann sighed and stood.

Each trio of obeliscos called a tribelisco, the three obeliscos stood eighty-one feet tall, their surfaces covered with ancient Gaelic, indecipherable even still. We speak variants of the language throughout the Orion Spur, he thought in irony, but we can't read the script.

He stepped between the central tribelisco and the smaller tribelisco to the left, only twenty-seven feet tall. Three-to-the-third feet tall for the outer tribeliscos, he mused, versus three-to-the-fourth feet tall for the inner tribelisco, nine obeliscos in all.

A small henge compared with Stonehenge, where thirty-five trilithons stood perpetual sentinel, and far smaller than Göbekli Tepe, a two-hundred stele henge with twenty circles of stones.

Culann stood behind the larger tribelisco and lined them up evenly in his vision. The obeliscos had been placed to provide the most expansive view of the coastline and the sea beyond, probably as a guard against sea-borne invasion, the mountains ringing Las Cogotas protecting it from invasion by land.

Just visible far out to sea was an island, too far to distinguish anything specific.

By now, Jamie had packed up and left, and even the villagers had retreated, none left at the low rock wall.

Again, Culann glanced up.

The three obeliscos punctured the air, sylphs suddenly swirling around them.

A funnel cloud looped down from the cloudless sky and swept him into the air, spinning him dizzily, and a mocking voice crackled, "Interloper, you die today and join me underground!" Two cloud-fingers held him upside down above a large, gray maw, which sucked the air from his lungs. Lightning crackled between cold white teeth. The mist-hand hurled him end-over-end at the ground, right at the sharp point of an obelisco.

Culann swept his arms together and clapped his hands. "Moura Encantada of Obeliscos a la de Las Cogotas," he declared in his best Galician, "yield to the henge of your origin and rescind this vision! Guard your obeliscos against true enemies!" And he pulled his spirit out of the vision and into the present.

Professor of Astral Physics Culann Penrose, forensic physicist, stared up at a quiescent sky beyond the tops of the central tribelisco, feeling a touch of vertigo.

Did that just happen? he wondered.

The birds sang as they'd always sung, the wind blew as it had always blown, and the sylphs were nowhere to be found.

He felt disoriented, as though numb or asleep or in a state of siege.

The mouras encantadas were said to wander their megaliths in similar states.

Culann shook it off, knowing something had happened, but not sure what.

As before, the obeliscos yielded nothing to his examination.

#

"Let him go, Officer," Professor Penrose told the constable.

"Eh, Señor? Are you sure?"

Culann stood outside the cell of El Druido Lubri, the bedraggled figure behind bars red-eyed from weeping, his remorse plain.

"I swear, Señor Profesor Penrose," the man had pleaded, "I didn't intend to make her disappear. I only wanted to scare her. Please, I beg you … "

All that he was really sure of, after his encounter with la moura encantada at the obeliscos, was that other forces were at work. El Druido Lubri couldn't have yanked Professor Ríoghan Tanguy into the gate, ropes and all, by standing outside of it. The other two disappearances at Stonehenge and Göbekli Tepe, likely of similar origin, attested to the work of some larger force—or a very nasty demon. I guess I'll see whether that bears out when I get there, he thought.

Culann was in his yacht and en route to Alcyone within an hour, under autopilot.

"Her lady the Ceannaire is busy, Professor," he was told when he tried to place a com to President Ceridwen Gwilym.

"May I talk with someone, please?"

"One moment, Sir."

And in the silence, Culann wondered what bureaucrat he was likely to get. The remainder of his crew was en route aboard a specially-equipped frigate outfitted by the Ministry of Investigation.

"Professor Penrose." The breathtaking woman on screen was almost as well known as the President. Her personal Druid, Sionann Lìosach, had taken the com. "Apologies for her ladyship's indisposition. She's asked me to assist you in any way you might require."

"Very kind of her lady to offer," Culann said, giving the woman a slight bow. "It's clear El Druido Arturo Lubri did nothing to cause Professor Ríoghan Tanguy's disappearance, and I've ordered his release. I'm en route now to Stonehenge on Alcyone."

"My old Proctor, Medraut Bhodhsa, presides at Stonehenge," Druidess Lìosach said. "Give him my regards, Professor."

"Certainly, Dame Lìosach. Be happy to do so." Culann pondered how to describe what had happened. "A curious thing occurred on Galicia."

"Oh, Professor?" Concern furrowed the bridge between her brows.

"A moura encantada, an enchanted spirit, attempted to pull me into el infierno, hell."

"Odd to hear an astral physicist speak of either, Professor." Sionann smiled, a look of mock bemusement on her face. "Such mysticism must be uncomfortable for you."

"On the contrary, Dame Lìosach. Physics and mysticism complement each other nicely. We're prone to seeking scientific explanations for all phenomena, even those which have none. Mysticism elucidates what science cannot."

"Thus the ancient tomes propound. You've studied the old sciences, it appears."

"Indeed, Dame Lìosach."

"I'll pass along your observations to her lady Ceridwen. As to that intoxicated simpleton on Galicia, it may behoove us to cite him for interference with an excavation, if nothing else. Anything to discourage these provincials."

"It may, Dame Lìosach." He didn't agree but wasn't about to say so.

"Prudent not to voice your disagreement directly, Professor. You've a subtlety to you I admire. Com me directly if there's anything you need."

"Graza, Dame Lìosach."

And the screen went blank. 'That intoxicated simpleton?' he wondered, staring for minutes afterward at the blank vidscreen. What the devil kind of Druid would speak of a fellow Druid that way? Was there no professional courtesy among the Druidry?

Chapter 3

Culann Penrose knelt at the base of the south gate at Stonehenge, inspecting the threshold, seeing no sign that the grass inside the gate had been disturbed.

The drag marks in the grass extended right up to but stopped at the threshold, two gouges the shape and size of sodhopper heels, both a foot long. Gnomes chattered nonsense at him from behind the pillars, peeking out only when he wasn't looking.

"What the bloody hell is a forensic physicist?" came a distant voice.

Culann grinned, the voice unfamiliar but the question expected.

Ignoring the incensed Druid now barreling down on him, Culann calmly inspected the left-hand post, running his eye up the edge. A gnome ducked behind it.

"What blasted Glaistig sent a necromancer like you?" the Druid exploded.

He stuck a smile on his face and stuck out his hand. "Professor Culann Penrose, Sir. Pleased to make your acquaintance. Druid Medraut Bhodhsa and Proctor to the young Llewellyn Gutraidh, I presume?"

"You'll not beguile me with yer demon thievin', I tell you! By what bloody right do you stand on sacred ground, eh?"

Bloody this and bloody that, Culann thought. "Ceri asked me here," he said, his hand ignored. He stuck it back in his pocket. "Lew a promising apprentice? He'd have to be for you to have accepted him. Your reputation precedes you. An honor to meet you, Sir."

"Eh? 'Ceri'? Who in Ifreann is that?"

The Gael Hell, a favorite of Druids everywhere, Culann thought. Does he expect me to be cowed and turn tail? Culann wondered. "No one in hell sent me, Proctor Bhodhsa, and I doubt the Ceannaire, the Lady Ceridwen Gwilym, would take kindly to being called a Glaistig. Further, she's quite concerned about restoring the Gates to use as soon as possible. She asked me to seek you out personally."

"Me? Really? Lady Gwilym mentioned me by name?"

No, not really, Culann thought, but it'll suffice that you believe it. "Said you'd proved helpful in the past in training some quite talented apprentices. Her personal Druid—"

"Sionann Lìosach, the only female I've ever proctored, comely lass," Medraut said, beaming.

"Breathtaking," Culann said. "What happened here, Proctor?" He gestured at the Gate.

"About three am, Lew commed me, said he'd seen something. I got dressed and joined him, and together we came up here. No sign of anything, and no residues of invocation, so I turned …back down the hill. Didn't notice till I'd reached the ring that he hadn't followed, and by then, he was gone."

Culann noted the hesitation, and in the eyes, he'd seen a moment of bewilderment. Further, the aura had shifted subtly, as though some essence had been drawn off. "What did he say he saw?"

"Just something, didn't say what. 'I saw something come out of the main gate,' he said."

"You inspected the gate about how long afterward?"

"Couldn't have been ten minutes—five to get dressed, two or three to walk up here. He's a good lad, Professor Penrose, didn't cross into the ring by himself, waited till I got here."

"Show me where you stood when you inspected the gate." He and his forensics crew had acquired astral-spectral images of the entire area. Anything they could record had already been imaged. "Jamie, get this, would you?" he said to his videographer.

The young man with a mound of electronics on his shoulder, a device bulging with multiple lenses, like an insect, positioned himself and nodded.

"Put me where Lew was standing," Culann told the other man.

Druid Medraut pondered a moment, stepped behind Culann to position him. "About there," he said, and then stepped to a position to the right of Culann, at the right post. "And then I asked him to describe what he saw."

"And what happened then?"

Medraut turned to look into the gate and hesitated. The gnomes hiding behind their posts began to snicker. "Well, we didn't see a thing, and so I thought for certain he'd been sleeping again, told him he'd have to serve slop for a week, and I ... left."

The look was of someone who'd forgotten all suffering and sorrow, and had become unaware of the passage of time. Again, that slight shift in his aura.

"Act it out, say what you said and do what you did."

"Eh? Repeat it all?"

"Please." Culann watched carefully as Medraut spoke and moved.

Again, that hesitation right before Medraut said, "It's nothing. You were sleeping again."

Culann thanked him and glanced toward Jamie, who nodded. He then looked at the gate, gnomes scattering as his gaze alighted on them. Stonehenge was home to the gnomes, and Earth was the monument's patron Elemental.

The one-foot wide stone posts, two feet in depth, eight feet tall, capped by a lintel one foot thick by two feet deep by five feet long, exhibited no detectible residue of invocation. Culann knelt at the base of the right-hand post, running his eye up the edge to where it intersected the lintel, the trilithon looking heavy and ancient.

Again, no residue.

Then he ran his eye across the lintel, his senses tuned.

What was that?

A blip, a spark but gone instantly, an anomaly in the ether.

He rescanned the lintel but to no avail.

Whatever he'd seen didn't re-manifest.

"What is it, Professor?"

"I thought I saw something," he said, then he turned to Jamie, who now had his astral-spectral imager off his shoulder. Too bad he wasn't imaging, Culann thought. "Guess it was nothing," he told the Proctor. "I'd like to speak with you later, Druid Bhodhsa. Find you at the Temple?"

"Er, uh, certainly, Professor, good day." And Medraut hurried down the hill.

A bit too fast for Culann's liking. As though to be shut of the place, he thought, odd behavior for a Druid who controls these very gates, the site at Stonehenge the most important of all the Gael Gates.

Culann looked up at the lintel again.

The cold stone slab yielded nothing to his gaze.

Not even a gnome twittered from behind it.

Deep in thought, he stepped to the next gate. Gnomes scattered at his approach. A minor trilithon, the gate exhibited a resonances indicating its pairing with Sterope, a small system within the Pleiades, the gate merely six feet tall, its lintel only two feet long, barely long enough to cap its two posts.

He saw that Jamie had packed his imaging equipment.

"See you back at the office, Sir," Jamie said.

Culann nodded, deep in thought, returning his gaze to the gate before him. The next gate was to Electra, another Pleiades sister, but beside that, a major gate to Tucana, where the Cisalpine branch resided, where nothing untoward had happened.

He stepped around the Henge toward the easternmost gate, that to Alrakis, in the constellation Draco, where a forest of two hundred stele known as Göbekli Tepe stood, where a battleship captain had disappeared simultaneously with the apprentice here and the archeologist on Galicia.

The east gate stood stoic as stone, not a single gnome around it.

Activated, it provided a direct portal to Alrakis, one system within a cluster of over forty stellar systems flanked by Ursa Minora and Majora. Quiescent, the Gate looked like a simple trilithon, its sarsen stones cold, lifeless, and eternal.

Like its sister gate, which had swallowed the apprentice Llewellyn, the east gate gave no indication of having been used recently, Culann detecting no residue of aura, not a remnant of ether.

He was tempted to activate the gate to hasten his arrival at his next destination, but President Ceridwen Gwilym had ordered the Gael Gates shut down.

Why these three? he wondered briefly, the Southern Triangle, Pleiades, and Draco comprising the relative vertices of the Gael domains, most the other occupied worlds strung in between.

He looked at the lintel, a megalith one foot thick, two feet wide, nine feet long, crossing the gap between the two posts, set seven feet apart, all the major gates the exact same dimensions.

The even-cut grass at his feet vibrated in the slight breeze.

The earth cleaved beneath his feet and sucked him into the furrow. Deeper and deeper he plunged, the tunnel opening before him and closing behind him, an earthen Alcubierre warp, the tunnel so narrow dirt smeared his clothes. He clawed at the earthen sides but couldn't stop his slide.

A face materialized in the tunnel wall even as it flashed past him. "Meddler in the old radiations, you die today and stay with me underground!"

Anu! he thought, the ancient manifestation of Anann, the Maiden Mother Earth Goddess.

The tunnel morphed into rock, scraping his shoulders and hips, the rock parting just enough for his body to squeeze between slabs, rumbling in complaint at his peristalithic extrusion.

Culann summoned the powers of the firmament. "Curse you back to Tír na nÓg, Anu! Lady of Healing, Airmid, Goddess of Tuatha Dé Danann, hear my plea! Beg thy sister, release me!"

The even-cut grass under his feet was reminiscent of his boyhood days, the east gate staring dully at him, unsympathetic to his plight. As though nothing had just happened.

He drew a breath and felt his shoulders, sure his hands would come away bloody.

His clothes were intact, his shoulders uninjured.

Culann shuddered, no longer doubting the wisdom of shutting down the Gates.

#

"I can't believe I did that, Professor," Druid Proctor Medraut Bhodhsa said.

Culann looked across the table at the dispirited older man. They sat in a pub in Amesbury, the closest town to Stonehenge, the old stone walls having seen far worse than a dejected Druid having failed an apprentice.

"It would *seem* that leaving Llewellyn inside the ring alone would be an unconscionable act for a man of your caliber," the Professor of Astral Physics said.

"Eh? Except for what? What in Tír na nÓg might justify or excuse such a negligent act?" The pint in front of the Druid stood untouched.

Culann's was half-empty, a skein of foam like a curtain of silk on the mug insides. "Would you mind, Druid Bhodhsa, if I were to invoke a spirit on your behalf, other than the one in that pint there in front of you?"

"Call me Bode, Professor. 'Druid this' and 'Druid that' annoys me terribly. What have you got in mind?"

"Thank you, Bode, and call me Cull." He rubbed his chin thoughtfully, brought his gaze up and grinned at the other man. "To all the spirits," he said, raising his glass.

Bhodhsa raised his too and downed a long draught. "Yer a fine man, Cull, good to see you're on this, much as my brethren malign you. It grates on us all, not having the Gates to get us around. Going to summon Belagog from the brew?"

Culann snorted and shook his head. "Nothing so large. And nothing that Gullveig the witch will take exception to." Seeing the man's desperation for something to relieve his torment, Culann summoned the healing elemental, water. "Help this man in my sight and help his mind to feel at right."

An undine wisp rose from Bhodhsa's brew and shrouded his head in a thin fog. Then the veil dissipated.

"I feel terrible what happened to Lew. You'll do your best to find him, Cull?"

"I certainly will, Bode."

"That's the spirit. I don't want to be hearing any more of that down-in-the-mouth talk from you, Laddie, eh? There wasn't anything a body could do to stop Lew from being taken; it couldn't be helped." Bhodhsa drained his pint. "You mentioned invoking some spirit? Not sure what for, but I'm willing."

"How about we belay that, Bode? Perhaps it's best not to stir the Elementals."

"Never should if it isn't needed. What do you think's happening with the Gates, Cull?"

"Too early to tell, Bode, but it isn't pleasant. By the by, I've another site to investigate. If I may, I'll be takin' my leave."

"An' leave a half-pint behind? Where's your stamina, man?"

"You've enough for us both, Bode. All yours." Culann nodded and stood, shook hands with the Druid and stepped out of the pub.

Bemused that he might so easily bedazzle a Druid.

#

"Twice now, it's happened, can't be a coincidence," he said to Druidess Lìosach. "I'll arrive on Alrakis in a day. I'd be grateful if you could meet me."

"All right, if you insist, Professor. Sounds as if you'd like me along when you investigate Göbekli Tepe."

"Aye, Druidess. Both times I was named the intruder—not an initiate into the mysteries. Your presence may discourage a third attempt."

"Attempt at what, Professor?" Sionann asked. "What were these spirits trying to do?"

"I think they were trying to kill me."

"But why? As you yourself pointed out, you're not an initiate. You've no power in their domains. You're a man of science, not a whit of magic about you."

Yet it had been magic he'd used to ward them off. "None so's you'd notice, now, is there?" he said anyway, disinclined to reveal over vidlink the other skills he possessed. "Thanks for meeting me there, Dame Lìosach." And he killed the connection.

Again staring at the blank vidscreen for several minutes, not moving.

"Alcubierre Warp Theory, onscreen."

His ship displayed an intricate schematic, far too detailed to read without amplifying it by sections. His hands flew across the tactiface; he knew what he needed. The space expansion/compression series, the heart of A-Warp. The Elementals sucking him into their spells had been redolent of A-Warp, a translight drive that operated in a manner analogous to an airplane wing.

That's not a coincidence, either, he thought.

A theorist grounded in the ethereal sciences, Culann possessed a cursory understanding of A-Warp, the equations reluctantly yielding their clues to his perusal. Who do I know who can help me with this? he wondered.

One of his ex-wives was a propulsion engineer at Nerolead Interstellar. He considered for a moment contacting her.

He split the screen between the expansion and compression sections, threads of each attenuating across the chasm as though the equations were stretched beyond their capacities to hold the theory together. The negative energy density of its exotic matter generator failed to attenuate the theory enough, and the instability introduced not a stabilized, traversable snake-burrow but a one-way tube-end, the three-dimensional equivalent of a box canyon. The A-Warp theory shredded to pieces in front of him.

Culann blinked, the expansion/compression sections unchanged before him.

Did I really see that? he wondered.

The phenomenology of Neo Druidry fell under the rubric of Astral Physics, its practice the subject of Culann's study for twenty-five years. He'd once studied their mysteries as a young man, but only his intractable perseverance in scientific pedantry had prevented him from advancing through their esoteric abstrusities. That, and Druidry's refusal to acquiesce to documented, scientific experimentation.

Culann had propounded to the Druid elite the benefits of establishing for posterity the scientific underpinnings of their mysticism, but they'd dismissed his pleas as heretical.

A-Warp lent itself as a model to Gael Gate operations precisely because the portals were traversable. Their obscure control by a cabalist group of elite Druids did little to enamor them to a skeptical public and an inquisitive academia. But just as conventional physicists dismissed the discipline of Astral Physics as quackery or worse, so too did Druidry dismiss it as a reductionist scheme to discredit mysticism.

Science and Religion had battled thus for centuries, Culann simply the current martyr that each side crucified in its attempts to legitimize itself, neither willing to accept the idea that both were simply points on a continuum.

He sighed, seeing little hope of bringing both sides together.

And now the Gael Gates were coming apart.

As the A-Warp theory had just now, in front of Professor Culann Penrose.

Chapter 4

Finnán Cadeyrn, Druid to the Potentate of Alrakis, Dylan MacAskill, met Professor Culann Penrose at the spaceport. "Fine fix we're in, isn't it? Not only that, but they send a soft-shoe apostate to investigate. Brewed any spirits in that lab of yours, Professor? Or just some fine Scotch whiskey?"

"Spirits haunting me wherever I go, Finn. Spirits, spirits everywhere, and not a bloody drop to drink." The two men threw their heads back and laughed, then fell into each others' arms. Other travelers glanced askance at them and wove their way around the two men.

Finnán held him at arms' length to look him up and down. "How are you, boy? A bit thin in the face and thick in the belly, but aren't we all, eh?"

"Comes from not enough good company, old man. Good to see you after all these years. You haven't changed a mite."

Finnán Cadeyrn stood six-four, was barrel-chested and hairy, beard to his belt. He wore his usual Druidry robes, the faint bluing of age to the black fabric, and a cravat with a stars-and-moon print tied under his beard. Brash did not do him justice. "Aye, but the Potentate keeps me busy, MacAskill does," the Druid said. "Come on, let's get to the Tepe. I'm itchin' to get my gates working again."

The two men headed for the hovers, banter bouncing between them, Culann trying to figure how long it'd been since he'd seen his old mentor.

As they left the spaceport, Cadeyrn pointed out the battleship Tylwyth Teg on the tarmac, the ship now legendary for its part in the battle at Eltanin. "Disturbs me, Culann, that her skipper was the one sucked into the gate. Captain Niamh Lozac'h is revered in Galatia, as fine a pilot as ever known. We're all worried about her."

"What was she doing on guard duty at the stele?"

"What she was supposed to be doing, Bag an Noz bless her—guarding the stele! Not one to shirk a duty, Captain Lozac'h. What'd you find on Galicia and Alcyone? Nearly simultaneous disappearances, I'm told."

"No trace of the victims, unfortunately. I ordered the release of Druid Lubri, whose only crime was trying to scare the archeologist."

"And drinking too much queimada," Finnán interjected.

"Which we've all been known to do," retorted Culann. "The gates bore not a hint of residue."

He and Finnán exchanged a glance, both knowing what that meant. Invoking the powers inevitably left residues of both the powers invoked and the Druid who'd invoked them.

"What the Uilebheist do you suppose is happening, Cull?"

"I wish I knew, Finn. I wish I knew." Culann sighed, watching the countryside. Göbekli Tepe stood some sixty miles south of the Capital, Ancyra. The landscape was sere and rocky, the desert planet more temperate nearer the poles. "Those incantations you taught me came in handy."

"Eh? You know it's blasphemy to use them. The Ministry will require a report." He threw a knowing glance at Culann. "What happened?"

Culann told him about being drawn into the air at Las Cogotas, and then into the earth at Stonehenge.

"Shielded yourself at both with an invocation?" Finnán asked.

"And if it's the Well, the Fire, and the Tree, then I've knocked out two of three. By the way, I've asked Druidess Sionann Lìosach here in case something goes awry."

"That sultry wench? She could make a man's cherries tingle if she could find a kind word in her. Probably waiting for us at the Tepe. What's her lens on events?"

"Didn't seem to have one, really, but then, she doesn't preside over her own gates, either. Doesn't seem to evince the same urgency for getting the gates back open as Lady Gwilym. Did my crew arrive all right?"

"They're out there, itching to crawl through the stele now. Five complaints already from the local cabal, but they're a fractious bunch of charlatans."

Minor Druids frequently helped the appointed stewards of the Gael Gates, no single person able to operate all the gates at any particular monument, and especially not the twenty gates at such a large installation as Göbekli Tepe, the easternmost terminus of the Gael Federation.

"What about the guard?" Culann checked his notes. "Cadet Phelan Brogimāros?"

"Regular bloke, enlisted a year ago from Delta Cephei II, three months out of basic."

"Anything unusual about his demeanor?"

"Eh? Unusual?"

Culann described Proctor Medraut Bhodhsa's anomalous responses when asked about apprentice Llewellyn Gutraidh's disappearance.

"Not that I noted. Sounds as bedeviled as that besotted clurichaun at Las Cogotas. Not like Mede at all. I'll bet he didn't take a liking to your arrival." The clurichaun was the equivalent of a drunken leprechaun.

"He was overjoyed," Culann said flatly.

Finnán bellowed a brazen laugh. "Here we are, through this culvert and up."

Several hovers like theirs sat parked at a set of low barracks, beyond them a gate with a heavy guard. All but two of the guards wore the green uniforms of her Lady's personal retinue.

"Druidess Lìosach is here, I see," Finnán said, a shudder working its way visibly up his spine.

Even though Lìosach was as feared for her influence with the Lady Gwilym as for her skills, Culann was glad she was here. Whatever had plagued him at the obeliscos of Las Cogotas and at the trilithons of Stonehenge might be wary to attack him at the stele of Göbekli Tepe.

Or so Culann Penrose hoped.

#

"What happened, Phelan?" They occupied a drab interview room the next building over from the barracks, the Spartan quarters at Göbekli Tepe lacking the slightest comfort. Behind Culann, observing, were the two Druids, Sionann and Finnán.

The young Cadet looked at him, blinking. Cadet Brogimāros had been confined to quarters for dereliction of duty, pending court martial.

Ironic, Culann thought, that his only dereliction was in leaving Captain Lozac'h alone inside the Ring. All the monument sites were sacred ground, never to be entered unless necessary, and never alone. One did not abandon one's peers in the Ring.

Phelan shook his head slowly, his gaze withdrawn. "It was cold, deathly cold, Sir. Captain Lozac'h asked me to walk the perimeter opposite her, and I …decided to stay. Then she commed me, said she saw something, and ordered me to meet her on the other side."

"Which way did you go?"

"West, Sir, opposite her. Before I got around the ring, she commed again, said , 'I saw something again, center ring, between the northernmost pair.' I found her at the north gate, Sir. While we each checked our weapons, we took turns keeping our gazes on the gate, and then we entered the ring."

Culann watched carefully, knowing Jamie was capturing the interview.

"We approached the center ring, and…" Phelan paused, his stare blank. "Just as we got there, she said, 'It was nothing. I was mistaken. Go on back; I'll follow in a moment.'" The blank stare fled, and Phelan looked at his interrogators. "She ordered me to leave her."

"What happened then?"

"I…when I got to the Ring, I looked back and didn't see her. That was when I commed base command, Sir."

Culann asked the young man to reenact the scene, using the wall as the center ring.

The Cadet positioned himself against the opposite wall, hand at shoulder ready with a mock weapon, his back to Captain Lozac'h. He moved across the room in a half-crouch. "We approached the center ring, and …" Phelan paused, his stare blank.

"Stop."

"Just as we got there—"

"I said, 'Stop,' Cadet," Culann repeated.

The gaze cleared, the face bewildered. "Sir? I mustn't have heard you."

Culann glanced at Jamie, who gave him a nod. The Cadet's aura had dimmed at the pause. "Thank you, Cadet." He glanced over at his colleagues, the two Druids. "Do either of you have questions for Cadet Brogimāros?"

Both of them shook their heads, their faces impassive.

"You're free to return to your quarters, Cadet. Thank you."

"Thank you, Sir." He saluted and left, the mystified look still on his face.

Culann waited a few moments, then turned to the two Druids. "Shall we go up to the stele?"

"What's the point, Professor?" Sionann asked. "It's clear he's guilty."

Finnán snorted. "It's clear he's innocent."

"Nothing's clear," Culann reminded them. "Three people are missing by means we still haven't divined." He looked at Sionann. "I'll be recommending that the charges be dropped, Dame Lìosach. It's clear a geis has been laid upon him."

"Geis or no geis, he left Captain Lozac'h in the Ring."

"And you'd also recommend similar censure for Druid Lubri and Proctor Bhodhsa?" Culann asked. "I know you've not an iota of sympathy for the provincial, but your own mentor?"

Druidess Lìosach stared at him. "Bode's an incompetent fool."

"The important question is, will Lubri cate himself to an early grave?" Finnán said. "We all find a way to take our departures, don't we, Cull?"

Chuckling at the pun, Culann stood and headed out the door, bemused by Lìosach. About five years his junior, she seemed fixed in her biases, not a good trait in a Druid.

He stopped at the guard kiosk, saluted the cadet and glanced along the ring to the east, the direction that Captain Lozac'h had gone.

The two Druids caught up with him, having a heated conversation, Jamie right behind them.

Culann gestured for silence, his senses tuned. "Sionann, Finnán, take the west perimeter, please. Cadet," he said to the guard in the kiosk, "would you accompany me to the east?"

"Yes, Sir!" The young woman muttered something into her com. "Alerting command is all."

"Keep your eyes on the center ring, in particular," Culann advised his colleagues. "We'll meet on the north side and approach the center ring just as the other two did."

They both gave him a nod. Jamie with his multi-lensed mega-arthropod on his shoulder also nodded to indicate his readiness.

Two hundred dun-brown stele stood sentinel like a parched, petrified forest. Ten stele to each ring, the twenty rings varied in size, one large ring at the center, five medium rings surrounding it, and fourteen small rings encircling them all, about half the stele having capstones. The afternoon sun blazed down upon already-baked stone, not a weed growing inside the ring, the slight knoll occluding the opposite side. Like its counterparts, ancient invocations kept the ring clear of obstruction.

Culann followed a path around the ring, worn there by hundreds of years of patrol, keeping his gaze on the center ring, where all the stele had capstones. The stele varied in height from ten to twenty-five feet, the capstones of proportionate size. But all the stones were one foot by two feet, a divine dimension.

At the eastern terminus, Culann stopped, sensing ... something.

The ghost of experience. Captain Lozac'h stopped here, he knew.

Cadet Phelan hadn't been able to tell them where she'd been when she commed him the first time, but Culann knew it was here, her resonance occupying the space where he stood.

He looked up at the stars, trying to pick out the other Henge systems—the Pleiades, Ophiuchus, Puppis, Gamma Doradus, and Tucana.

Why am I trying in daylight? he wondered. "Did you feel that, Cadet?"

"Sir?"

"What's your name, by the way? I'm Culann Penrose."

"Cadet Ensign Piritta Quemener, Sir, at your command."

"Any magic in you, young lady?"

"Not by half, Sir. I couldn't get a spell to arrange its own letters, Sir."

Culann nodded. "And you've no sense then that anything took place here, on this spot? Not to worry, Cadet." He looked through the stele toward the center ring, dun-brown stone on soil of similar color. He blocked out the glare of afternoon sun with his hand.

The edge lines of megalith defined where the stele were, inert, without residue of invocation.

He continued on around the perimeter.

As he approached the north gate, the other two approached from the other side. "I sensed where Captain Lozac'h stopped to com Cadet Brogimāros," he told them.

Druidess Lìosach pursed her lips as though to object to something.

"In good time, Druidess, you'll see why you're needed here." He turned to his videographer. "Jamie, keep imaging until we've all left the Ring, eh?"

"Yes, Professor," Jamie replied, his bug-eyed machine fixed to his shoulder like some parasitic alien.

He looked at Cadet Quemener, saw how she was armed. "Finn, all the guards here armed that way?" he asked the other Druid.

"Aye, Cull. We thought it prudent ever since the Eltanin tribes poured through these gates."

"But you've had no trouble from them in the meantime?"

Finnán grinned. "Not after Captain Lozac'h pounded their planet, we haven't."

"Finn, you and Cadet Quemener watch from here. Dame Lìosach, come with me. Let's enter together."

"Eh? Enter the Ring with an apostate like you?" she sneered. "I'd sooner hack out my own kidney with a spoon than condone your tainting sacred ground."

"Nothing sacrosanct here, Nann," Finnán said. "The ancient prohibition merely specifies that no one's to enter the Ring alone. Captain Lozac'h and Cadet Brogimáros entered the Ring together, and neither's an initiate."

Culann was glad of Finnán's presence. As the presiding Druid at Göbekli Tepe, Druid Cadeyrn was final arbiter over who could and couldn't enter the Ring.

"Then there bloody well should be some prohibition against apostates." Sionann raised an eyebrow at Finnán, and then looked at Culann. "You'll answer for anything that happens, Professor."

"One of my intentions in asking you here is that nothing does. Shall we, Dame?" He gestured.

Together, they entered the ring, stepping over the narrow stone ridge.

"There, no lightning from a cloudless sky," Culann said, trying to disguise his relief and trying not to grin at Sionann. He stepped toward the central ring of ten stele, fixing his gaze there, where the main gates were.

"By all the gods of Tír na nÓg, old man, I'll flay you alive if this is all a fool's errand," she muttered, her gaze too on the central ring.

"So, I'm to be punished if something happens, and flayed alive if it doesn't." Culann disliked having to keep his gaze on the innermost ring with the Druidess right beside him. Much too tempting for her, he was sure.

The two of them skirted a small outer ring. The sensations from it were redolent of transits to minor worlds in the Ophiuchus and Puppis constellations. The next ring they passed was one of the four middle rings, these ten stele having five caps among them. Two capped stele exuded traces of recent transits, these to Tucana, the stele of a size to rival the smallest megaliths in the innermost ring.

"No recent transits to the Pleiades or Gamma Doradus," Sionann muttered.

He'd wondered if she too could sense recent ethereal activity, the skill somewhat rare even amongst the Druidry. Culann heightened his awareness as they approached the innermost ring, the two northernmost stele among the tallest, easily topping twenty-five feet, their capstones nearly touching across the ten-foot gap between them.

"Now there's an oddity," she said. "No traces of essence at all."

As they sidled closer, Culann couldn't detect any either. The solid stone blocks exhibited no residue of invocation, not of Captain Lozac'h's disappearance, nor of any transit before that, despite the innermost ring having the most active gates of the twenty rings at Göbekli Tepe.

He'd wanted to ask Finnán about the number and frequency of transits, and had forgotten. He turned northward to wave the big Druid in.

A whirlpool sucked Sionann headfirst into its maw, guzzling thirstily, and Culann lunged for a foot. A calfskin boot slipped from his grip but he cast a hold with his will and stopped her slide into oblivion, the funnel of water slurping off toward the gate itself. He followed its spiral into the distance, an interminable distance.

Air, earth, water, he thought. "Otherworld Elementals, belay, I say! Unhand this maid to me today!"

And the water reversed course and inundated him, pushing her into him and sending them both sprawling, awash in water and spluttering for air.

"Ye blasted brollachan!" Sionann spouted, blowing mist from her mouth. "Are you possessed? What in the devil's name did you douse me for?"

Culann sat up and wiped the water off his face to look at her. "Twasn't me, Nann. The Elementals nearly siphoned you off to nowhere."

Finnán and Quemener came running up, splashing through the small flood. "Are you all right?"

Culann nodded.

Getting to her feet, Sionann snarled, "Of course, I'm not all right! Oh, dear Cridwen, look at me!" Her blouse and skirt clung to her form and left little to the imagination.

Finnán gave her a thorough glance, perusing her up and down and grinning ear to ear.

"Don't look at me like that!"

"But you just said—"

She shook her fist in his face. "Don't tempt me, Druid! My boots are ruined! Soaked through and through! What the bloody hell are you laughing at?"

But Culann too was holding his sides and loosing his laughter to the sky, the prim Druidess pouting over her calfskin boots a risible sight indeed.

Finnán helped him to his feet, the Cadet attending to the Druidess.

Sionann pointed a finger at Culann. "You'll pay for this, Apostate!" And she stormed off south, toward her hover, threading her way between the circles.

"I'll talk to her," the Cadet said, adding over her shoulder, "What can she do, turn me into a newt?"

Culann and Finn both laughed, shaking their heads. Then Finnán looked him over. "You look intact, Cull. You'll live, I daresay."

"Glad to hear it, Finn. You see what happened?"

"Did indeed, young man. Don't worry about Nann; she'll recover too. How about some dry clothes?"

"First, let's get Cadet Brogimāros out of confinement, eh?"

Chapter 5

Earth, Water, Air, and Fire. Aboard his yacht, Culann considered the four major Elementals.

The four classical Elementals, with their corresponding mythic beings—gnomes, undines, sylphs, and salamanders—had been studied for centuries, their various schools feeding frenzily upon subtle differences of power between the Elementals.

Don't forget the fifth, he told himself. Aether, more often spelled without the initial 'a,' wasn't very influential, had very few proponents or even advocates, was rarely invoked or contemplated, and as such remained much of an enigma even within the enigmatic sciences of Neo Druidry.

An irony that it's the most plentiful Elemental, Culann thought.

Also known as quintessence, ether was the space between worlds, the material filling regions unoccupied by matter. Early astral physicists postulated that ether permeated all available space, even that occupied by matter, providing the medium for light to travel through vacuum. Particle physics had soon disputed that postulate, proving inductively that light was both wave and particle. Wave physics too unstable at the time to oppose their particulate colleagues, this supposition soon became dictum, and ether faded in relevance from physics as a specialization. Further, dark matter and dark energy—the components of ether—were known to constitute together a full eighty-five percent of the universe, the other four Elementals combined making up the remainder.

All superfluous, this study of the Elementals, in Professor Penrose's view.

The four schools of Neo Druidry were four blind people describing an elephant, Culann mused to himself, the A-Warp theory equations splashed across the screens in front of him. Consider in their enormity, the equations occupied the mathematical equivalent of the universe.

That, too, Culann found amusing.

And what mythic being might correspond to the enigmatic fifth Elemental, Ether? he wondered.

He didn't know, and he found the thought overwhelming.

Further, he'd been attacked within the media of three elements: Air, Earth, and Water.

But not Fire.

Not yet.

Or had they been attacks?

Culann didn't know. They'd certainly felt like attacks, and he'd been able to defend himself from each as though they'd been attacks. But if so, then that presupposed an attacker, one with intent to harm, motivation to destroy.

Which begged the question: Why?

The first series of three attacks—victimizing a Druid apprentice, a starship commander, and an archeologist—had appeared random, inflicted spuriously, for no other reason than wrong place, wrong time. The latter series of three, all victimizing him, hadn't been random at all, had appeared to target him, an Astral Physicist. Theories of criminal behavior didn't describe either series of crimes well at all. The nature of the attacks required the attacker to harness a technology little understood by physicists or Druids.

A simile in fiction was Deus ex Machina, Culann thought, or "God from the machine." We know how to turn on the machine, but we don't understand the principles of its operation. Nor am I likely to be rescued at the last minute by some fantastical plot device, the physicist thought.

Ergo, the logic gates of his mind told him, three possibilities are at work here:

One, someone is using the Gates to wreak havoc.

Two, these anomalies are spontaneous, natural phenomena.

Three, a flaw in the technology is causing malfunctions.

"Incoming com," his yacht told him.

He mentally bookmarked his thoughts. "On screen," he said.

The face of the Ceannaire, Lady Ceridwen Gwilym, President of the Gael Federation, appeared before him. "You should be ashamed of yourself, Cull, attempting to give a dirty Druid a bath."

He threw his head back and laughed. All he could do was hold his sides to keep from busting a gut or blowing a hernia.

A smug smile on her face, Ceridwen waited until his mirth subsided.

He wiped away the tears and shook his head at her. "I couldn't resist, Lady. Ignorance tempts the learned to impishness, doesn't it?"

She shook her head at him. "I'm afraid I need to ask a favor, Cull, one not much to your liking."

His amusement settling down, he wasn't surprised, the President known to call on people quite at random to get things done, often placing the com herself. "As long as it doesn't involve bathing more cats, all right?"

"Precisely what it does involve, Cull."

He sobered and nodded. "Well, out with it, Ceri. What do you have?"

"Well, I can't convince my Druid that you had nothing to do with that inundation. Not even the vid you so prudently sent me could convince her otherwise."

He'd anticipated a vitriolic report from Druid Sionann Lìosach, maligning him to the Gods, so he'd commed Jamie's vid of the incident at Göbekli Tepe to President Gwilym. On it, a watery whirlpool engulfed the Druid from inside the gate and clearly would have devoured her without Culann's intervention.

"And how can I help, my Lady?"

"Forever the sycophant, aren't you?"

"Without a whit of irony."

The President snorted at him. "Cull, I need you to take her with you. Bring her fully into your investigation, even to the point of making her your lieutenant, if need be."

Culann's intuition alerted him. "Get her out of your hair."

"She's irrepressible—downright obdurate! Won't let up for a heartbeat! Demands that I fire you every few minutes. If I had an open Gate to assign her to, I'd do that, just to get her out of the palace. I can't get anything done! Cull, help!"

He grinned at the President's discomfiture. "And if she interferes with my investigation?"

"You have my permission to paddle her backside raw."

Again, Culann burst into laughter, and by the time he'd recovered, President Gwilym had thanked him and switched off.

First she asks me to do the impossible, the physicist thought, and then she asks me to manage the unmanageable.

The pity is she knows exactly how much she can ask of me, he thought, guessing it would push him to his limits.

#

Druidess Sionann Lìosach took one look at his yacht and said, "We're taking mine."

Culann raised an eyebrow at her and looked across the spaceport toward her ship.

Hers wasn't a yacht. A squat, powerful, patrol-class vessel surrounded by guards sat menacing in its own corner, as though eager to attack any who approached. "A gremlin," he said, the brand familiar. "How fitting."

"Thank you," she said. "Let's go."

They crossed the spaceport tarmac of the Capital planet, Alcyone, its primary of the same name among the dimmest of the seven sisters of the Pleiades. Culann had returned to the Capital in his ship, having wondered what Sionann had in mind for their travel.

A small valise in hand, Culann followed her. The ring of guards parted for them, and they walked up the ramp. The inside was plush, thick carpet woven from the wool of Esankios sheep, walls paneled with Zizonti wood slats, brass-mounted hand-rails of Aleites reeds, light fixtures molded from Sleitom crystal. The materials exuded their origins, their essence emanating brightly, as if proud to serve the Druidess Lìosach.

All of it, Culann realized, of Celtiberian origin.

"Your quarters are that way, Professor," Sionann said, gesturing down a corridor. Beside her, a spiral staircase carved from the core of a giant Uerzoniti cephalopod wound its way upward. "My quarters are the next level up, and above them are the galley and the cockpit. Make yourself at home, Professor. I understand we're in for a journey."

"A few minutes to settle in is all I'll need. Meet in the galley in ten minutes, perhaps?"

She shrugged at him. "As you wish." And she slipped up the stairs like a wraith.

Culann stepped into his stateroom, appointed as lavishly as the corridor. A small desk sat opposite a compact kitchen. Beyond that, a portal opened onto the bedroom and lavatory, which but for its modest dimensions was palatial in all other ways. He sensed that the desk was a last minute addition, put in place of what had been a small dining area, a concession to Culann's propensity for frequent study.

He set his valise on the desk. "Import data files," he said aloud.

The desk lit up, the screen brightening. "Confirming identity, importing data. All data uploaded, Professor. Welcome aboard."

So at least he could resume his cogitations, and do so in luxury.

Having been attacked by three Elementals, Air, Earth, and Water, but not by the fourth, Fire, indicated where they needed to go next. In the day it'd taken him to return to Alcyone, Culann had drafted a summary for the Druidess Lìosach, she who'd become his unwilling investigative partner. She had to know what they were facing.

The vibration under his feet was so subtle, Culann might have missed it. Liftoff? he wondered, a slight shift in weight the only indication they'd launched.

He stepped into the corridor and over to the stairwell. Up twice around deposited him into a short corridor, one way the cockpit, the other the galley.

"Welcome aboard, Professor," said a voice from the cockpit.

He poked his head in. "Thank you."

"Captain Bébinn Nankivell, at your service, Professor." She grinned at him from around her chaise. "Just call me Bébe."

Stars streaking past on the display behind her indicated that they indeed were on their way already. "Pleased to meet you, Bébe. Nankivell, eh? Solid Cornish name, like my own. Out of Taygeta Five, like myself?"

They shook. "No, Sir, Alcyone Six, but my in-laws are from Newquay, my wife born on Taygeta, in Perranporth."

"Ah, across the berm from me own hometown, Mevagissey. Call me Cull, Captain."

"Yes, Sir. Pleasure's mutual. Your work's admired all over Taygeta." She winked at him. "Your reputation precedes you."

"Which reputation is that?" he asked, winking back. They shared a laugh.

"Where we off to, Cull? Always wanted to see Canopus, myself."

"Well, I can't help you there. Tucana, is my thought, where our Celtalpine brethren practice the Druidry of heat."

"So it's Fire we're after, eh?" Druidess Lìosach said behind him. She beckoned him into the galley.

"Set course for Tucana, Lady?"

"Yes, Captain, Tucana, it is."

"Aye, course set, Lady. I hope the Golaseccans and Cisalpines have settled their little dispute."

The two branches had been skirmishing over Fire ideology since their origins from Celtalpine Gaul on Terra before the Diaspora, one declaring the supremacy of cold, the other propounding on the dominance of heat. Not unlike the doctrinal differences between Lilliput and Blefuscu over which end of the egg to crack at breakfast.

Culann retreated to the galley with Sionann, where he saw she already had his summary displayed. He looked at it, bemused, as he hadn't provided her with it.

"I took the liberty of—"

"Invading my privacy," he said, indignant.

"Becoming conversant with our objectives," she finished. "Rather interesting possibilities that you've come up with. A technological flaw causing malfunctions seems the least likely of the three."

He wondered what other personal areas of his life she'd availed herself to. "I'm partial to the spontaneous natural phenomena, myself."

"I think someone's using the Gates to wreak havoc, frankly."

"Well, at least, we'll have plenty of lively repartee, won't we?"

"I can't say I've ever felt impoverished in that respect."

"That was my impression." Culann tried not to grin.

Sionann had a slight wrinkle to her brow, as though slowly arriving at the conclusion … "I think I've just been insulted."

"There was one subject I failed miserably at charm school," he quipped. "How to insult people without their knowing it."

"I've always abided by the dictum, 'If you can't say something nice, make up something nasty.' "

"Not part of the curriculum, if I recall. Oh, but that wasn't charm school you went to, was it?"

"Certainly wasn't."

The two of them looked each other over, a Lilliputian and Blefuscucian at odds over ends.

"I'm not here because I want to be," she said.

"A livid Ceannaire is quite an addition to your curriculum vitae, eh? I've a long list of incensed Druids on mine. Care to join them?"

"Done."

"We'll get along fabulously."

#

Culann stepped off the Sughmaire—the odd name Sionann had given her ship—onto the tarmac at Tucana Prime, a brittle planet a mere half-AU from its spectroscopic binary, Alpha Tucanae. Its two suns, an orange subgiant and a red dwarf, both operated at a combined temperature of 4.3 Kelvin, barely enough to heat the innermost planet. The remaining twenty-two planets were uninhabitable balls of ice. Tucana Prime wasn't exactly a tropical world either. Snow-capped mountains towered over the spaceport, piles of stone and ice so forbidding they threatened to fall upon the tarmac.

Culann pulled his parka tight, a light dusting of snow whipping across the ground at his feet. Sionann was right behind him, like him hurrying for the terminal.

A trio of thick-robed Druids scurried out to greet them.

"Scathach Ogham of the Exalted Martyrology," the woman in the lead said, her robes brown. She gestured at her colleagues. "Armel Gallou of Golasecca and Óengus Tàillear of Cisalpina, respectively." The Golaseccan wore robes of red, his Cisalpine brother robes of white.

"Armel!" Sionann said, stepping past Culann and throwing her arms around the smaller of the two Druids behind Ogham. "You're looking well, my friend. I haven't seen you since we pestered Proctor Bhodhsa with questions at Stonehenge. Let's get inside before the frost bites our asses."

"Good to see you too, Nann," Armel said, flourishing a hand at her. A glowing lizard leapt from his hand to her shoulder. "There, is that better? Nothing like a little fire spell to beat back the cold."

Of course, Culann thought, and he conjured a penumbra of warmth for himself.

"Much better, Mel, thank you. I was wondering how everyone here tolerates the cold."

After handshakes all around, they repaired to the terminal anyway, such spells transient, Culann's dissipating quickly.

"What brings you and Druidess Lìosach to Tucana, Professor?" Druidess Ogham asked.

"The Fanum at Montefortino di Arcevia, in the Province of Ancona," Culann said.

"Our paradise in the Appenines," she replied. "Haven't divined why the ancients put our Gates way up in the mountains, but there they are. No surprise the salamander is our constant companion, eh?"

The modern plasteel and glascrete terminal seemed packed, passengers jostling each other in long lines at check-in kiosks and baggage terminals. Many of the travelers looked piqued and anxious.

"You'll get the gates up and running soon, won't you, Professor?" Druidess Ogham asked. "I don't know how long we'll be able to withstand this crush. Aren't enough interstellar flights. Half the people here are on standby."

Culann had seen similar crowding at other spaceports. The increasing public outcry at the inadequate number of flights, the crowded terminals, the delays, the lost luggage, and the sudden economic slowdown were putting tremendous pressure on the government to open the gates.

We'd better find our three missing citizens soon, Culann thought, their families frantic.

The large hover at the curb was already weighted down with their luggage, behind it the equipment van with Professor Culann's investigative team ready to follow.

He settled himself into a seat. "Are all three of you coming with us to the Fanum?" he asked the trio of Druids. "Fanum" was the ancient word for "sanctuary."

They looked amongst themselves. "Any time we get a visiting dignitary," Druid Gallou said, throwing a smirk at his Cisalpine colleague. "We live there, Professor."

"It's an uncomfortable arrangement," Druid Tàillear added, "having our three factions represented every time an interstellar luminary deigns to visit."

"Golaseccans and Cisalpines and who else?"

"The Senones," Druidess Ogham said. "We operate the gates at Montefortino di Arcevia."

The triumvirate is the most unstable of political structures, Culann thought. If any single one of them fails, the structure falls apart. He watched the scenery around them through the light, brittle mist. Pine forest eked out nutrients from rocky escarpments. The road between blocky, ice-capped boulders looked barely wide enough for the hover.

"Any untoward activity at the gates?"

"Nothing like the events elsewhere," Ogham said, shooting him a glance. "Why here?"

"Earth, Air, Water, and Fire," Culann said. "The other three gates correspond to the first three Elementals, their Druids proponents of that element. Montefortino is a Fire Gate. Any missing persons reports, Druidess Ogham?"

"Call me Scathe, Professor. No need to be so formal. Let me check on that, would you? Given the environment, we're bound to have a few missing persons. Proctor Gwrtheyrn Jézéquel hasn't been seen in a few days, but that's not unusual. She's practically in her dotage. You're asking about persons reported missing at or near the Sanctuary, though, correct?"

Culann nodded, adding, "About the time of the other occurrences."

The Druidess mumbled something, her hand to her ear.

"Inevitably find them during a thaw," Armel said.

"Can't get them to wear emitters," Druid Tàillear said. "Golaseccans want to live in the Stone Age."

"Speak for yourself, caveman," Armel retorted.

"Contain yourselves, gentlemen," Scathe said, glancing between them. "I've placed a request for missing persons reports for all of the Appenines. I'll have them cull the unlikely ones."

The ride wasn't very comfortable, despite the smoothly operating hover.

"Scathe," Sionann asked, "how's the Druidry taking the shutdown?"

"Not well," Druidess Ogham said, "Idle hands salt the stew with deviltry."

Culann grinned at the adage. "How many gates at the Sanctuary?"

"Nine megaliths in three trios, twelve gates total. One of the smaller Henges, to be sure, but serving the entire constellation. We're nearly cut off without them, Cull." Druid Scathach Ogham frowned, glancing first at Armel Gallou and then at Óengus Tàillear.

Neither of the other two Druids met her gaze.

Culann exchanged a glance with Sionann.

#

They stood just outside the ring.

The Henge exuded power, nine megaliths of divine proportion arranged in divine geometry. Each stone measuring one foot by two feet by nine feet, three megaliths spaced nine feet apart, each making a triangle, and each triangle placed nine feet from the other triangles at the vertices of a larger triangle. The Ring was encircled by a low, foot-wide, knee-high stone wall, which but for its cap of snow, looked perfect for sitting. Inside the Ring, bare triangular flagstones tessellated the ground. Beyond the Henge was dense, impenetrable forest, the jumbled landscape of boulder hushed under its perennial blanket of snow.

Culann counted the gates again, beholding the geometric wonder of manifesting twelve gates from nine stones.

Inside the ring, half-a-dozen salamanders scrambled around, hissing at wisps of cold. The slim fuaranders were a pure-white antithesis to their reptilian counterparts, but identical in size and shape, like antimatter.

Suddenly, Culann understood the local schism.

The brown-robed Senones mediated the long-simmering conflict between the red-robed Golaseccans and the white-robed Cisalpines. Never mind that they're all Druids, he thought.

Behind him was the monastery where all the Druids lived. The round, domed structure was painted three different colors.

Not unlike the schism between Magic and Science, Culann thought, bemused, glancing at Sionann, who'd been uncharacteristically quiet.

"You're not proposing to enter the ring, are you?" Druidess Ogham asked.

"Not without proper escort."

"But you can't," Druid Gallou said.

"You've not been initiated," Druid Tàillear said.

"Well, at least Golaseccan and Cisalpine agree on something," Professor Penrose said.

The two Druids looked at each other, as though mutually offended.

"Ready, Jamie?" Culann glanced over at his videographer.

"Aye, Sir." Jamie stood nearby, his bug-eyed alien vidgear consuming his shoulder.

Culann nodded to Sionann, and the two of them stepped into the Ring. Immediately, his senses focused, and the traces of a recent transit lay apparent to his senses. Unlike the other three Henges, where he'd detected no trace of the transits that had snatched three innocent souls into oblivion.

"There it is," Sionann said.

The shape itself was in the central hexagram. Culann extended his hands toward the shroud, and a face manifested. The vestiges of destination were absent from the energy, as though the person had gone nowhere.

Or nowhen.

"No destination, as though the person just disappeared into the ether," Sionann said.

Culann glanced at her. He'd not shared that portion of his Elemental theory with her, that the fifth Elemental, Ether, which comprised eighty-five percent of the universe, might itself be the force at work in the Gael Gate abnormalities. "You're remarkably intuitive," he murmured.

And he gestured that they approach the gate.

"I forbid it!" Druid Óengus Tàillear rushed into the Ring and stood between them and the gate, the white-robed Cisalpine spreading his arms to block their approach, white fuaranders skittering frantically around his feet.

"You have no authority to do so, Druid," Sionann said. "Step aside, or face Ministry censure and Federation prosecution."

"Your muddy furrow stinks of miasma, succubus!"

"Your microscopic obelisk spouts green, putrid slime, incubus!"

Culann put his hand on her arm. "Is it my presence you object to, Druid Tàillear?"

"Apostate blasphemer, you'll meet Arawn anon and suffer all the torments you deserve!"

"Druid!" Scathach snapped.

His gaze whipped toward her.

"Professor Penrose is here to get the gates open. Stand aside, man!"

"I'll not, I tell you! This—"

"Take my place, Druid Tàillear," Culann interrupted.

The gaze whipped back to him. "Eh? What'd you say?"

"Take my place, Druid, and investigate this wraith yourself. I don't mind." Culann stepped back and invited the Cisalpine to stand where he'd stood. "Druidess Lìosach, accept his presence for mine, please."

"Certainly, Professor." Sionann smiled at Tàillear, a cat at a mouse.

Druid Óengus Tàillear glanced between Culann and Sionann, between the devil and the deep blue sea. "All right," he said, his chin up in challenge to Culann, "I will!" He hiked his white robes and stepped to Sionann's side to face the gate.

Together, the two Druids stepped forward.

A funnel of Frost and Fire swirled out of the gate and plucked Tàillear from where he stood, his scream already distant.

"Ether delay and Druid stay!" Culann blurted, already too late. The portal was closed, and only an afterimage was left of Frost and Fire, wind gusting around the Henge.

Sionann crumpled beside the megalith.

He and Scathach rushed to her side. She was barely breathing, her pulse faint. "Help me," he said, and the two of them carried her from the Ring.

Druid Armel Gallou stepped past them into the Ring, mouth agape, his gaze fixed to the Gate. "Gnomes, undines, sylphs, and salamanders, give back my brother Tàillear, whom you claim too soon!"

Culann and Scathach lay Sionann on path outside the rim.

"Armel, no!" Scathach said.

Druid Gallou stepped up to the gate. "Return my brother, I say!"

"Ether, no, spare Gallou," Cullen muttered, extending both hands toward the figure.

Another funnel swirled ominously in between the megaliths, fuarander and salamander spinning furiously, a blizzard gusting above the Henge.

Culann felt the pull, the whorl making a nimbus around the Druid, mesmerizing.

Druidess Ogham stepped up beside him. "Elementals all, give way and leave be." She twirled both hands above her head and then thrust them toward the ground, palms down.

The funnel of Frost and Fire subsided, retreated into the gate, and vanished.

Druid Gallou turned on them. "I almost had him back, you fools!" He was still the only one inside the Ring. He turned as though to try again.

"Armel, no!" Scathach said again.

Druid Gallou vanished in a flash, the funnel there and gone.

Culann knelt, dismayed, sure they'd both been taken to the other side. "Arawn, take them to Tír na nÓg forthwith, I pray."

Sionann raised her head and looked around. "What happened?"

He stepped to her side to help her up.

"Another two souls have been taken by the Gael Gates." Scathach said, staring forlornly at the Henge.

Chapter 6

"That's Procter Gwrtheyrn Jézéquel," said Druidess Scathach Ogham of the Exalted Martyrology of the image Culann pointed to.

"Yes, that's the person I saw," Sionann corroborated.

They'd repaired to the monastery scriptorium, where disciples of all three orders had quickly gathered, grim at the terrible events that had just taken place, not one but two of their brethren, principal Druids both, obliterated by a whirling dervish of fuaranders and salamanders.

Acolytes had brought them bound volumes containing registries of their fellow practitioners.

"I thought she'd gone on sabbatical," said one Druid, his brown robe synched with a blue sash. He stood at a podium, a quill poised above a scroll, beside him a basket of bleached vellum, ready for his scrawl. Shelves towered nearly to the ceiling around the room, placed at haphazard angles, many with ladders leaning against them, bound volumes in leather on the shelves, the essence of aldehyde scenting the air. "I'm Proctor Seznec, Yezekael Seznec," the man said.

"Pleased," Culann said. "And Proctor Jézéquel has been gone how long now?"

"Three, four days," Seznec said. "She was wont to wander, somewhat senescent, didn't have assigned duties, not at her age."

"Inclined to folly, at all?" Culann asked.

"Disinclined, if anything," Scathach said, "the picture of propriety." She glanced at Seznec, drawing her black sash tight.

Seznec nodded in agreement.

"Druidess Lìosach and I will return to the Henge alone." Culann held up his hand to the numerous objections. "No reason any of you should risk your lives.

We now have six disappearances into the Gael Gates, and death disregards all doctrinal differences."

"You can't go out in that," Druidess Ogham said, pointing to the upper windows of the Scriptorium.

Beyond frosted panes, snow swirled with zeal, eager to devour those unwise enough to venture forth. Fuaranders frolicked just beyond the glasteel panes. The storm had descended even as they'd retreated from the Ring.

"We'll have to," Sionann said. "I'll fashion us a cloak, and not of salamander."

The red-robed Druids around the room glanced among themselves, as though guiltily.

Culann and Sionann headed toward the door. "Perhaps you'd better stay inside, Jamie," he told his videographer.

"Are you certain, Professor? It's not far to the scriptorium entrance."

"Druidess Ogham, do you have a rope?"

Scathach gestured at an acolyte and glanced at Proctor Seznec.

Standing just inside the glasteel door, the cold drawing all warmth from the area, Culann tried to see the Henge just a hundred feet away. A blurry wall of withering white was all that hung outside.

"Professor Penrose, a word if I may?" Scathach asked.

Alone, he divined. Culann gestured at Jamie and Sionann, their parkas already up over their heads.

"Forgive me, Cull, but we've not been completely forthright."

"There are undercurrents here to undermine any foundation. But go on," he added with a smile.

"Procter Jézéquel and Druids Gallou and Tàillear were dabbling in other elementals." She looked down and away. "Initially, with my permission. But when they began to fuse them—and not just fuarander and salamander, but across elemental—I objected and demanded that they cease."

"And you think they carried on in secret." It wasn't a question.

"I do, Cull." She looked side to side, pursing her mouth, her brows drawn.

He could see she was frightened. "There are three other disappearances, Scathe."

"But three of them here alone. And Procter Jézéquel …" Her voice became faint. "She wasn't right."

"Proctor Seznec mentioned senescence."

"Sharper than tacks, she was, but bent." She glanced out the door. "It's begun to hail." Knuckle-size balls of ice smashed on the flagstones outside the door and drummed on the roof.

Culann brought his gaze down from the ceiling. "Bent, as in determined?"

"Warped, the fabric of her thoughts so wrinkled that her mind had begun to fray."

Taken aback, Culann looked at her quizzically. "Compressed in front and attenuated behind?" he said, intuiting from her imbalanced aura what she was trying to say.

"That's it exactly," Scathach said. "Much better than my own analogy."

A-Warp, he thought, puzzled it should come to mind at all. He looked out toward the Henge, still invisible behind the scree of storm. The fundamental mechanics behind translight travel, Alcubierre Warp Theory was also thought to govern Gael Gate operation, but physicists had failed to establish its articulation, no matter what their discipline. Even Astral Physics, Culann's specialty, had been unable to prove experimentally that the Gael Gates operated on A-Warp.

Not that they don't, Culann reminded himself, just that we haven't proved it. "And you think their experimentation ..."

"Yes, Professor, I do."

And you feel guilty you weren't more proactive in stopping them, he thought.

"I suspected they'd continued, and I wish I'd done more to stop them."

Culann saw Druidess Lìosach had been listening. He'd have done the same. "An odd pair, Druids Gallou and Tàillear?"

"Devout defenders of their own sacraments, and yet able to collaborate in apostasy."

"Thank you, Druidess Ogham." Arguing about angels dancing on the heads of pins, he thought.

Sionann stepped toward them. "Does the weather always get so bitter?"

An aggregate of hail cemented the walk outside the door, but the hail itself had ceased falling. The frolic of the fuarander had subsided somewhat.

"No, not like that," Druidess Ogham said, another worry adding itself to her brow.

Culann pulled his parka hood forward, meeting gazes with Sionann and Jamie.

Together, they stepped to the door.

The Order of Exalted Martyrology certainly seemed adroit at creating martyrs.

#

The storm had ceased the moment they'd stepped from the scriptorium.

"As if it knows we're coming..." Sionann said.

Culann raked his eyes across the sky. Among the ancient texts in the scriptorium behind him were encyclopedic canticles devoted to the worship of weather—and how it might be influenced. Volumes so anachronistic he'd often wondered what value such a medium still held. And yet such scriptoriums thrived.

His thick, fur-lined sodhoppers did little to beat back the cold. He invoked a salamander to warm his feet.

"Is that wise, Cull?" Sionann asked, raising an eyebrow at the creature underfoot.

"Wiser than frostbite," he quipped, looking ahead.

The megaliths stood like frozen spikes in the crisp afternoon air. No snow touched them, as if nothing could stick to the polished stone surfaces. The inside of the ring was clear of snow as well, the tessellated flagstone looking dry despite the heavy snowfall moments ago. The forest beyond was a jumbled wall of white splashed with shades of gray.

They stepped to the knee-high perimeter. He glanced back.

Behind them, the multi-lens trained on them, Jamie gave Culann a single thumb up.

"What are we looking for, Cull?"

"I'm not sure, Nann. You heard what Scathe said?"

"Every word. Sorry for eavesdropping."

"No, you're not, and I'd have done the same, Lass."

She threw him a grin. "Last I was called 'Lass' was at my initiation."

By some crusty, traditionalist Druid probably, Culann thought. "Procter Jézéquel began to fuse the Elementals."

"What do you think Scathe meant by that? Rendering each into its component parts, or forcing the Elementals to mix their fundamental substructures?"

"Not sure, but I inferred the latter." He turned to face the Henge, summoning his strength.

Swirls of fuarander and salamander appeared between all the gates, twelve small funnels of chaos.

"I don't like the look of this, Cull."

"A welcoming committee," he said.

"As if they know," she said.

He expanded his sphere to include her, inviting her to merge her powers with his.

"You're not supposed to have magic, Apostate."

"Imitation is the highest form of flattery. Help me, Nann."

He felt her essentia infiltrate his being, and he knew they were a formidable pair. She was the Druidess extraordinaire, as fine a pick to serve the Ceannaire Lady Gwilym as any. Further, their male-female complement comprised as redoubtable an alchemy as the pairing of matter with anti-matter, of light with anti-light.

"Cull," Jamie said from behind them, "I'm picking up something else above the Henge."

Sionann gasped.

Culann saw it too.

A massing of raw … something. Some visceral entity, too insubstantial to register on any of his five basal senses, something nearly invisible to his magic receptivity, something diaphanous and ethereal.

Of course! he thought, knowing suddenly. "Behold, for we now see before us the mighty Ether," he declared, voice sonorous, arms outstretched as though to welcome some prodigal child.

Druidess Lìosach beside him, Professor Culann Penrose stepped into the Ring.

#

The curious sensation of floating was the first thing to reach his awareness.

Culann couldn't have said what came afterward as reality rushed to fill the void. The ascetic cold of the hospital, the noise of a busy emergency room, the smell of antiseptic battling back the stench of illness, the blaze of lights from banks on the ceiling, the taste of defeat.

He tried to sit up but hands held him to the bed.

"Not so fast, Professor," said the white-coated physician, with a sharp glance at her colleagues.

"Sionann?"

"She's safe, two beds over, just coming to, like yourself."

He relaxed and let them minister to him, trying to recall what happened.

And failing.

He wondered if his videographer had recorded everything. "What about Jamie?"

"The young man with the camera?"

Culann nodded.

"Three beds over, a bit bruised, a broken shoulder, but otherwise intact."

Shoulder …? he wondered, fearing the worst. Whatever it was had wreaked havoc, reaching beyond the Ring to injure Jamie too.

"The others are going to be all right as well, once they're treated." She looked him over. "All the local emergency rooms are overwhelmed. You and Druidess Liosach are damn lucky, you know."

"Eh? Others?" he asked.

"The monastery collapsed, and everyone within two hundred yards sustained some type of injury," the Doctor said.

"But not us," Culann supplied.

"But not you," she confirmed. "Doctor Blodeuwedd Chynoweth." She stuck out her hand.

He shook, feeling drained. Intact, but drained, as though sucked dry of energy. He laid his head back and closed his eyes, as if to sleep. "And the Henge?" He peeked at her.

"Gone, Professor. Disappeared as if sucked into another dimension."

Culann stared at her, disbelieving.

"Or at least, that's what Druidess Ogham tells me."

"Is she all right?"

"A few lacerations to the face when the glasteel shattered, but otherwise unhurt."

He began to get up. Under hospital blankets, he wore only a gown. "Where are my clothes?"

"You're not going anywhere, Professor," Doctor Chynoweth said.

"But I have to go back. I have to see what happened." He looked around for his clothes.

"I can get your cooperation, or I can use restraints. Which would you prefer?"

The Gael Gates on Tucana torn from reality, and the insufferable physician wasn't going to let him leave. "I could order you charged with interfering with a federation investigation, Doctor."

"You *are* the subject of a federation investigation, Professor," she retorted.

He looked over her shoulder. Beyond the ring of orderlies, two armed federation troopers stood sentinel at the curtain. He groaned. A forensic physicist and Lead Investigator arrested for destroying a sacred site.

"But I'm sure it's a formality, at least until they get statements from everyone." She excused herself and was gone.

He couldn't have got very far anyway. His body felt drained, as if he'd run a gauntlet or a marathon. Even the little effort of trying to get out of bed had left him enervated.

What in Eiocha's creation happened up there? Culann wondered. Even the glasteel had shattered.

The two guards stepped aside for a bedraggled figure. His right arm was welded to his side, in a cast. Jamie grinned at him. "Glad to see you're all right, old man."

"And all the feckless farnacle to you too, spritely pup."

Jamie laughed and shook his head. "So you already know they're not going to let us go any time soon. The department's in an uproar."

"Presumptuous bastards, who do they think they are, Federation Investigators?" Culann chuckled, without the energy for heartier laughter. "A mighty uproar, is my guess. You all right?"

"It's just a flesh wound." Jamie gestured at his shoulder.

"You had your bug-eyed camera mounted on your shoulder."

Jamie nodded, grimacing and meeting his gaze. "No word whether it's been recovered."

Culann wondered at the mass of visceral energy that had gathered above the Henge, poised for battle, and directly under it, funnels of Frost and Fire sprouting from each Gate. "You've video'd the essence of hundreds of things—"

"Thousands," Jamie interjected.

"Ever come across something like that?"

Jamie shook his head.

"Ever turn that camera on a ship moving into A-Warp?"

The young man's gaze narrowed. "Are you getting warped, too, like Procter Jézéquel?"

Culann shook his head. "It's long been suspected that the Gates operate in one fashion or another on A-Warp. What we saw above the Henge certainly exhibited the quintessence of an Elemental, but none we're familiar with. I suspect it was a wasn't."

Jamie blinked at him. "A 'wasn't'?"

"An incongruity in space, either a compression or attenuation."

"By 'attenuation,' you mean it was being stretched?"

"Or expanded, yes," he said, frowning. "Perhaps even ripped."

#

"A 'wasn't'?" Sionann looked at him as if he'd lost his mind. Once he'd explained what he meant, she seemed able to assimilate the concept.

"The quintessence of an Elemental, but neither Earth, Water, Air, nor Fire, eh? Where'd you get this Ether idea, anyway?" Sionann asked, staring at him from her wheelchair. She'd felt as enervated as him, but had negotiated her way out of her hospital bed to come see him, the hospital staff insisting she use the wheelchair. "Probably the only way I was going to get here," she'd said.

Beyond the curtain, the bustle of the emergency room seemed subdued. The two federation guards still stood sentinel, joined by the pair assigned to the Druidess.

"On Earth in the late 19th century, physicists postulated that Ether permeated space—all space, even that occupied by other Elementals—providing the medium for light to travel in a vacuum."

"So we're reverting from our thirtieth-century theoretical fundamentals to our thirteenth-century superstitions, wiping out the intervening scientific advancement as if it didn't exist?"

"Well, evidence for the presence of such a medium was never substantiated through experimentation," Culann replied. "But astral physics has since established that dark matter and dark light make up eighty-five percent of the universe. I suspect those experiments overlooked this quite considerable part of the cosmos, which they hadn't known about to start with."

The level of activity beyond the curtain rose considerably.

Sionann shook her head, glancing over her shoulder. "All right, Professor physicist, break it down for me. How's Ether causing the Gael Gates to malfunction?"

"I don't know yet. Only a suspicion." He couldn't see the cause of the surge in activity, the curtains occluding his view.

The federation guards suddenly stiffened and saluted.

"At ease," said a gravelly female voice.

An aide whipped aside the curtain.

Ceannaire Lady Ceridwen Gwilym, President of the Gael Federation, regarded Culann from within a ring of attendants. Her bent form and wispy hair took little away from the steel gaze. "By Goayr Heddagh, you've got the balls of a goat to destroy an entire Henge, Cull. Not the reason I sent you, if I'm recollecting events, now, is it?"

"Nay, your Ladyship, not the reason at all." Culann bowed the best he could from his recumbent position.

Druidess Sionann Liosach turned her chair and bowed as well. "Your Ladyship."

"Nann, child, did you ever get that apology this pesky apostate owed you for the dunking?"

"Never did, your Ladyship."

"The curmudgeon was always good at evasion. What happened here, Cull? The Henge is gone, just a pit in the ground where it used to be."

Someone brought her a chair and placed it near the foot.

Culann regarded the old battleaxe, wondering how much to tell her. "Do you want it all, your Ladyship?"

"I traveled all the way here from Alcyone; I damn well *better* get it all."

He shot a glance at the spectators, among them at least twenty people from the Fanum. How many journalists were among the observers, he didn't know.

"Clear the room," she said, her voice low and gruff.

Doctor Blodeuwedd Chynoweth stepped forward. "Forgive me, your Ladyship, but—"

"You've an emergency room to run, of course." The Ceannaire turned to her aide. "Find the three of us someplace private to talk." And she grinned at Cull. "I want to hear every word."

#

"Is she always like that?" Culann asked.

"Always," Sionann replied.

He'd met her on occasion, but'd never for an extended conversation. After his initial soliloquy, in which he'd disclosed the three possible explanations and elaborated upon his Elemental theory, Ceannaire Gwilym had grilled him with questions for another hour.

"And what was the reason, by Gwitihn, that you and Nann entered the ring again?" she'd asked near the conclusion of the interview.

"To sense for myself the forces at work in the Henge, I suppose."

"You suppose? You don't know?" The Ceannaire's voice had been full of scorn.

"Of course, I don't know. Do you always know? The ambiguity of what we face challenges all our assumptions about how the universe operates, your Ladyship. We've come up against the limits of our knowledge. How the hell am I supposed to know?"

"Aye, the very question." And then she'd taken her departure, tottering away like the ancient witch she was purported to be, all bent spine and spidery hair, lacking only a pointed, black, wide-brimmed hat.

"She didn't dismiss you outright," Sionann said.

"That's a comfort." He looked around the conference room where they'd wheeled his hospital bed, a nearby table stacked with the remains of their meal. During the extended interview, they'd been brought meal trays, bland, tasteless hospital food, but filling even so.

Not the kind of cuisine a President was accustomed to, Culann was sure.

He lay back, the spirit sucked from him again, this time by an Elemental just as deleterious as Ether itself, this one going by the title of Ceannaire.

Chapter 7

Just a pit in the ground where the Henge used to be.

Culann stood looking forlornly over the destruction, the monastery half-crushed as though the ithyphallic giant Cerne Abbas had smashed it with a club.

"What now?" Sionann asked.

"How the hell am I supposed to know?" He couldn't help but think he'd caused it, despite knowing he hadn't. He turned to look at her, feeling her stare.

"Saying that a lot, lately, Cull. People are going to think you're daft."

"Eh? Well, maybe I am, at that." He shook his head at her. At the hospital, he and everyone present at the monastery's destruction had been asked to give statements and provide contact information. The Ceannaire and her cortege had already left for Alcyone by the time he and the Druidess had been released on their own recognizance.

"You want to come with me?" He gestured at the pit.

"You can't be serious," Sionann said, snorting skeptically. "And bring down the wrath of Ether again? Not for all the gold in Tír na nÓg."

"Tisn't gold I'm offering," he retorted. "It's eternity."

"Uh-huh. And while you languish in eternity, I'll live out my life in peace. Just give me enough time to get clear of the area, will you?"

He snorted back at her, shaking his head. "See you at the spaceport." He watched her leave, wondering at her stare. The hover lifted off and found its way through the snowy wood along a road framed by tangled tree and blocky boulder.

All the monastery personnel had relocated to the nearby town, the Fanum uninhabitable. And without the Gael Gate, there was no reason for them to stay. Restoration work was set to begin in another day. To his knowledge, there was no restoring the Gael Gates, however. They would attempt to recover as many vellum texts as possible, but the Fanum was unlikely ever to regain its former glory, the site now deserted.

Except for him.

Forensic physicist Culann Penrose, Professor of Astral Physics at the University of Cardiff, looked down into the pit, Ceannaire Gwilym's question from their interview ringing in his head.

"And what was the reason, by Gwitihn, that you entered the ring again?"

Culann knew he'd be asked that.

Folly? Blatant disregard of danger? Prurient curiosity? He didn't know.

All he did know, and all that had ever governed his every act, from his toddler years when he'd exhibited the ability to harness the fundamental forces of the cosmos, was that he had to find out.

It's just a pit, he told himself.

Jagged-toothed tiles stuck out over a precipice, bits of foot-wide, knee-high perimeter still clinging desperately to the edge. The strata of underlying rock laid bare the geologic forces which had formed these Apennine Mountains, where tectonic upheaval had thrown horizontal sedimentary plates into a nearly-vertical position. The jagged slopes around the sanctuary all jutted at similar angles, a hardy pine-like tree having spread its seedlings throughout the forbidding rock escarpments. The hemispherical pit was symmetrical, like a bowl carefully carved from the earth by some gigantic scoop.

Culann looked for a place to climb down inside. One piece of knee-high perimeter had fallen part way down, far enough to give him ingress. It seemed willing to hold his weight as he tested it. At its lower end, his head was level with the surrounding ground, and the pit was easily twenty feet deeper.

He stepped off.

Into oblivion.

He stood on a strand of stars, awash in space on either side. Above him was empty abyss, the nearest galaxy, Andromeda, just a pinprick. The stars under his feet glittered like grains of sand, the Milky Way. He stood on the edge of the galactic disk.

I called it a 'wasn't,' he thought, chagrined, and now I stand at the edge of nowhere, atop a strand of stars that can't possibly be supporting my weight.

Culann thought about the impossibility, and concluded he didn't have the theoretical background to understand where he was, how he'd arrived there, or how he continued to stand there.

Maybe there isn't a theoretical background, he told himself.

Maybe, it just is.

The physicist part of him insisted that there had to be an explanation.

The wonder-filled child in him drank in the glory of the galaxy beneath his feet.

If I'm truly here, he thought, then I could be anywhere. All I need do is choose it.

The Pleiades, he thought, where the clans known as the Insular Celts resided, where Alcyone shone brightest, the sixth planet in that system being the Capital of the Gael Federation, and where the sister sun, Celaeno, bathed its fourth planet and Stonehenge with its pale, blue light. And his point of view shifted, the seven sisters swirling into view.

How about Gamma Draconis? he wondered, home constellation to the Galatians, where on the sere planet Alrakis sat the stele of Göbekli Tepe. And the galaxy under Culann shifted again, bringing the planet into view.

And Galicia? Home constellation in the Southern Triangle to the Galicians, the double-star Gamma Doradus, where the obeliscos of Las Cogotas thrust into the sky. Stars streaked past him as his position shifted there.

And back to Tucana, where the Senones mediated the constant feud between the Golaseccans and the Cisalpines on Tucana Prime at the Montefortino di Arcevia Fanum, whose once proud triple stands of megaliths had now been replaced by a hole.

Culann stood at the edge of that hole, looking down into a bowl of stars. Whatever striated sedimentary bedrock had once lined the bowl was gone.

Only stars and space remained.

That's impossible! the physicist in him thought.

That's wonderful! the child in him thought.

And Culann knew he was looking at a universe whose fundamental rules had changed.

#

"You look as though you've seen the face of God," Sionann said, looking at Culann over her shoulder from the copilot's seat.

Captain Nankivell swiveled in the pilot's chaise to give Culann a once-over. Her eyebrows shot up on her forehead.

Culann had returned placidly to the spaceport, wonder and awe buoying his step like a cloud under his feet. He stood in the short corridor between the cockpit and the galley, oblivious to the stars streaking past on the viewscreen.

He didn't know where they were going, and somehow, it didn't matter much.

"Follow me, Professor," and Sionann stepped past him into the galley. "Sit," she ordered.

Culann followed her obediently sat.

She wrestled a hot cup of tea from the beverage dispenser, pulled a steamy meal from the sustenance synthesizer, sat across from him, and shoved them both toward him. "Eat."

Other than the filling if tasteless food at the hospital, he'd had nothing.

"You walked all the way from the Fanum to the spaceport?"

"Is that far?" he mumbled around a mouthful of food.

"Through the cold?"

"I didn't feel cold." He remembered something about the climate of Tucana Prime, and how cold Alpha Tucanae was, the binary star barely able to sustain life on the planet.

She examined her prefrontal lobes from the insides of her orbital sockets. "What happened at the pit, Professor?"

"Do you want me to eat or talk?" he asked without irony. He smiled blithely, happy to do whatever she bade him.

"Eat first and then tell me. If you're as weak as I was after that penile Elemental smashed the Henge into the ground, you'd better eat. Surprised her Ladyship didn't fire us outright for all the destruction we caused. And Culann, why the Annwvyn did we go back into the Ring? Don't answer me—just eat. If I'm going to assist you in this investigation, I have to know what I'm up against. It looks as if the spectral hounds of Annwvyn have been unleashed upon us, the way the Fanum was destroyed."

He tried to tell her through mouthfuls of food that no, the Henge itself hadn't been destroyed, just moved to another dimension, and that the sudden vacuum had created a vortex whose backlash had pulverized the monastery at Montefortino di Arcevia. But she wouldn't let him speak and finally took the fork from his hand and fed him herself, until he was so sated that he felt sick.

By then the weight of fatigue put the blear in his eyes and forced his lids closed. Gentle hands carried him to his cabin, two women's voices mixing together in his dream as the gentle swaying turned the corridor lights into arcing suns. Darkness snapped into place, and Culann knew no more, the universe snuffed from existence.

#

"Another dimension? You're talking astral physics, Professor, a language I don't speak."

Culann looked blankly at Sionann, the two of them hunched over the remains of their breakfast in the galley, the ship just entering orbit over Alcyone, the Gael Federation Capital, where Ceannaire Lady Ceridwen Gwilym, President of the Gaels, had summoned them.

The disaster at Montefortino di Arcevia had made galaxy-wide headlines. As a result of the publicity, physicists of every discipline and charlatans of every stripe converged on ice-bound Alpha Tucanae.

After the fall of the Proto-Gaels, the Gate technology had never been replicated, and the Druidry had always concealed their operation behind a façade of wizardry and incantation. Thus, the Gates had never been used by non-Gaels, except in the instance of betrayal, the Eltanin invasion of Alrakis via Gael Gate one example.

"She's in damage control, you realize," Sionann said of the Ceannaire.

"Damage control? You're talking public relations, Druidess, a language I don't speak." As astute as he was in both physics and metaphysics, Culann was a public relations babe in the media woods.

"And just because you know quarks, you can use snarks?"

He grinned and apologized. "So what does she want from us?"

"Some reassuring words to a frantic public. If you can walk on the Milky Way, you can surely find something comforting to say to its inhabitants."

Culann considered a few things he might say. "Sans my usual babble of leptons and bosons?"

She rolled her eyes. "Please!"

"Let me think about it," he said. "We've got about two hours?"

"Two and a half."

Culann retreated to his cabin to prepare himself, both to scrub himself thoroughly and dress his best.

The patrol-class gremlin landed at the Durouľ̃ernon spaceport amidst tight security, a cordon of Federation elite surrounding the ship, members of her ladyship's personal guard. A limoflitter whisked them away, their hovercade of twenty vehicles making a swift beeline through the streets of the ancient city to the palace.

Originally a Brythonic settlement called Durouľ̃ernon, or alder stronghold, it was renamed Durovernum Cantiacorum by pagan conquerors in the 24th century. Upon its independence, the city took its Anglo name Canterbury, itself derived from the Old Anglo Cantwareburh, later shortened to Kent. After the Kingdom of Kent's forced conversion to Christianity in 2597, its first Archbishop founded a Piscopalian See. With the spread of the Proto-Gaels in the 27th century, their marauding forces augmented by the Gael Gates, the original name was restored to its Brythonic roots. Throughout its multiple names, Durouľ̃ernon had somehow maintained its air of ancient dignity, at least in its core, modern technology having surrounded it with soaring glasteel suburbs.

The rib vaulting, pointed arches, and flying buttresses of Durouľ̃ernon Cathedral grew larger as their hovercade approached. The sight of it inspired Culann to awe and reverence.

At the archipiscopo east entrance, where spires of the arched portico on either side pierced the sky, Professor Penrose and Druidess Lìosach ascended a cascade of steps through a gauntlet of reporters battering them with questions. "Keep a smile on your face and a 'No Comment' on your lips," Sionann had warned him. Of course he'd had little enough time to consider what he'd say and no time to review it with Sionann, who'd been on her com during the limoflitter ride. The blizzard of questions stripped away any illusion of welcome, warmth, or safety.

At the top of the steps, the podium displayed the Ceannaire's crest, its top sprouting a scintillion scintillating microphones. Behind the podium were the soaring Cathedral doors themselves, as regal a backdrop as might be had. On these steps in 2644, the apostate Thomas ą Becket had been martyred by the King of Kent, Henry II.

Culann wondered idly if he too might be martyred for his apostasy, his recalcitrant beliefs a different creed altogether from that of Thomas ą Becket.

The Ceannaire stepped from the Cathedral just as Professor Penrose and Druidess Lìosach reached the top. Her coif was a tidied web of spider silk, and her bent form barely cleared podium and its bouquet of microphones.

Culann and Sionann took up positions on either side of the President of the Gael Federation.

She spread her arms, her royal robes cascading from her outstretched arms like wings.

The silence was instant.

"Federation citizens, fellow Celts, Cisalpines, Gauls, Galicians, Galatians, and Gaels, we face a challenge as a nation unlike any since Eltanin invaders poured through our Gates. These Gates were what gave our mighty navies their tactical advantage when they conquered the Orion Belt in the 27th century. These Gates unite us in our beliefs and bring the blessings of Tír na nÓg into our lives in the here and now.

"Strange events a week ago prompted our closing the Gates, and in the investigation, further portents have inaugurated great difficulties for us all, culminating in the disappearance of the sanctuary at Montefortino di Arcevia. Let me assure you that every resource in our power is being brought to bear to restore the Gael Gates and our hegemony over the Orion Spur.

"Our Eltanin foes would like nothing better than to see us cede Draco back to them, but they are the least of our concerns.

"We are a people of the Elementals, disciples of Earth, Water, Air, and Fire. A new Elemental now encroaches upon our mastery of these four ancient disciplines, one for whom we have no disciples, and therefore no means to manage. Professor of Astral Physics Culann Penrose, a forensic physicist from the University of Cardiff, can explain."

Culann found himself shoved in front of the microphones bristling from the podium. The lenses of a hundred cams peered at him like insects. The eyes of a voracious media devoured his image. The ears of a parched public sought to slake their thirst for reassurance from his every utterance.

"A new Elemental, Ether, beckons us with its call," he said. "The Druidry has been our intermediary with the Four Elementals for a thousand years, operating the Gael Gates in devoted service to the Federation. Now, these gates have begun to function in ways we don't understand, placing our citizens at risk. The Gates have channeled us across the Ether between worlds since Proto-Gael times, and we, blithely ignorant of the Ether all around us, have utilized its fluidity to expand our domains and enhance our lives. Like all Elementals, Ether is now asking for its fair due.

"The means to manage this new Elemental are being developed as we speak, and the Gael Gates will return to their normal operations as soon as possible." Culann stepped back from the podium as questions erupted from the press corps below.

"The Professor isn't in a position to elaborate at this time," Sionann said, taking the podium, the Druidess so well known that she needed no introduction.

Culann watched her take several questions adroitly, which she answered without any kind of specificity. Several of her responses reassured even Culann, who knew how grave the circumstances were. Ceannaire Gwilym nudged him to follow her, and they edged backward into the Cathedral.

The soaring doors closed on the noise, and the celestial silence of ancient reverence enveloped them. If the exterior inspired awe, the interior evoked reverence.

"No time to stop for admiration," President Gwilym said. "Call me Ceri, by the way—I hate Ceridwen. So where are these 'means' you spoke of? Aye, I thought you might have been confabulating. Can't say I blame ye, Laddie." She grinned at him from beneath a spidery halo.

They walked between the soaring columns in the central nave companionably.

"Tis said in low whispers that Thomas ą Becket was secretly a Druid."

"Where'd you hear that load of dreck?"

He grinned at her and shook his head. "Does a rumor repeated twenty times become a fact? I'm not inclined to believe it, either. Soon, it'll be said that I am, too."

"Denounced as apostate by Neo Druidry for two decades, Professor Culann Penrose becomes a Druid of the Ether!" The Ceannaire threw her head back and cackled.

And yet …

"Ceri, if you'll pardon, I've a visit to pay to Stonehenge," he said, the urge emergent.

"You do, my boy." She winked at him. "It's why I asked you here."

Chapter 8

She's an Elemental unto herself, she is, Culann thought, staring up at Stonehenge, the night sky beyond the edifice brilliant, a full moon leeching the stars of all their luster. Crickets chirped their nocturnal rhythms in counterpoint to the night bird songs. The scents of grass, flowers, and trees wafted to him on a chill wind.

He examined the Henge in the moonlight.

Thirty smaller trilithons surrounded five large trilithons, all thirty-five post-and-lintel structures built from the native sarsen stone. Four stones at the edge of the ring marked the monument boundaries, two station stones to the east and west, the slaughter stone to the south, and the heel stone to the north.

The blue brilliance of several sisters outlined Stonehenge, the Pleiades Constellation all young stars, their multiple suns bathing sibling planets with muted blue light at all hours. Perched atop the largest trilithon, its lintel easily twelve feet long, was the pulsating star Pleione.

The sight had never ceased to inspire Culann.

"Tis a sight, isn't it, Sir?" Near the slaughter stone stood an apprentice.

"Indeed," he said. "Culann Penrose." He stuck out his hand. "And you?"

She grinned at him. "Everyone knows who you are, Professor. Brígida Mosquera, apprentice Druid of the Sylphs. Shall I alert Procter Bhodhsa that you've arrived, Sir?"

"Not necessary, apprentice Brígida. I'd like not to disturb him further, something my presence tends to do. Your name sounds Galician. Are you Celtiberian?"

"I am, Sir, from Nemetobriga."

He saw even in the dim light how comely she was. "Tragic events there, eh? Call me Cull, by the way."

"Pleased, Cull, and if you've a mind, I like to be called Gida."

"Pleased, Gida." He gave her a slight bow.

"Quite the tragedy, Cull. I know Professor Tanguy's family. They're frantic, don't know whether to search for her, give her up as missing, or give her the last rites in corpus absentia."

Something triggered a memory for him about the region. "Isn't there a tradition …"

"Indeed, there is, La Romeria de Santa Marta de Ribarteme, a tradición apostólica to show gratitude for life and health where a person in a coffin is carried on a pilgrimage to the cemetery and mimics being buried. They've considered this ritual, too. If I may ask something on their behalf, Sir?"

"Certainly, Gida." He grinned at the fluid ease with which she transitioned between Gaelic and Spanish, Galician a rich mixture of the two languages.

"Bring Professor Tanguy back, somehow."

He saw the plea in her gaze. "I'll do everything I can, Gida." He looked up the hill, at the Henge bathed in both starlight and moonlight. "At the obeliscos of Las Cogotas, I was attacked by sylphs."

"At Druid Lubri's behest?"

"No, thank Arawn. While I was in the Ring, examining the obeliscos."

"I can't imagine sylphs having any antipathy toward you, Cull. You've such a kind and gentle manner."

"Thank you, Gida." He didn't remember the last time someone had said something nice to him. Too much time around the acerbic Sionann, he thought. "I doubt it was me they were after. There were undines at Göbekli Tepe and gnomes here, too."

"And salamanders at Montefortino di Arcevia?"

He admired how sharp she was. Stonehenge was a good place for her apprenticeship. While Proctor Medraut Bhodhsa was narrow-minded at times, the pool of expertise among the thirty Druids at Stonehenge was deep indeed. She'll benefit greatly here, he thought.

"I've delayed long enough, I suppose." He looked toward the hilltop.

"Delayed what, Cull?"

"My fate here tonight."

"Muy mórbida, Profesor. Why such talk, eh?"

Culann shook his head. "No matter, Gida. It's been my destiny for a long time, coming here tonight."

She looked at him quizzically. "What are you going to do?"

"Give myself up to the undines, of course."

She glanced toward the towering trilithon capping the hilltop above them, looking suddenly afraid. "Señor?"

"I'll be fine, Gida. Oh, and no need to alert anyone just yet. If I don't come back by morning, that's the time to raise the alarm."

"You're going up there alone, Cull? But ..." The Henge was sacred ground, never to be entered unless necessary, and never alone.

"There are times, Gida, when the ancient prohibitions must be trespassed upon. The future of the Gael Gates depends on this."

"Are you sure? I'd be honored to go with you."

"Thank you, Gida, kind of you to offer."

"Would it interfere, my coming with you?"

He nodded. "The Druidry will be nobler for your becoming a member."

She dropped her gaze in modesty. "Thank you, Professor. I'll see you when you come back. Hasta luego."

Culann smiled and turned to the Ring, the only boundary being the even-cut grass, three inches tall, all the time, all year round, kept that way by ancient invocation. He stepped across the near-invisible boundary, the dewy grass quickly drenching his sodhoppers. The full moon lit his path. He circumvented the smaller trilithons, heading for the main gate at the hillcrest.

Eighteen feet tall, the trilithon gleamed in the bright moonlight. Its lintel was a foot-thick megalith ten feet long and two feet deep.

He knew Brígida was watching from below, despite how little was visible in the low light. He considered summoning the gnomes and propitiating their help, but they knew he was here. And why.

Culann raised his gaze to the lintel stone.

He plunged feet first into the earth and kept plunging, as though pulled under by some cryptid beast purported to troll underground caverns. The earth scraped past on all sides, opening under him and closing above him, dirt smearing his clothes. Where before he had clawed at the earthen sides of the tunnel, now he willed himself to relax.

A gnomish face materialized in the tunnel wall even as it flashed past him. "Meddler in the old radiations, you die today and stay with me underground!"

This time he refrained from incantation. "I am yours, Arawn, to be taken to realms where I'm needed."

The tunnel sides changed from earth to rock, the thick sarsen stone of the megaliths themselves. Screeching in complaint, the rock parted just enough for his body to squeeze between slabs, scraping his shoulders and hips.

Suddenly, he was extruded into a chamber and fell onto his backside.

Picking himself up, he checked his scrapes and scratches. The shoulders of his jacket had been shredded by the rock and hung in tatters down his upper arms. He stomped to shake off the thick coat of damp soil from his legs. Dirt sifted out of his hair, and he brushed himself off as best he could.

The chamber was even-cut and cubic, its sides of the very same megalith sarsen stone as the monument above him. He counted ten of the two foot-wide stones along one chamber side. They appeared to emit a luminescence, the light in the chamber without apparent source. Along the south wall was an arcane set of symbols. Proto-Gael runes, Culann saw.

He stepped to the symbols, which covered the wall from floor to ceiling.

The obeliscos at Las Cogotas on Galicia were etched with Celtiberian runes all the way to the top, the script still indecipherable to modern linguists. A script nearly identical to this.

Culann felt the runes begin to work on his brain, his first instinct to summon an incantation in self-defense.

Give yourself over to the process, he told himself.

Even as he watched, the runes changed shape and reorganized themselves. Mathematical symbols snarled their tendrils around numbers. Letters grew appendages and settled into lines. Slowly, meaning began to emerge.

A-warp.

He blinked at the rune-covered wall. The runes themselves hadn't changed, he realized, only his ability to interpret them. A comprehension invocation? he wondered, having never heard of such. Paleographers, archeologists, and Druids alike had been attempting to decrypt the ancient runes for centuries. And here they were, in a chamber far beneath Stonehenge, decrypting themselves for Professor Culann Penrose, noted apostate and blasphemer.

This chamber was the Gael Gate engine, he realized, the place that activated the gates themselves. And the A-warp equations, despite being written in the Proto-Gael script, articulated how a stationary object might be brought into contact with a place many thousands of parsecs away.

Of course! Culann thought.

If A-warp operated by compressing space in front of an object and stretching space behind it, why couldn't the A-warp engine compress and stretch space enough to make the distance negligible?

Close enough to step across, like a threshold.

And how did the Druids operate them? he wondered, their secrets shrouded in the esoterica of ritual and incantation.

He worked through the equations, the runes morphing as he went, each symbol changing from its Proto-Gael form to modern Gaelic as his eyes alighted upon it, and back to Proto-Gael as his gaze moved on.

How …?

In astral physics, there were mysteries whose mechanism eluded comprehension, consciousness a prime example of one such mystery—especially its etiology. Astral physics attempted to extrapolate across the chasm between the existing fields of particle physics and the rather arcane and fuscous field of metaphysics. The acceptance of these mysteries as fundamental components of a unified field theory was a necessary assumption in astral physics, on the presumption that the study of these mysteries would ultimately illuminate their enigmatic mechanics.

And how did the Druids operate the Gates? he wondered, convinced that that long-standing mystery was nearly within his reach.

Two-thirds of the way through the A-warp equations, he saw an anomaly.

An equation whose symbols didn't assemble in quite the right way.

At first, it pricked his awareness like a mote in his eye. He first thought it some sort of visual distortion deriving from the invocation that allowed his mind to decipher the runes. As he tried to examine the anomaly further, it slipped like a wet bar of soap out of comprehension. Analogous to an optical migraine, the distortion was only apparent when he didn't look directly at the equation. He gazed at the symbol preceding it, then the one after it.

In its reverted Proto-Gael runes, the language that had eluded understanding for centuries, it looked oddly like a normal equation, but not part of the A-warp sequence. How could that be? he wondered. If written by the ancients, they wouldn't have had a contemporary alphabet to construct the equation with. A few symbols were analogous between the two, their morphology traced from the Proto-Gael runes to the modern alphabet.

He committed the equation to memory. He'd have to have a colleague in particle physics examine the equation. Although he was conversant with its general ideas, the mathematics were too abstruse for him to decode without assistance.

He traced the sequence through to its end, then reexamined the anomalous equation.

It was gone.

Blinking as though to clear his gaze, Culann looked again.

Not there.

The equations before and after, which he recognized from his prior study of A-warp theory, but not the equation that had eluded comprehension.

He retraced the sequence from the beginning, faster this time, and upon reaching the point two-thirds of the way through, he found nothing unusual or enigmatic.

With a nearly eidetic memory, Culann couldn't wait to consult with one of his erudite colleagues in the more prosaic branch of physics. He wondered what one of his ecclesiastical colleagues would think, convinced it'd be excoriated as apostasy.

Culann smiled.

He looked around the rock-lined chamber, wondering how he'd get back to the surface. Airmid, Goddess of Tuatha Dé Danann, had interceded at his propitiation the last time a gnome had sucked him underground. Stepping to the middle of the chamber, Culann summoned the powers of the firmament. "Goddess Airmid, blessed be. Hear my favor and bring me up to Stonehenge thus."

Nothing happened.

He took a deep breath. The air here did not have that stale quality of long enclosure, at least. He wondered how it was ventilated. Again, he concentrated on bringing the forces of the universe to bear, and he spread his arms toward the ceiling. "Take me to Tír na nÓg, if that be your plan, Goddess Airmid, but leave me not in this luminal limbo."

Again, nothing happened.

"Arbiter of Healing, Goddess Airmid, beg thy sister, Anu, to release me!"

The rock stared at him, as though biding its time.

It occurred to him to be as rock and bide his too, but he'd be dust long before the rock tired of him. I'm not meant to leave yet, he thought, because the chamber isn't finished with me.

He looked over at the rune-covered south wall. What did I miss? he wondered. With a heightened awareness, he looked at the remaining three walls. On the north wall was the faint outline of a vaguely-humanoid being.

Odd I didn't see that before, he thought, stepping toward it.

The figure looked to be about the same height and breadth as Culann himself. Further, the effigy looked positioned just as Culann was.

He raised his arms.

The effigy raised its arms, sparks flying from the hands, leaving lighter streaks.

Culann backed away, and the figure faded.

He stepped toward it again, and the effigy returned. On a whim, he gesticulated through an elaborate set of gestures.

Streaks on the wall marked the movement of his hands.

Druidic prestidigitation!

He giggled, giddy with the discovery.

Their elaborate gesticulations when summoning a Gael Gate actually served to communicate the gate's destination to the A-warp engine, like semaphore. He'd always thought these gestures an elaborate means to befuddle the uninitiated observer, serving no other purpose.

Backing away lest he inadvertently open a gate to nowhere, Culann lowered his arms. The figure on the wall receded into the sarsen stone.

On the south wall, Proto-Gael script that decoded itself for its viewer, and on the north wall, a sarsen stone surface that reflected and interpreted its user motions.

What surprises will I find on the east and west walls? he wondered.

A column of rock descended from the ceiling, enveloped him, catapulted him to the surface, and dumped him unceremoniously on the threshold of the main gate.

Culann threw his head back and laughed.

Two figures came barreling up the slope, the sky pale and the blue sisters now the only stars visible.

He'd been underground far longer than it'd seemed.

Proctor Medraut Bhodhsa and apprentice Brígida Mosquera slowed as they approached. "Ysbadaden Pencawr guards our gates too well, it appears," Druid Bhodhsa said, his voice thick with scorn. In the ancient legends, the giant Pencawr guarded his nine gates against infiltration by Culhwch, who desired to marry his daughter.

Brígida glanced askance at Proctor Bhodhsa and helped Culann to his feet. "Are you all right, Profesor?" She spoke the blend of Gaelic and Galician with the ease of someone bilingual from birth.

Chuckles still shaking him, he nodded. "I am, bless Arawn, I am." He made a feeble attempt to brush the detritus of his journey from his clothes. He knew he looked a wreck, his jacket shredded at the shoulders, his slacks caked with dirt, his hair filled with sand.

"Who the hell let you up here by yourself, eh?" Proctor Bhodhsa asked, his gaze ready to excoriate.

"No one, Proctor," Culann replied. "I slipped past Apprentice Mosquera with un conjuro para oscurecer, an incantation to obscure."

Bhodhsa stepped up to Culann, his face florid. "You'll bring down the wrath of Tír na nÓg with your meddling, Apostate!" the Proctor frothed, spittle spattering Culann. "What're you aiming to do—take all the gates into oblivion?"

The Professor groped his pockets for a handkerchief and wiped his face. "I'd rather not, Proctor," he said, keeping his voice nonchalant. "Somewhat of an inconvenience that'd be, eh?"

The Proctor looked ready to explode, apoplectic.

"Forgive me, Proctor," Brígida said, going to a knee. "It was my fault. I should have been more vigilant." She lowered her head.

"Two weeks serving the slop for your lapse, Apprentice," Bhodhsa fumed. Then he turned and stomped down the hillside.

"Sorry about that," Culann said. "I'd forgotten he could be unreasonable. And thanks for the diversion."

"Certainly, Profesor, a pleasure. Thanks for *your* diversion. The old codger would have tacked my hide to the slaughter stone if he'd known I let you up here."

He looked up from his feeble attempts make himself presentable and grinned at her. "Mutual it seems and better that way, eh, Lass? Ah, but my gratitude would be complete if I had a bath and change of clothes."

#

A pleasant lassitude upon him, Professor Culann Penrose waited in an anteroom outside the offices of the Ceannaire, Lady Ceridwen Gwilym. The palace in Durouĭˉernon was a sprawling complex not far from the Cathedral.

It was early evening, and he'd slept most the day, his nocturnal visit to the underground chamber not unlike a sojourn to Tír na nÓg. Apprentice Brígida Mosquera had secured him a bath, a change of clothes, and a place to rest. He'd tried to decline the additional comforts she'd offered, but she'd insisted.

He was still puzzling through the enigmas he'd found.

Runes that deciphered themselves, and stone that interpreted motion.

The Proto-Gaels had been more advanced than their descendants knew.

The runes had been on the south wall, the effigy on the north.

Slaughter stone to the south, and heel stone to the north. Some correlation with the above-ground Henge? he wondered.

He'd commed a colleague in particle physics with the equation he'd seen on the rune wall, the equation whose symbols hadn't assembled in quite the right way. He'd not yet received a reply. What did it mean that the equation had later disappeared?

Gael Gate operation now less of a mystery, Culann still hadn't resolved what was going wrong with them, why six people had been whisked off to oblivion, why an entire monument now sat inside some liminal limbo, why the four Elementals had suddenly become rebellious.

"Professor Penrose?"

He looked up.

A secretary was beckoning.

Elaborate mahogany molding framed a door thick with the gravity of the presidential office. Filigree fabric papered the walls between sconces where in olden times lanterns once resided. Plush pile carpet underfoot also glinted with filigree and silenced his every step.

"Cull, so glad you've returned," Ceannaire Gwilym said, stepping around a large desk to greet him, her hair a matted nest of spider-silk, her hunched frame lending an air of frailty that she didn't have. She bade him to sit, a carafe and cups on a service cart nearby.

"Tea, Madame?" the secretary asked, his prim, precisely-creased slacks like twin pillars to the floor.

"I'll serve, James, thank you," Ceridwen said, and the secretary retreated with a bow. The Ceannaire turned to look at him, really look, and then sat beside him. "There's an unexpected vitality to you, Cull. What mischief are you brewing now?"

He laughed softly, not surprised at her observation but knowing it comprised of many discoveries, not just those in the chamber. "I gave myself up to the gnomes, Ceri."

"Gave yourself up? The release and relief are plain in your manner, Cull, more so than I'd expect. Some momentous discoveries?" She poured them both a cup, amber disks of hot brew rising in the porcelain.

"I know how the Druids operate the gates."

The Ceannaire smiled, pushing a cup toward him. "Complaints of trespassing have been lodged with my office from the Ministry of Druidry. How should I respond, do you think?"

Culann grinned. "Invite them to investigate the disappearances themselves."

"Out of the question, of course." She waved at the fresh-cut lemon, the light and dark sugars, the small pitcher of milk. "Did you really sneak up to Stonehenge in the dark of night? Sounds like some school-boy prank."

After adding a dab of milk, he inserted the teaspoon at the "6 o'clock" position, and then gently moved it to the "12 o'clock" position. When done, he placed the teaspoon on the right side of the saucer. "No, no, of course, I didn't sneak up there. I stopped to chat with the apprentice on guard. Proctor Bhodhsa is just upset I didn't take him with me. I'll bet he complained I violated the sanctity of his gates, now, didn't he?"

Her eyes came up from his teacup, as though she'd been watching. "What happened up there, Cull?"

Taking an occasional sip, he told her, leaving nothing out, up to his being dumped unceremoniously just outside the main gate.

Ceridwen shook her head. "So all that elaborate song and dance actually has a purpose! Who'd have thought?"

"Nothing you couldn't have asked, Professor."

He looked up, startled to see Druidess Sionann Lìosach, standing there as if having listened to his entire narrative.

Her jaw rippled and her brow was furrowed. "No, not Professor Penrose, Doctor of Astral Physics at the University of Cardiff. Much too privileged to do something so simple as to ask. Beneath him completely."

"Might you have told me about the chamber, Nann? Might have been useful to know."

She wore her robes of office, the long black outer robe with the bright yellow trim, a kelly-green sash synched at the waist. In her hand was a staff as gnarled as the Ceannaire, Druidess Lìosach looking too young to wield so ancient a talisman. "Why should the Order tell you anything, Apostate?"

"A spot of tea, Nann?" Ceridwen asked. And she began pouring without waiting for an answer.

"Oh, certainly, Ceri, thank you." She sat across from them, leaning the staff against her chair, within easy reach.

Culann watched her, wondering whether she knew the ancient tradition of commensality. Breaking bread with an adversary held a universal significance that stretched across race, culture, custom, and language.

"And don't think, Professor, that my taking tea with you will in any way defuse my animosity. You're a thieving scoundrel out to obliterate the Druidry, and you'll burn in hellfire for all eternity for your futile efforts."

"You mean I won't be going to Tír na nÓg or Annwvyn?" He put his hand to his chest dramatically. "Thank Arawn I'll be spared that eternal boredom."

"Cull!" Ceri said.

"Forgive me, your Ladyship. My apologies, Nann. I goad you for no better purpose than my own amusement. Scoundrel I am." He paused and looked at both dramatically. "Out to obliterate the Druidry, I am not."

The other two looked somewhat mollified, exchanging a glance.

He reminded himself he was the intruder in this domain, the collaboration between Ceannaire and Druidess many years old, the newly-invested Ceannaire Lady Gwilym having whisked Sionann at age twenty-three from her matriculation ceremony into her service.

It had been a remarkable move, the Druidess a political neophyte to the internecine squabbles that plagued any government, the Ceannaire taking her witch broom to a bureaucracy thick with centuries of cobwebs, grime, and the detritus of prior administrations.

Of course destroying Neo Druidry seemed his intent to them. His discipline was on its face antithetical to their metaphysical beliefs. The explicit purpose of Astral Physics was to bring together the divergent realms of particle physics and metaphysics, to render the mysteries of all faiths into articulate principles and reproducible results. To remove the mystery from their mysteries.

The Protestant Reformation on Earth more than a millennium ago had threatened to eviscerate the Catholic Church similarly, having removed the clergy as sole arbiter between God and the faithful. Catholicism had survived, and so would Neo Druidry.

"If I may, Dame Lìosach, I would love to have your company when I return to Göbekli Tepe and Las Cogotas."

Culann tried not to laugh when Sionann nearly choked on her tea.

Chapter 9

"I don't begrudge it a moment," said Druid Finnán Cadeyrn, counselor to the Alrakis Potentate, walking beside Culann toward Göbekli Tepe. "Oh, a lesser person might, being swept aside by the new Ceannaire like that," Finnán added, and then he gestured at the sight above them. "And I'd have never come here if she hadn't booted me out the door." The six-four, barrel-chested Druid wore the same old robes he'd always worn, his favorite cravat tied under his beard.

Culann swore he'd wear them until they fell, threadbare, from his considerable girth.

The stand of two hundred stele dominated the hilltop above them like an alien forest. The area looked deserted. Not two weeks ago, it had been a bustling center of travel. Now it was deathly quiet. I can almost hear the rocks growing, Culann thought.

The sere, hot landscape on Alrakis was a startling contrast to the wet, verdant downs of Salisbury, where calcareous grasslands gave the gentle hills a manicured look. A sirocco blowing uphill buffeted them with dust, and a small devil twisted across their path.

Druid Cadeyrn gestured as if summoning an invocation. "Never let a dust devil cross your path without crossing yourself."

Culann and Sionann had arrived at Alrakis that morning aboard her Gremlin.

"What's his Honor, the Potentate, think about all this?"

"Dylan's miffed at Ceri's high-handed edict, but what Potentate wouldn't be? Impotent Potentate—nice ring, no? What's he Potentate for if it means being rendered impotent by her Highness the wench herself?" He looked around as if to insure they were alone. "I didn't say that aloud, did I?"

"The sound of a falling tree when I wasn't there to hear it." Culann grinned at Finnán; Druidess Sionann Lìosach was still at the spaceport, tending to her ship, the Gremlin. She'd asked that he await her arrival before entering Göbekli Tepe.

"So you cracked a chamber, I'm told."

"Eh? More lies from the mouths of babes? Who might've told you that?" The Professor didn't need to look over his shoulder toward the spaceport.

"She might be young, but her soul is old. Don't underestimate her, Cull. I'm probably preaching to the choir, but I've talked with many a former colleague at the Ministry of Druidry—scathed to the person, the lot of them, some reputations ruined completely."

The political infighting that had followed the new Ceannaire's investiture had left blood splattered on the Cathedral walls. Even the ivory towers at Cardiff had been speckled by the spray, Culann having managed to steer clear. "Thanks for the warning, Finn. I've had a bruise or two, already."

"So what brings you back, Cull?" Druid Cadeyrn stopped at the Ring. A narrow, inch-high stone ridge marked the Ring here at Göbekli Tepe. Even without it, the demarcation would have been clear. The coloration and consistency of the soil within the Ring seemed different, as if the sand and grit were sifted for purity.

Culann felt the power of an ancient invocation at work, so subtle that it barely registered on his senses. He wondered how much to tell the Druid. Years ago, when he'd been young and foolish, Culann had entered into an apprenticeship under Druid Finnán Cadeyrn. "You remember why I failed as an apprentice?"

Finnán grinned. "How could I not, man? It was a most spectacular failure."

At his matriculation ceremony, Culann had denounced the order as the fatuous lot of charlatans they were, disgusted with the graft, nepotism, abuse, and general chicanery that were rife throughout the order. He'd been credited with bringing down Ceannaire Gwilym's predecessor, and then he'd been accused of being her puppet, banished from the order, and very nearly crucified. Only direct intervention from the Ceannaire's office had stopped his execution, further fueling rumors he'd done her bidding.

Finnán had been one of the few who'd eschewed the traditional "perquisites" of office generally accorded the Druidry and thus had been spared the worst of the purge that'd followed. Except for being removed unceremoniously from office and being replaced by Druidess Lìosach.

"Well, Finn, seems there are some scientific underpinnings to the Gael Gate operation." He'd received an excited com from his colleague in particle physics that morning.

"Eh? Of course, there are. None of us ever said there weren't."

"No, but you did your very damndest to obscure it and swindle us all into believing in your hocus-pocus."

"And you're going to air our dirty laundry in public again, eh, Apostate?"

"If I could find some that's clean, I'd consider airing that instead, Finn."

The other man chuckled. "Maybe we've worn out our welcome, given ourselves so deeply over to pride, presumption, and pretension that we deserve to be brought down a notch. None better to do it than you, Cull."

He looked over at Druid Cadeyrn, a good fifteen years older than he was. About to retire, Culann suspected, and exhausted by the infighting, the backbiting, the cloaked hostilities, the snide asides. There were dark circles under the Druid's eyes, and his cheeks sagged as if he'd lost weight recently.

There were reasons that Druid Cadeyrn was Chief Druid here at Göbekli Tepe, at the eastern edge of the Gael Federation, and no longer the Presidential Druid, serving the Ceannaire at Durouĩernon on Alcyone—not the least of which was his having proctored Culann. As one who'd proved incorruptible, Finnán had been roundly despised by his brethren. But after ousting him, Ceannaire Gwilym had sliced apart the Druidry with a scalpel, and had cut it clean of its necrosis.

Finnán looked up the hill and sighed deeply. "We're put forth as eidolons of human comportment, and we can't keep our robes synched closed or our fingers out of our parishioner's pockets. What have we learned since you denounced the order? How to hide our concupiscence better. Nothing more, Cull, nothing more."

Culann heard the hum of an approaching flitter. That'll be Sionann, he thought, seeing Finnán's glance over his shoulder.

"Smart as sin and old as gold, Cull. Never forget that about her, eh?"

"Thanks, I won't. So where's the technology malfunctioning, Finn?" He'd hoped to get an answer from the Druid before Sionann's arrival.

The older man gave him hard look. "You're the physicist; you tell me."

"Wish I had the answers, I do." Culann had to decide whether Finnán knew and wasn't saying, or whether the old Druid truly didn't know. Finnán was too subtle to tell him directly. "There are equations in the Gael Gate's A-warp that aren't in a spacecraft engine. What do the equations do, Finn?"

Finnán chuckled. "That's what I'm talking about. You tell me, Cull."

"Tell him what, Cull?" Sionann asked, climbing the gentle slope. "The Apostate telling the Cabalist the secret of everlasting life? That'd be a laugh."

"Nann," Finnán said with exaggerated flair, "we both know everlasting life can only be found in the bottom of a pint, by god. Even a sober bastard like Cull knows that, don't you, boy?" And Finnán threw his head back and laughed.

Sionann looked at them both suspiciously, she the intruder in this domain.

Culann gestured vaguely up the hill. "Shall we, before the place crumbles with age?"

"Lead on, fearless Apostate!" Finnán declared, as if he'd had one or two already.

#

He hadn't intended, in stepping onto the stage at his matriculation, to denounce Druidry itself, just its corrupt members.

He stood alone among his fellow graduates, thirty of them, the only one without the blood-shot, glassy eyes, the hoary breath, the spinning head, the nauseated stomach. Culann evinced plenty of wreckage from the bacchanal the night before, but not from overindulgence in drink.

The night before, they'd celebrated their anticipated graduation with gallons instead of pints. Like any fraternal organization comprised of nine males to every female, licentious behavior with the opposite sex was one of those "perquisites" frequently shared among the brotherhood.

But the two young women who'd had a few with the rowdy crowd had become scared, and the boys, infatuated with their own importance, hadn't known when to stop. But abstemious Culann had known and saw the two young women struggle, trying to fight off the intoxicated young men.

And it had been only him against the rest, even the proctor assigned to monitor the goings-on unable to keep his robes closed. The only way to stop the rapine had been to assault them, and at thirty against one, they'd beat him roundly.

As his comeuppance, he'd wired a vid feed of the saturnalian night to the overhead viewscreen, all of it, and had sent the same vid to local media outlets, as well as the University Provost and the village bobbies.

His only regret was that they hadn't awarded him his sheepskin before the vid went on.

The forest of stele around him, Culann felt again like the lone soul amidst a crowd of lesser beings. As before, it was he who was apostate, the disbeliever, the standalone, he who took the road less traveled.

Then he shook it off. Arawn forbid I should think I'm special, he thought. Down that path lay dereliction in hubris. I'm a scientist out to solve a mystery, nothing more, he reminded himself.

And the majestic stele around him became again a place of ancient wisdom and reverence.

The twenty rings of stele were a small forest of two hundred pillars, about half of them with capstones. Varied in height from ten and twenty-five feet, all the stele were identical in width and depth, one foot by two feet, the divine dimension. Ten stones each, the twenty rings varied in size, one large ring at the center, five medium rings surrounding it, fourteen small rings encircling them, and a narrow inch-high stone strip surrounding it all.

He brought his gaze to the central ring of stones capping the hilltop. There, all the stele had capstones, whose lengths were proportionate to height. While the capstones appeared to balance precariously atop the stele, their weight alone gave them permanence and stability.

The trio threaded their way between stele rings toward the center, ten stele each with a capstone, this decalith among the most ominous of all the monuments. The two northernmost stele where a funnel of water had nearly sucked Sionann into oblivion were among the tallest, easily topping twenty-five feet. Their capstones nearly touched across the ten-foot gap between them.

Undines, Culann saw, played at the base of the stele, the little creatures splashing about in their self-made pools, which manifested wherever they went. Many of them postured at the human approach, the females thrusting their voluptuous mini-bosoms at him, the males waving their tiny tumescent members at Sionann.

"Yeah, just try and please this with that!" she snarled, parting her robes and thrusting her hips at one cavorting undine male.

The undines tittered and scattered, Culann averting his gaze.

Finnán just shook his head in laughter. "I'd say we pissed off the undines enough the last time we were here, eh, Nann?"

"Wasn't an undine that tried to suck me into oblivion, Finn," she retorted, letting her robes fall back into place. And then she turned to Culann, "All right, Professor, what now?"

"Now comes the tough part, Nann. You and Finn need to let the whirlpool take you under."

"Are you daft?!" Sionann asked.

"Let myself be drowned? In water?" Finnán snorted. "Make it a whirlpool of brew and I'll jump right in!"

Culann had been expecting resistance. "It's what I did at Stonehenge. I let the gnomes take me underground."

Sionann and Finnán stared hard at each other. "You know this prankster better than I do. What do you think?" she asked.

"He's daft, all right, and ethical even to his own detriment, but well meaning for all that. My gut says we trust him."

"Your gut calls you a glutton, Finn, that's no endorsement."

Finnán's girth strained the aging black fabric of his Druidry robes. He patted his barrel-gut appreciably. "Stocky I am."

"That's all fat, Finn." She snorted and shook her head. "So the gnomes at Stonehenge took you into the chamber, eh, Cull?" She looked at the gate looming above them, the two capstones twenty-five feet above them, and then brought her gaze back to the astral physicist. "Four days ago you saved me from drowning, but this time, you're willing to drown with me. By Maighdean Uaine, I don't know why I do the things I do."

The Green Maiden invoked by Druidess Lìosach was a half-goat, half-woman sea creature who waited at stream-side and begged travelers to help her across, often leading them astray.

Finnán stared at Sionann. "You'll help this Green Maiden Cull to cross this stream and lead you astray? Not I, Dame Braveheart, not I! I'll be happy to watch from over here. Besides, what if you don't return? Who'll raise the alarm?"

"Why the cold feet, Finn?" Culann asked, thinking the other man had already acquiesced.

"Lad, it's been a long journey, and I've been looking forward to retiring for a few years now. I'd like to spend my dotage in peace."

"Finn, you've been in your dotage since we met," Sionann said.

"Facile-tongued wench, let's have it out over on yon hilltop and see who's the more adept Druid, eh?"

"Sorry, Finn, you're not my type. Let the coward stay, Cull."

"He's right, though." Culann tried not to smile at their easy banter, the both of them brash and audacious. And cowardly, Finnán was not. "We do need someone to sound the alarm if something goes awry." And he acknowledged that Finnán did indeed look tired.

Sionann nodded, conceding the point. "Very well. And the old goat's right, you know."

"Eh?" Culann asked.

"You're a good man, Cull."

I'm a scientist out to solve a mystery, nothing more, Culann thought again. Even so, hearing such from the Druidess Sionann Lìosach, advisor to the Ceannaire Lady Ceridwen Gwilym, President of the Gael Federation, was high praise indeed, especially since she seemed to have nary a word of that for anyone. He shot her a smile and turned to the Gate itself, the northernmost pair of stele towering above him.

Druid Finnán Cadeyrn stepped back, synching his robe and tightening his cravat as though expecting a spell of bad weather. "Arawn guide you both," he said.

"Thanks, Finn." Culann sensed no residue from the incident four days ago, an oddity in itself. Such an event was sure to leave its essence.

"You don't see it either, do you, Cull?"

"You mean what happened the other day?" Finnán asked.

It didn't surprise him how well she could read him, Finnán's assessment of her both astute and insightful. In a lot of ways, she was quite like him. "I suspect we're pushing the boundaries of A-warp into unknown realms. You ready, Nann?" He looked over at her and saw her avert her gaze.

"Aye, Cull, I am." She readied her stance beside him.

Professor Culann Penrose raised his arms. "Undines of Göbekli Tepe, heed my call, bring on your vortex and wrap us in your embrace."

A column of water snaked out and slaked its thirst upon them, sweeping them both into the gate.

#

They landed in a chamber, a soaking wet pile of limbs and clothes, tangled together by the whirlpool of spinning water.

"Cull, look!" Sionann disentangled herself from him and pushed herself to her feet.

One wall of the chamber was a vortex. The whole wall, spinning relentlessly, a constant slurping whirlpool on its side, defying gravity. The other three walls were the native metamorphic sandstone, two of them shimmering, as though somehow insubstantial.

The whorl was mesmerizing.

Culann tore his gaze away and stood, looking down at his dripping clothes. "Sorry for the dunking."

"*Now* I get an apology."

They grinned at each other, both looking as flummoxed as wet cats.

"I don't imagine invoking a dry-spell would be prudent at the moment." Her robes clung to her like glue, leaving few of her contours unrevealed.

He gestured her to go ahead. "This place has withstood invocations for fifteen hundred years. Another little dry spell in the desert won't harm it."

While she conjured something, he looked at the walls adjacent to the whirlpool. On one, he now saw their shapes replicated in vague outline. On the opposite wall were runes, the indecipherable runes, which deciphered themselves as he looked at them. He traced the equations through to the anomaly, the one that was there, and that wasn't there.

Culann's mind stumbled. An anomaly that was there, and that wasn't there. Like some Wonderlandian enigma, a Cheshire smile, a Schrödinger's cat.

Of course he saw the equation. And when he looked away it was no longer there.

"It's not there if you're not looking at it," Sionann said. "Why is it doing that?"

He hadn't realized she was standing beside him, completely dry. His clothes had dried without his noticing. "Did you do that?"

She shook her head, her gaze fixed to the runes. "No, and I didn't invoke a spell either. I started to, and then noticed I was dry."

He looked at the opposite wall, now completely blank, and approached it. "You saw this as well?" he asked, his own form appearing in outline.

She stepped up beside him, and her outline manifested on the wall. "A mirror stone, we call it." She gestured with her hand, and streaks appeared where her hand had been. "Yes, our gesticular interface, the way we Druids operate the Gael Gates."

He thought back to the chamber beneath Stonehenge. There, two walls had been in use; here, at Göbekli Tepe, three. Pondering the difference, he caught a glance of the fourth wall.

Plain sandstone stared back at him.

Culann knew it did something. He knew it.

It stared back, as if daring him to find out.

"No, Cull, not yet."

"Eh?" Startled, he looked at her. "What did you say?"

"You're not ready to do that yet." She stared at the wall, her gaze fixed, her face blank.

"Nann!" he said sharply.

She looked at him, her face full of bewilderment. "Did you just say something?"

"What did you just say?"

Now, Sionann looked befuddled. "I didn't say anything, Cull."

" 'No, Cull, not yet. You're not ready to do that yet.' "

"I didn't say that. I didn't say anything."

Now, Culann was sure that the two blank walls at Stonehenge served a purpose. He took his bearings in the chamber beneath Göbekli Tepe, and then stepped toward the whirlpool wall, the north wall.

"What's going on, Cull?"

"I wish I knew, Nann."

#

When they got back to the Gremlin, Culann showed Sionann the vids Jamie had made. The interview with the guard Phelan Brogimāros here at Göbekli Tepe, Proctor Medraut Bhodhsa's responses at Stonehenge, and Druid Arturo Lubri's answers at Las Cogotas obeliscos.

They were in Sionann's suite aboard the Gremlin, Druid Cadeyrn behind them, and watching from the doorway was Sionann's pilot, Captain Bébinn Nankivell. The suite though posh was crowded with four people.

"That's what you looked like down there," Culann told her.

"The fairy changelings of Finistère!" she said, her gaze vacant, this time in shock. Le Scour's account in the annals of Ancient Druidry of three changelings he saw in one family at Finistère was often cited as evidence of early demon possession.

"This isn't a demon, Nann," he said.

"What in Tuatha Dé Danann is it, then?"

"I don't know. A new Elemental is my best guess, one we've somehow neglected."

"This 'Ether'?" Finnán asked.

Culann nodded, looking over his shoulder. "It makes up eighty-five percent of the universe, and yet we know nearly nothing about it. Particle physics hasn't studied it much, and Neo Druidry lends it no credence. Eighty-five percent of the firmament as manifested around us—studiously ignored."

"How is Ether related to the gates' malfunctioning?"

"I can't quite make the link, but I sense that it underpins all of what's happened, even the random snatchings."

"Hardly seem random, Cull," Finnán said. "They have the feel of something intentional. Remember, there's Procter Gwrtheyrn Jézéquel at Montefortino di Arcevia, too, whom we didn't find out about until much later. One per Elemental, Cull. That's not random."

"I'll cede that to you, Finn. That's a lead we need to follow. Nann ..."

Sionann looked doubtful. "Dossiers on all four? Not sure I see the sense in that. On the apprentice Lew Gutraidh and the Druidess Jézéquel, certainly, but the battleship Captain and Archeologist? Not a touch of magic to either one. In fact, wasn't Professor Ríoghan Tanguy somewhat outspoken in her opposition to the Druidry?"

"She clashed with Druid Arturo Lubri on a few occasions," Culann conceded. "Still, it's an area I've neglected, and if I start poking my nose into Druidry archives to build dossiers—"

"The Ministry will scream bloody character murder," Finnán finished for him. "Better let me do that."

Culann looked at Druid Cadeyrn. "You're sure, my friend? You've no official capacity in this."

"Aye, but a former Presidential Druid still has a bit of weight to throw around, Laddie." He pointed a finger at Sionann. "And you leave that one alone, young lady."

She was biting her tongue and trying not to laugh.

"Thanks, Finn." Culann realized he'd dismissed this line of inquiry for precisely the reasons that Sionann had cited. Unlike him to miss something as significant as that.

What else have I been missing? he wondered.

Chapter 10

"Me cago na cona que te botou!" Druid Arturo Lubri said, recoiling visibly at Professor Penrose's request.

Culann's Galician wasn't that good. "Perdón?"

The Druid threw a glance at Sionann over his shoulder and immediately apologized. He drew his cape tighter, despite its being tied at the base of his throat. "Forgive me, Señor Profesor Penrose, I forget myself. This has all been so difficult." He gestured vaguely in the direction of the obeliscos. "Dame Lìosach, I humbly beg your forgiveness. The filth that spews from my mouth has fouled your ears. Arawn will deny me Tír na nÓg for my offenses."

"Druid Lubri," Sionann said, "times are difficult for us all, right now. There's nothing to apologize for. What did you say?"

She acts as if she didn't understand, Culann thought. He'd asked the Druid to accompany them to the obeliscos, forgetting momentarily the animosity between the now-missing archeologist and the local Druid. Culann Penrose, like Archeologist Ríoghan Tanguy, was a fully-tenured university professor. Further, Culann was infamous for his apostasy.

"It was nothing, Dame Lìosach, and does not bear repeating. As to your request, Profesor, forgive me but I must decline."

They stood in the anteroom of the Druidic Temple in Las Cogotas, just outside the main worship hall, where the village faithful gathered. And no one in Las Cogotas was unfaithful.

Galicia was something of a cultural enigma. At the very southern terminus of the Gael Federation, the Southern Triangle constellation was relatively isolated, Gamma Doradus some distance from the major space lanes. Exacerbating its isolation were its linguistic and cultural insularities. The derivation of Galician from Gaelic and Spanish had resulted in a language whose morphology and phonology were unique, long since having become a distinct language, and no longer just a combination of its roots. Further, their tradición apostólica, or apostolistic traditions, such as La Romeria de Santa Marta de Ribarteme, gave the region a unified set of cultural practices which fit within the Gael Federation like a square peg in a round hole.

The region talked constantly of seceding. Without the Gates, Culann guessed, they'd have long since left the Federation. And now that the operation of the Gates had been suspended...

He frowned, the implications clear. He glanced at Sionann, who'd expressed contempt at least of the local Druid, Arturo Lubri, if not of the region as a whole.

Behind Lubri through a doorway was the temple itself. Hues of its soaring stained-glass panels filtered through the door around the Druid's feet. The anteroom itself appeared to be a combination reception area, waiting room, and conference room, private booths on one side and open sitting areas on another, with a small side bar serving tapas and bebidas beside the vestibule door. The temple nave was as much a town hall, a chamber of government, a convention center, and a chamber of commerce. To the villagers of Las Cogotas, it was the center of town, the center of life.

If he hadn't been in jail, Druid Lubri probably would've objected to my entering the ring on my first visit, Culann thought. *Ironic that I ordered his release.* "Please, Dom Druido Lubri, it's vital to our investigation." He decided not to add that getting the Gates back into operation was of utmost priority. He suspected their remaining shuttered wouldn't displease the other man.

"It is a matter of principle, Profesor. Los Obeliscos are sacred to the Druidry and to Galicia. Their purity and integrity must remain unsullied."

"I'll protect Los Obeliscos, Dom Druido, upon my life," Sionann said.

"Perdón, Doña Lìosach, but you have not been purified properly to enter the Ring, either. Request denied."

She dropped to a knee and bowed her head. "Dom Druido, forgive this abominable sinner her iniquities and profanities. Show this humble supplicant how she may cleanse herself in the tradición apostólica."

Culann knelt as well. "Unbeliever that I am, I too wish to be cleansed in the ancient tradition."

Druid Arturo Lubri took a step back, his eyebrows jumping up his forehead. "I will consider your request, Doña Lìosach, Profesor Penrose. For now, I must pray. If you'll excuse me?" He waved his hand in front of his forehead in circular motion as though wiping sweat away, and then turned and retreated into the nave. Without awaiting a reply.

#

"That went well," Culann said, their sodhoppers scraping on the cobblestones. The narrow streets of Las Cogotas felt as wide as the boulevards of modern Durouï ̄ernon, the buildings on either side no more than three stories tall.

Sionann snorted. "I could invoke Federation authority, if needed."

"Kind of you to offer, Nann, but I think not. I'd rather get his cooperation. What did he say, by the way?"

She glanced askance at him with a shudder. "It truly doesn't bear repeating, Cull. You don't want to know."

"I guess I'll trust you on that, Nann. None too pleasant, judging by your reaction. This way," he said, indicating a pub on the corner, a small clapboard sign indicating its name: A Cova Céltica. The strains of a Celtic-inspired folk song threaded its threnody from a dark interior.

"Queimada, por favor," Culann told o camareiro, the waiter.

"La bebida is best served warm, Señor, if I may so recommend?"

"Sí, Señor, graza. And you, Señorita?"

"I'll have what he's having," she said, looking around the interior.

Memorabilia dating back several centuries festooned its walls, several sets of gaita, or bagpipes, among the decorative ensembles.

"Profesor Penrose, no?" asked a short, dark man dressed in the colorful local garb.

"Sí, Dom—"

"Ontonio, Belenos Ontonio. Good to see you, Profesor."

"Ah, good to see you, Dom Ontonio. This is Druid Sionann Lìosach, from Alcyone." To her he said, "Dom Ontonio led the excavation crew under Professor Tanguy."

The two greeted each other.

"La Druida Lìosach is as beautiful as she is famous," Belenos said, bowing over her hand.

Sionann colored slightly.

Culann didn't know she had the capacity for embarrassment. "I imagine there's been no work at the excavation site since La Profesora's disappearance?"

"No, Profesor, none. I secured the site as she would have desired and made provisions for the crew to be paid, but I fear valuable artifacts left half-exposed will be vulnerable to thieves."

"El universidade has not made arrangements?"

Dom Ontonio shook his head.

O camareiro brought drinks, the scents of lemon, herbs, and cinnamon wafting to Culann from the steamy beverage. "One for Dom Ontonio, por favor," Culann said.

"Perdón, Profesor, but I must decline." The man shook his head at o camareiro. "El Druido's liking for la queimada has soured mine," he told Culann.

"Can we see the site?" Sionann asked, her face half-eclipsed by the mug.

"By all means, Doña Druida, sí. It is to the south, just over the ridge." He looked at their footwear. "You will need heavier calzados, I think."

Culann glanced at her, the warm beverage coursing through him. "What are you thinking?" He realized that a slight change intonation might imbue his question with quite a derogatory emphasis.

"I suspect Professor Ríoghan Tanguy wasn't simply a victim of circumstance."

#

A tor marked the excavation site at the base of a mountain whose slopes soared into the clouds. The tor itself was a free-standing rock outcrop rising abruptly from the forest floor. Holly, fir, and pine covered the upper slopes of the mountain, and around the excavation were oak, birch, and alder. Further down slope, toward the sea, was a much milder clime, one prone to cold mists from the chill currents off the coast. Here, at the mountain base, a thousand feet above sea level, the sun was bright, almost harsh.

Culann had seen the tor's aura as soon as they'd come over the pass, looking like a gigantic flame to his ethereal senses. He'd stopped to admire the sight.

"Druid Lubri was right about its being a sacred site," Sionann had said.

Belenos had tried but couldn't see how the tor glowed with magic.

"We had awnings above the areas where we were digging," Belenos said as they entered the area. Around the tor were carefully manicured pits. The tor itself, a granite outcrop about twenty feet in girth, rose nearly forty feet straight up, its sides scarred by erosive forces, but remarkably uniform. Sylphs of the Air circled its peak in haphazard formation, throwing suspicious glances toward these visitors.

Kneeling at one excavation pit, Culann saw the glow of two half-exposed artifacts. One of them appeared to be a ladle, as might be used to serve queimada. He counted at least fifteen places around the tor where the soil had been excavated. "I see two artifacts here, in just this one spot. Is this a rich excavation, Dom Ontonio?"

"Sí, Profesora Tanguy could barely contain herself. We excavated hundreds of items and sent them to el universidade to be cleaned and catalogued. And she ... " Belenos looked down and away, then shook his head. "She admired the site very much."

That's not what he was going to say, Culann thought, the man's aspect changing as he watched.

"It was more than admiration, wasn't it, Dom Ontonio?" Sionann asked.

Belenos Ontonio nodded. A slight smile alighted on his face, and then was gone. "Sí, Doña Druida. One day, I arrived early, and La Profesora bade me to wait back here while she finished her ablutions." He waved his hand in front of his forehead in circular motion as though wiping sweat away, a motion oddly reminiscent.

"Eh?"

"She had a collapsible shower, and before each day of work, she cleansed herself inside it. Occasionally, we would get glimpses ... Under those drab work-clothes, she was quite attractive, Profesor, but she always performed her ablutions alone. It was almost el devoción a la relixiosa."

A religious devotion.

Such an odd ritual bewildered Culann, particularly given the mostly-male excavation crew. He and Sionann exchanged a glance. Had her excavation of this sacred site led to her being abducted at the obeliscos? If so, then the two sites shared a connection, somehow.

"Dom Ontonio, La Doña Druida and I would like to try something, but we want to insure that you're safe. May I ask you to stand over here?" Culann gestured to the edge of the clearing, some fifty feet from the tor.

"What will you and La Doña Druida be doing, if I may ask, Profesor?"

"My question, exactly," Sionann said, drilling him with a look.

"Invoking the magic of the tor." He gestured at the granite pillar.

"El Profesor is also El Druido?"

"No," Culann said, chuckling softly, "but I studied with the Druidry when I was younger."

"Mixing science and magic must be confusing, Profesor."

"Not at all, Dom Ontonio, although it may seem so. By the way, may I ask about a gesture I saw you make?" Culann waved his hand in front of his forehead as Belenos had done. And as Druid Lubri had done when he'd dismissed them.

"This, Profesor?" Belenos repeated the motion.

"Sí, Dom Ontonio. What does it mean?"

The man shrugged. "It is a gesture common to Galicia, is all I know. Profesora Tanguy also asked me about it when she first arrived. Everyone does it here."

Culann nodded, his curiosity piqued. "Well, I'd suggest you wait over there, Dom Ontonio. That would be safest."

The man backed away while Culann turned to join Sionann at the tor.

"Ablutions, eh? Odd, wouldn't you say, particularly for a skeptical archeologist?"

Religious devotion in an archeologist. He supposed that his own beliefs in the unified physical and metaphysical realms might seem equally incompatible. He nodded, looking up at the ponderous rock spire towering above them.

The sylphs circling the top had gathered at its rim, peering down at them and twittering amongst themselves, as though sensing the visitors' intent. "Not very inviting, are they?"

"Did he say where she did her ablutions?"

Culann shook his head, looking around. He found a small area just at the edge of the excavation, holes spaced a few feet apart. He looked to the top of the tor and gauged the angle.

"A peep show for the sylphs?" she asked.

"One way to propitiate them, eh?"

Several of the male sylphs on the rock ledge above them gestured obscenely and waved anatomical parts at the humans below, the female sylphs watching with mischievous smiles.

"Not something I'd recommend you do," he told her quickly, her behavior at Göbekli Tepe coming to mind.

"Not considering it. What are we after here, Cull?"

"I'm not sure. The place pulsates with energy."

"So if the sylphs attack us, we just let them, eh?"

"That's the idea, Nann."

"Gruagach help me," she muttered.

"Those long-haired, naked little men with broad shoulders aren't going to help you here. Strictly household chores. Ready?" He looked at Sionann.

"As ready for chaos as I'll ever be."

Culann raised his arms. "Paralda of the sylphs, grant my plea. Show me what there is to see."

The sylphs leaped from the tor, pounced upon them, and hurled them high into the sky.

#

"How'd we get here?" Sionann asked.

Culann looked around, trying to determine where "here" was, an eerie ululation piercing the air. The last he remembered was the breath being sucked from his lungs as they were flung skyward.

The ululation was coming from one side. There, just outside the gate, a line of villagers behind him, the village itself a backdrop, Druid Arturo Lubri gesticulated wildly, the otherworldly voice of a banshee issuing from his mouth.

Straight above them soared three obeliscos, forming a perfect triangle.

They were inside the main tribelisco at Las Cogotas.

Sionann helped him to his feet. "What the hell is he doing?"

Druid Lubri looked to be summoning an invocation, his face a rictus of ecstasy, his hair stringy with sweat, his robes flying with every contortion. A ring of villagers all in bright clothing surrounded the tribelisco, holding hands and chanting in counterpoint to the Druid's mantras.

What *was* Druid Lubri doing? Culann wondered, the Ceannaire having ordered the gates idled. Furthermore, Culann had no idea what would happen if a gate were invoked when people were inside the tribelisco. "Stop! Not when we're inside!" He waved at the Druid, not twenty feet away, facing them.

Druid Lubri seemed to be ignoring them.

"Cull, look at that woman!"

As he watched, a young woman in drab, dun-gray digs, garb meant for the dirty work of excavation, joined the ring. "Is that Professor Tanguy?"

"Looks like her from the dossier Finn sent me."

"But ..." His mind stumbled on the anomaly. How could Professor Ríoghan Tanguy be here again?

"They don't see us, Cull."

All the villagers stood in a ring, facing the tribelisco. None evinced any indication that they noticed the pair inside the stone pillars.

He was beginning to understand. "We're not here, then, are we, Nann?"

"No, Cull, we're not. And this isn't happening now."

Lubri spun, flaunting his cape as though taunting a bull, his eyes glazed in ecstasy, a froth of fine spittle at the corners of his mouth.

Tanguy giggled, loud enough for Cull to hear.

The Druid froze, his gaze fixed to the archeologist. "We have an infidel in our midst! She who mocks the sylphs and desecrates our sacred sites!" He launched an arm in her direction. "Seize her!"

Multiple villagers converged on Tanguy.

"Bring her here," Druid Lubri commanded. "A rope!"

They overpowered her, dragged her between two obeliscos, and tied each limb with rope, legs apart, her arms suspended at forty-five degrees overhead.

Lubri stuck his face into hers. "You'll desecrate no more, Infidel! You'll meet the sylphs face to face, and then you'll believe!"

The scents of lemon, cinnamon, and spices wafted past Culann. Queimada!

"What are you doing, Cabrón?!" she spat, struggling against the ropes.

He backhanded her, and her head flew to the side. "Perra pequeña! Cona! Back in position, everyone! Let's send this succubus to moura encantada!" He backed away and resumed his chants and gyrations.

"Dom Ontonio, help me!" she called to someone in the ring.

Belenos Ontonio kept his place in the circle, sweat pouring off him, his eyes wide.

Lubri whipped his cape from his shoulders, grasped it with both hands, thrust it to the ground, and knelt at Ríoghan's feet, ululating stridently. Then he abruptly straightened and flung the cape back over his head.

A thunderclap split the air, and Ríoghan vanished.

Then all the villagers and Druid Lubri vanished too, replaced with solid, white-quartzite rock. The obeliscos formed pillars at the corners of the three-sided room, Celtiberian runes glowing on the columns.

"All right, Cull, you've done it again." Sionann's tone was as congratulatory as it was scornful.

"Damned if I do, et cetera," he quipped.

"What do you think that was? A time-warp, a recording, a glimpse of the past?"

He shook his head, looking around and up. The quartzite rock on three sides looked somewhat eroded, like the tor, but still too uniform to be natural. The walls like the obeliscos soared above their heads to eighty-one feet, where a triangular aperture of sky peered down at them. No way we're getting up there, he thought idly.

Culann looked at the glowing Celtiberian runes on the obeliscos. As before at the two other sites, these runes deciphered themselves as he looked at them, revealing the same A-warp equations.

On the third obelisk, the runes lit up in red. These aren't A-warp equations, he thought. Further, the columnar shape prevented him from seeing them fully.

As though sensing his thoughts, the runes spread themselves across the quartzite wall.

With a near eidetic memory, Culann did his best to fix the image in his mind. He ran through the equations one time to reinforce the memory.

He turned to look at Sionann and was surprised to find her right beside him.

"I wish we could read those, don't you?" she said, her gaze on the red runes. "We need to have Finn look at that scene, Cull." The Druidess gestured at the wall that had shown them what happened.

"Why's that?" Don't the runes decipher themselves for her? he wondered.

"I may be a Druidess, but I'm not a Gael Gate operator. I don't know what gestures conjure what destinations. But Finn does." Chief Druid at Göbekli Tepe, Finnán Cadeyrn knew the gesticulations necessary to align a Gate with the desired destination.

Culann stepped to what appeared to be the mirror stone. His shape manifested in the rock. "Step back, Nann. I want to try something."

"Clear the room. El Profesor is about to experiment." She grinned at him. But she also retreated to the obelisco opposite the mirror stone.

He brought to mind Druid Lubri's wild gesticulations. And repeated them.

The quartzite wall between the obeliscos dissolved, revealing a vista of rolling grassland plains, tree-capped knolls, and meandering streams. The landscape glowed, the grass a bright emerald green, the sky the azure of aqua, one or two raveled clouds lined with silver drifting lazily past, birds singing happily.

"Where is it? *What* is it?"

"Tír na nÓg?" he wondered aloud. "The supernatural realm of the terrestrial fairies, everlasting youth, beauty, health, abundance, and joy?"

The grass at his feet just beyond the threshold was matted, as though trampled by many feet, or flattened by … someone sleeping on it?

Culann knelt and examined the area more closely.

A stick sharpened on one end leaned against a tree. Over a branch hung a mat woven from the three-foot grasses. Trails led toward and away from the tree.

"Someone's living here," Sionann said over his shoulder. "Professor Tanguy?"

He suspected such and stood. "Shall we see?" And without waiting for an answer, he tried to step across the threshold.

And bounced off the solid quartzite stone, hitting his nose.

"Something we're not supposed to do, looks like," she told him, trying not to laugh.

#

"Druid Arturo Lubri," Culann said, a bandage across the scrape on his nose, "you're under arrest for murder. Anything that you say can and will be held against you. You have the right to a counselor, even if you can't afford one. Before la condestábela detains you, I have a few questions."

Druid Lubri stared at him with the fury of the righteous. "Anda que che den pelo cu!"

Culann glanced at the constable. Culann and Sionann had conjured their way out of the triangular stone chamber with a simple sylph spell. Belenos had gone straight home, while Culann and Sionann had retrieved the village constable. All four of them stood in the vestibule of the Druidic Temple in Las Cogotas.

"Did he say he's not going to answer questions?" Culann asked the constable.

The bright red face of the young woman told him his answer. "Uh, sí, Profesor Penrose, he refuses."

"Perdón, Doña Condestábela, but my Galician is somewhat rusty. Could you translate what he said, por favor?"

She ran her finger around her collar. "He, uh, invited you to receive pleasure in your back passage, Profesor."

"It sounded somewhat stronger than an invitation, but no matter." Culann turned to Druid Lubri. "Think back to the moment before Profesora Tanguy's disappearance, when you took off your cape."

Bewilderment replaced rage. "Eh? I didn't take off my cape. I never take off my cape." He wore it now, tied at the base of his throat.

"Several villagers attest that you did, Dom Druido. They also say you slapped her, called her 'perra pequeña' and 'cona.' Did you or did you not do these things?"

Again that bewildered look. "I did not call her names, Profesor, I swear. Those who accuse me of thus do not know the remorse in my heart at La Profesora's disappearance."

His repentance is nearly lugubrious, Culann thought. "Tell me what happened."

Druid Arturo Lubri bowed his head, seeming on the verge of tears. He looked up at Culann, blinking rapidly. "I … was leading an invocation. It was the procession of la borriquita, a local holy day. I led the village faithful from the Temple up to los obeliscos. I didn't intend to activate the gate, Profesor."

"Tell me what happened next, por favor," he said gently.

"It was all very strange. I saw her approach the ring of villagers, Profesor. I thought it odd that she would join us, but we are a welcoming peoples. She took a place in the ring beside Doña Noba Pacem. And then she laughed, Profesor. She laughed." Druid Lubri stared at the ground, shuffling his feet, his jaw rippling.

"What happened then, por favor?"

The Druid froze.

"Dom Druido?" Culann asked softly.

No response, the gaze fixed to the ground, the posture completely still, as though Druid Lubri had entered some catatonic fugue.

Culann exchanged a glance with Sionann, who'd been uncharacteristically silent.

"Arturo!" La condestábela said, shaking the man gently.

"Eh? Perdón?" Confusion replaced catatonia, and the Druid looked between them. "What did you ask me?"

"What happened after Profesora Tanguy laughed?"

Druid Lubri stared at Culann. "I don't know, Profesor."

#

The triple tips of the tallest tribelisco thrust like horns above the rooftops, made surreal by the distortion of the beveled Cathedral glass.

He and Sionann stood in the nave of the Druidic Temple, its serenity helping to settle his disquietude.

"The fairy changelings of Finistère at work, again." It was the first time she'd seen that response live, rather than a vid.

"So it seems, eh?" He looked directly at her, easing himself to a pew. "Are there invocations which might render a person incognizant of his or her actions?"

"Demon possession? Or just suspended volition?" She sat beside him companionably, leaning back in the pew.

He shook his head. "Somewhere in between, Nann. One that gives control of the victim over to the will of another."

She snorted at him, shaking her head. "Sounds like possession, Cull."

"But not by demons," he added.

Her gaze narrowed, her brow furrowed. "We'd need to consult with a modern-day Dark Disciple."

He stared at her blankly, for a moment. "An adherent of Ether?"

Her jaw dropped open. "Somewhere in my studies at Stonehenge ..."

"Go on."

"I was researching a transmigration spell, one of the arcane ways to enter Tír na nÓg without having to die. Fabled invocations, to be sure, never reproduced among the Druidry, or not in modern times, anyway. And I came across Amyntas, once King of Galatia, purported to have drawn the wrath of Eltanin by summoning the dark light."

" 'Dark light'? Bit of an oxymoron."

"Captain Niamh Lozac'h wasn't the first to fight off an Eltanin invasion."

Culann nodded. "Go on, sorry for interrupting."

"The dark light was sometimes referred to as 'ether.' According to legend, Amyntas was the last of the Dark Disciples."

"Eh? He was King of Galatia *and* a Druid?"

"In those times, they weren't constricted by the same ethos as we are now. The separation of terrestrial from ethereal powers is what really defines Neo Druidry from its antecedents."

There it was again, a reference to Ether. Utterances conveyed a great deal of information about a speaker in addition to his or her semantic, cultural, and historical background. Druid Sionann Lìosach was descended from the insular Celts, whose Druidic beliefs had suffered centuries of separation from the Galatian, Celtiberian, and Cisalpine Druidic communities.

On Alrakis, center of Galatian Druidry, as everywhere throughout the Gael Federation, the separation of powers was sacrosanct. Druid Finnán Cadeyrn might wield colossal power by being the arbiter of the Gael Gates at Göbekli Tepe, but his influence was eclipsed by that of the Potentate of Alrakis, Dylan MacAskill. Similar separations of power governed the hierarchies on Alcyone, Galicia, and Tucana Prime. Even the President of the Gael Federation, Ceannaire Ceridwen Gwilym, respected the demarcation between the firmaments and practiced no magic.

One of the reasons that he, forensic physicist Culann Penrose, Professor of Astral Physics at the University of Cardiff, was widely regarded as apostate. He believed in the predominance of science and practiced Druid-style magic in spite of nearly universal restrictions prohibiting non-initiates from doing so.

If he ever ran for political office, he'd have to foreswear magic entirely.

He regarded Sionann, wondering whether she'd detected her own reference to the dark Elemental.

"Why are you looking at me that way?" She looked embarrassed, flush creeping up from her neck.

"Where might we find a Dark Disciple?"

Chapter 11

Professor Culann Penrose eased the Meave to the tarmac at Newport on Alcyone, the towers at the University of Cardiff visible in the distance. Good to be home, he thought.

The Meave, a lithe, wily yacht loaned to him by Druidess Sionann Lìosach, was appropriately named after the Queen of the Underworld, L'annawnshee, which translated from Proto-Gaelic as literally, Underworld Fairy. Its snazzy design and perky performance made it the best-selling Nerolead Interstellar model.

Druidess Lìosach had suggested he start his search for a Dark Disciple at Stonehenge, and then had loaned him the Meave—not so much to assist him as to rid herself of him.

Not that he blamed her. He knew he could be overwhelming at times, his two divorces attesting to that. He'd seen how flustered she'd gotten under his interrogation in the nave of the Druidic Temple.

And he expected his stay at Cardiff to be relatively short, here only to consult with his colleague in particle physics, the expert on A-warp to whom he'd submitted the strange equation he'd found in the chamber at Stonehenge. The professor, Clíodhna Ròsach, didn't know the surprise he had for her.

Of an age with him, Professor Ròsach was as fastidious in dress and speech as Culann was disheveled and disorganized. She claimed to exist "purely for the numbers," and found his Astral Physics daunting, impenetrable, and superfluous.

Her office and laboratory occupied a high-ceilinged, two-story hall at the east edge of campus with a marbled, Romanesque exterior. Its most striking feature was the east-facing rotunda lecture theater, where the Professor held her symposiums. The rich mahogany and scents of leather in her office were redolent of ancient history, her walls packed with tomes whose information in Cull's view was better stored and accessed from the many electronic devices available. Why she kept these outdated volumes of calfskin and sheepskin, he didn't know. One wall was given over to another kind of sheepskin, a wall cherished by professors everywhere, their curriculum vitae. Fifteen diplomas, plaques, credentials, warrants, and awards graced the wall.

He'd checked her schedule en route to make sure she wasn't in lecture, but when he appeared at her door, he saw she was occupied.

"I've a surprise for you, Cull," she said to him in the hallway from inside the office.

"Then it's mutual, darling," Culann replied.

The two students across from her glanced questioningly between them.

"You're such a scad, Cull, planting rumors like that. If I didn't know better, I'd say you're taking lessons from my sister." She turned to the students. "Professor Penrose claims that his Astral Physics bridges the gulf between the corporeal world and the metaphysical realm, but it's a bridge kept aloft by hot air alone. I'll see you both at seminar."

The two students excused themselves, one of them giggling at the two professors.

"Come this way, Cull, let me show you what I've done with that equation you commed me." She stepped to a door with a frosted glass pane and opened it.

"And that hot air, Clio, is my breath, I presume?" He followed her into the small laboratory beyond.

"You named it, Cull." Professor Ròsach indicated a holoboard taking up the far wall, twenty feet long, eight feet high, where equations were scrawled in multiple layers and colors.

He picked out the patterns he knew to be A-warp, but that was just the first two layers. He counted three more beyond that. He saw a magenta holopen on the opposite counter and picked it up. "Clio, if I may?" He held up the pen. "How is your sister, by the way?" He and Professor Ròsach's sister, Cathasach Bolloré, an A-warp engineer at Nerolead Interstellar, had had a brief but torrid marriage.

"Scandalous as ever, Cull. You know Satch, can't keep a level head or a civil tongue." She made some adjustments with a small device, and a clean holoboard layer appeared in front of him, sans the other layers.

"Pardon, while I concentrate." Culann closed his eyes and brought forth from memory the slate of symbols he'd seen inside the tribelisco at Las Cogotas, the runes that had peeled themselves from around the obelisco. He began to transcribe them, blessing his near-eidetic memory, slowly filling the holoboard with symbols in magenta.

Clíodhna watched in silence, for which he was grateful. At the odd moments he glanced at her, her gaze transfixed to the slowly-filling holoboard.

"Tea?" she asked at one point.

"Thank you, yes," he'd replied, and delved right back in to the intricate symbols. He was grateful he'd stepped through the sequence while the equations had hung in front of him, reinforcing his eidetic recall. Imagery stored along neural assemblies tended to fade as other information saturated the senses. Further, the physiological limitations of human memory allowed for the storage of only three objects in unassociated, unsequenced memory. Beyond three, the human brain began to associate additional items with external data and with a datum's relative position to other data in sequence.

His tea was cold by the time he finished, and he stood looking at the scrawl-filled board, his armpits soaked and arms like lead. "I feel as if I've just run a race."

Clíodhna was silent, staring wide-eyed. Somewhere, a chime tinkled. She started, as though waking from a dream. "Tá aiféala orm, Cull. I have seminar."

"Apology accepted, Clio. I'd have one too, if I weren't on sabbatical."

"Join me next door?"

"Sure, why not? I may learn something." He followed her through the door opposite the one they'd entered, and down a short corridor to another door with a frosted glass pane.

The rotunda theater, its tiers packed with students. Bright young faces followed Professor Clíodhna Ròsach around to the lectern. Cull took a seat at the lowest level to one side.

"Today, Laddies and Laddesses, I have a special presentation on Alcubierre Warp Theory, or A-warp for short, the principle means by which the human race achieved space travel and the functional mechanics by which our Gael Gates are posited to operate. Or did operate.

"First, I'll describe the basics of A-warp, the history of its discovery, its current implementation in our hyperlight vehicles, and why it is supposed that it operates the Gael Gates.

"In a few simple sentences, A-warp compresses space in front of an object and stretches space behind an object to create a draw much like aerodynamic lift to pull the object across space faster than light. And to utilize the warped space, it's always been assumed that an object has to be moving across that compressed space." Professor Ròsach paused dramatically.

"As all are keenly aware, the Gael Gates have been idled by a series of incidents which called their safety into question. The lead investigator into these incidents is the University of Cardiff's own Professor of Astral Physics Culann Penrose. In the course of his investigation, he sent me an equation whose significance he didn't understand." She flicked her wrist, and the equation appeared behind her in red ink, a holoboard superimposing itself upon a projection area. "An equation that, on its face, appears to resolve the translation of an object across space compressed to an infinitesimal degree."

Several conversations began among the students.

"But Professor," said one young woman, sitting half-way up the tiered gallery, "isn't that theoretically impossible? Infinitesimal compression of space is thought to induce a collapse across all space, one analogous to a reversal of the Big Bang."

"Precisely, Pryderi," Professor Ròsach said, "you have named the conundrum, based on the assumption that within the context of general relativity, A-warp depends upon the displacement of exotic matter. Using the Arnowitt-Deser-Misner formalism of relativity, A-warp posits that space-time is described by a foliation of space-like hypersurfaces of the constant coordinate time, taking this general form." And she flicked the device in her hand, spilling another equation across the screen, this one in fuchsia. "Where the inversion of torsion forces between foliations displaces exotic matter in equal proportion. Because the energy density is negative, the displacement of exotic matter then pushes the object across the compression threshold and into the new location. Sustaining the displacement of enough exotic matter to keep a gate open long enough to facilitate faster-than-light travel was long thought in pre-Diaspora times to be the inhibiting factor to A-warp's practical implementation.

"Here," she added, gesturing at the screen, "is the sequelae to the equation supplied by my colleague, Professor Penrose." And two superimposed holoboards in different colors appeared. "The first, in blue, is the mathematical induction of torsion foliation taken to its infinitesimal extreme, and the second, in green, is its reverse engineering."

"But they're different!" said one student.

"Precisely, Gobán, which we all know to be a contradiction. How is it possible that a reverse-engineered induction yields a result at odds with its origin?"

Professor of Astral Physics Penrose was long since lost, the discussion far beyond his expertise.

"Here's how," Professor Ròsach said, motioning. Behind her appeared the layer in magenta that Culann had just transcribed in Clíodhna's laboratory.

But I just transcribed it! he thought, bewildered even more.

"Some of the symbols aren't rendered quite accurate, as this was transcribed from the memory of someone not conversant with the actual mathematics. But I believe it's legible nonetheless." She stepped to the right side of the theater to let them study the holoboard.

"What's it mean?" Culann asked her quietly.

"Let's see if my students can tell you." She turned to the class. "Anyone care to speculate?"

Pryderi raised her hand. "I believe what it's describing is the displacement of exotic matter in excess proportion to its infusion between foliations. But if torsion inversion between foliations displaces exotic matter in equal proportion, doesn't excess displacement indicate the elimination of that excess?"

"And by elimination, you mean …?"

"The destruction of exotic matter," Pryderi said, looking bewildered. "But matter isn't ever destroyed, not even exotic matter. It's converted to other forms, typically to energy."

"Basic principle of conservation, exactly. In contradiction of general relativity, these equations posit that exotic matter is destroyed in the excess displacement in the torsion between foliations."

"Who transcribed these equations?" someone asked.

"Professor of Astral Physics Penrose, just an hour ago, in my laboratory." Clíodhna turned to him. "Would you like to describe where you found these equations, Professor?"

Culann stood and joined her at the front of the theater. "Good day, all, a pleasure to be here." He was sure to send the Druidry into a frenzy when he disclosed where he'd seen these equations. But he wasn't averse to doing that. For centuries, the runes on the obeliscos had been indecipherable to initiate and non-initiate alike.

"In my investigation into the disappearances of three individuals into the Gael Gates on a single day, I found myself inside a sarsen-lined chamber beneath Stonehenge, where I happened upon the first equation shown you today, the one in red.

"At a later point in the investigation, on Galicia, I found myself inside the main tribelisco at Las Cogotas. Anyone here familiar with Galicia?"

"I'm from Galicia," said Pryderi. Several other students also raised their hands.

"Las Cogotas is my natal village," said Gobán.

"The nine obeliscos are arranged in three triangles, two sets of smaller obeliscos twenty-seven feet tall on either side of a taller set of obeliscos eighty-one feet tall, each set of three known as a tribelisco. I was inside the tallest tribelisco, but I'm not sure I was at Las Cogotas proper. Instead of open air between the obeliscos, what surrounded me on three sides was stone wall, made from the quartzite common to the area. One quartzite surface changed in front of me, revealing vistas of distant places. Another manifested the equations in magenta behind me, which were transliterated from the runes inscribed on one of the obeliscos. Runes that have heretofore eluded deciphering for more than a millennium." He smiled at Clíodhna.

"How did you decipher the runes, Professor?" Gobán asked.

"I didn't. I've no more knowledge of Proto-Gaelic than I do of particle physics. Less, actually. The runes decrypted themselves for me, as though by incantation." He knew he was talking a language that they had no basis for understanding, students whose indoctrination into the physical sciences contravened their ability to understand.

"Today, Professor Ròsach in her analysis of these equations has provided me valuable clues in my investigation, hints of a possible conclusion, and perhaps the resolution that will finally reopen the Gael Gates. Thank you, Professor."

#

A few blocks away, on St Andrews Place, in a pub on the ground floor of a refurbished brick building, Culann eased himself to a chair by the fireplace, a happy pseudoblaze sending licks of flame up a faux chimney. The chill of the walk sent a shiver up his spine as he shook off the last of the cold.

Clíodhna sat beside him, her pint in hand. "Cheers!" she said. Across the room was Pryderi, her nose in a holotext. She waved briefly at them and returned her attention to her studies.

The two professors clinked glasses, and Culann drank deeply. The cold brew initially exacerbated his chill, but as its warmth worked into his veins, he began to relax. "Helluva lecture, Clio."

"Mutual, Cull. Certainly left them bedazzled, didn't we?"

"Did me too, matter of fact. Leicester University researchers must have felt something similar when they discovered dark matter axions streaming from the sun's core, producing x-rays as they slammed into Earth's magnetic field." Their discovery on twenty-first century Earth had led to the harnessing of A-warp and thus to interstellar travel.

"It's the next leap forward in A-warp, no question about it. You mentioned hints of a possible conclusion?" She looked at him directly. "Where'd all those people go, Cull?"

"That vista I mentioned? Not sure where it was, looked like some grasslands planet, a few species of scrub tree or bush. I'll be taking a former mentor there to see if he can recreate a sequence ... " Culann leaned close to Clíodhna. "The sequence of motions used by Druid Arturo Lubri to send the archeologist there."

Her gaze narrowed. "You'd have to have a witness with an extraordinary memory or a vid of the incident."

"Neither. We saw the whole scene replayed, Nann and I."

She shook her head. "Replayed?"

"We were inside the tribelisco, Clio, but it wasn't the present."

"You're sure, Cull? You know what that means?" Her gaze left his face to focus on something behind him. "Gobán, good to see you." She gestured at the chair across from them. "Have a seat. Professor Penrose, this is Gobán Feijóo, one of my thesis students."

Culann half-stood, extending his hand.

Which was refused, the young man trembling with rage. "El Druido Lubri is innocent, Cabeza de nabo, may you rot throughout eternity in ten times the torment you've inflicted upon him!" He spat on the floor and walked out of the pub.

Culann fell back into his seat, looking toward the door, the exterior chill returning redoubled.

"What the hell?" Clíodhna said.

"It appears I've offended a Las Cogotas villager. Not to worry, Clio. Won't be the last person I offend." He grinned at her.

"Even so, that was completely inappropriate. I'll have to have a word with him."

Pryderi stood before them. "Perdón, Profesores, I saw what happened." She glanced at the door Gobán had taken. "Please, Profesor Penrose, you must be careful. Don't believe those tourist brochures about Galicia with gaita-playing gallegos dancing Celtic dances. The reality is dark and sinister. It is Los Caciques, the bosses, who control Galicia, and they're not happy with El Druido Lubri's arrest."

"Thanks for the concern. Grazas, Señorita." Culann saw she had her study materials clutched under one arm. "Are you on your way somewhere? Perhaps I could accompany you?"

"Certainly, Profesor, I'd be honored."

"I have to get back to work, anyway." He took his leave with Professor Ròsach, putting a fiver on the table for the draught. Outside, he wrapped his coat tight against the chill, looking up and down St Andrews Place.

"You needn't have come with me, Profesor, I'll be fine. It's you who should be worried."

"Eh? Me? Call me Cull, by the way." He stuck out his hand.

"Pri," she said, shaking it and smiling. "Gobán is involved with El Caciquismo, the drug traffickers. The large Galician cities, such as Corunna, Santiago de Compostela, and Vigo, are rife with drug-fueled feuds. El Caciquismo and their powerful patronage networks have compromised local law enforcement and El Xudicial, the Judiciary."

They turned onto Boulevard De Nantes, where traffic was somewhat heavy, flitters whining past constantly. They faced oncoming traffic, the wind of their passage exacerbating the chill. Cull walked on the street-ward side of the walk, a slim strip of bedraggled shrubbery between them and the heavy traffic. "I've heard recent efforts to interdict the drug trade have been relatively successful."

"El Caciquismo obeys the laws of conservation, too, Cull."

"Displaced elsewhere, eh?" He laughed and nodded. "Well put, Pri. But what's Gobán's connection with them?"

"His Pai, Señor Breno Feijóo, he is the go-between."

"His father? Go-between? Between whom?"

"El Druido Lubri and El Caciquismo."

Culann almost stumbled, the implications clear, Druid Arturo Lubri using the Gael Gates to help Galician drug traffickers. "You're sure?"

Pryderi nodded, shooting him a glance. "And the local constable looks the other way." They came abreast City Hall, its precisely manicured lawns opening to their right.

Culann thought back to the constable who'd assisted with the Druid's arrest. She'd seemed the picture of propriety, even looking embarrassed at the Druid's foul remarks. "La Condestábela didn't appear to be influenced or compromised."

"You can bet El Druido Lubri didn't stay in jail for long, Profesor."

A hover veered from the traffic lane and Culann leapt aside, pulling Pryderi with him. The vehicle corrected and went on its way, leaving the two pedestrians sprawled on wet grass.

His heart hammering, Culann watched the hover flitter away, noting the make and model but unable to get its license. He helped Pryderi to her feet. "You all right?"

She nodded, regaining her feet and brushing herself off. "Thanks, that could've been…"

He looked at her when she didn't continue.

She was white as a ghost. "It wasn't an accident, I'm afraid."

"Eh? Of course it was. Couldn't have been …" He stopped, shivering and not from cold. "El Caciquismo?"

Pryderi nodded. "I suspect so, Profesor."

Chapter 12

"Good to see you, old friend," Druid Finnán Cadeyrn said, greeting him in the anteroom of his office in Ancyra. Across the street was the Capitol, the twin pillars of its erzurum cifte minareli, fluted minarets, crowning the monumental façade.

Culann grinned at his old mentor. "Thought you'd heard the last of me, eh?"

"Rumors of your death are constantly being exaggerated, Cull. Who's killed you now? Druidry in its entire, and now the Galician El Caciquismo? What's next, Mala del Brenta on Tucana?"

He shook his head at the barrel-chested older man. "Just my lot to upset the applecart, isn't it?"

"All of academia, too! How dare you expose us Druids as charlatans, as if you hadn't already? Professor of Astral Physics, Culann Penrose, forensic physicist, University of Cardiff, the curse that keeps on cursing. What mischief are you stirring up here, *this* time?"

"I've come to ask a favor, Finn."

The old Druid suddenly looked older, the dark rings around his eyes darker. "Expose our secrets, and then come begging us to tell you more? What herdhe you have, my friend."

The word, spoken with guttural fricative phonemes full of glottal stops, sounded like an expletive. "And those are?" He didn't even try to pronounce it.

"Testicles, Cull. Braver man than I, someone once said. What are you wanting this time?"

Culann admired Druid Cadeyrn's forbearance as he described what he and Sionann had found inside the tribelisco. The wide publicity given the transcribed runes had incensed the Ministry of Druidry, their secrets now writ large in both scholarly journals and scurrilous tabloids.

"That's phenomenal! You didn't tell anyone about the scene, did you?"

"Just Professor Ròsach, a colleague of mine in particle physics at Cardiff."

"A fellow academic. And Nann was with you, too. Only way for three people to keep a secret is if two of them are dead." Finnán chuckled mightily, stroking his beard.

The Druid's office walls were accented in mosaics, ancient scenes of Hittite history depicted in tile, sets of shelves alternating with mosaics. On the shelves were objects of historical value, among them pottery shards from Seljuk and urns from the Sultanate of Rum. On nearly every shelf, a sylph or undine frolicked, salamanders skittering up and down walls, gnomes trolling the floor.

Culann had dodged one or two coming in, trying to avoid stepping on them accidentally. "Why all the Elementals, my friend?"

"It's what happens when the gates are closed, Cull. The blocked energy causes them to accumulate. Soon, I'll have to open a caravanserai. So what did you have in mind for me at Las Cogotas obeliscos?"

He told the other man about the grasslands vista, the signs of occupancy just beyond the threshold.

"You think it's the archeologist? And you tried to step through the portal? I was wondering about your nose. Thought you might've had a bit of a row at the pub. And you want me to duplicate El Druido Lubri's summons and fully open that gate, eh?"

Professor Penrose smiled. "I'm expecting interference from El Caciquismo, of course. The tor under excavation was unattended. Who knows what's been plundered from the site."

"But that's not the kind of interference you're concerned about."

"No," Culann said, "it's not."

"And what about the other sites?"

"Exactly my thought." He met the other man's gaze. "Were the other victims transported someplace similar? Six people gone, Finn, and no one knows where they're at."

#

Finnán Cadeyrn behind him, Professor Culann Penrose approached Göbekli Tepe, the forest of stele on the hilltop above him looking ominous and foreboding.

He'd considered trying this particular experiment first at Nevalı Çori, another henge on Alrakis but of lesser importance, a smaller stand of megaliths with fewer gates. On Tucana Prime, the disappearances of Druids Gwrtheyrn Jézéquel, Armel Gallou, and Óengus Tàillear, and the apparent destruction of Montefortino di Arcevia, had really brought home to Culann the potential for disaster.

The terrifying fundamental forces at work were nothing to be trifled with.

"Think Nann will be miffed if we do this without her?" Finnán asked.

Fundamental forces weren't the only hazard. "Of course, Finn. But last I spoke with her, she was eager to have me gone. Loaned me her Meave just to be rid of me."

"Probably not what you think, Cull."

Culann stopped at the Ring, that raised one-inch perimeter of stone encircling the Tepe. It was early evening, the sun having just set. In the west, cloud flamed with the last of the day. He wondered about the trafficking at Las Cogotas that Pryderi had told him about and glanced at Druid Cadeyrn. Among the two hundred stele here at Göbekli Tepe, giving over a gate or two to other purposes might not seem much of an inconvenience. But Finnán operated these gates here on Alrakis with a cadre of Druids under his command. Las Cogotas in its isolation must have been far easier to compromise, only Druid Lubri operating those gates.

"Who goes there?" said a familiar voice.

Culann turned to look.

Ensign Piritta Quemener and Cadet Phelan Brogimāros approached.

The four of them exchanged greetings.

"Last I heard, Professor, you had a passel of undines chasing you underground," Ensign Quemener said.

"About drowned, we did," Culann replied, shaking his head.

"Wait till you hear his latest debacle, Cadet," Finnán said, chuckling. "By the way, there are indications the gates at Las Cogotas have been compromised by the local drug traffickers. Keep an eye out here, eh?"

"Yes, Sir," both cadets said, glancing at each other.

"Ready?" Finnán asked, gesturing at the ring.

Culann nodded, and the two men stepped into the Ring together. Undines ran in circles around their feet, seeming more numerous than on prior occasions.

"Aye, there's more of them," the other man said, when asked. "It's the Gates being closed."

The sere ground at their feet crunched dryly, the fine dust kicked up by their passage settling quickly, no hint of wind, not a whisper to speak of.

Culann looked back the way they'd come and saw that their tracks in the dirt disappeared within seconds. The aura of an ancient invocation tinged the ground. The art of everlasting spells had long since been lost, ancient Druidry legendary for its audacious wizardry.

"There's a story going round locally," Finnán said as they approached the innermost circle of ten stele, "that Captain Niamh Lozac'h's was inducted into an elite cabal of ancients who govern the spirit of our Tepes, both here and at Nevalı Çori."

"Superstition, do you think?" He looked up at the ponderous capstones, twenty-five feet above him, the edges of two nearly touching.

"Not like Alrakians to cloak their ignorance in fantasy, Cull. Perhaps her being held in high esteem before she disappeared…"

Culann nodded. "Saved Alrakis from the Eltanin."

"And lost most her family in the war, a brother and sister, at least. Known for her sacrifice." He looked at the Professor of Astral Physics. "It'd be a blessing to have Captain Lozac'h back. You'd have earned the gratitude of all Anatolia."

He was surprised to see the big man blinking back tears.

The undines at their feet had stopped playing, and now stood stock still. Each six inches tall, they stood in a formation that mimicked the stand of stele itself, one ring of undines surrounded by five more rings, and fourteen rings around those, twenty rings total.

"Searbhan help us," Finnán muttered, his brow furrowed. One of the Fomorians, Searbhan was a mythical giant among the insular Celts possessed of redoubtable magic. In one ancient tale, Searbhan had proved indomitable, until felled by his own club.

"What are they doing, Finn?"

"Protecting the Tepe, I'd say."

"As if it needs protecting from you?"

Finnán swung his gaze at Culann.

"Touché," Culann said. The Henge at Montefortino di Arcevia now occupied some liminal limbo, neither there nor here, after a visit by Culann and Sionann.

By habit, he examined the stele for residue of transits. Tinges of his and Sionann's passage lingered on the stone, wisps of their spirit still detectible only because no one else had come through this gate since then.

"Undine unbind," Culann said. "Escort us into your chamber."

An undine the size of the big Druid appeared inside the gate, water dripping down its eidolic shape. "Unbeliever!" An arm rose and aimed a finger at the Professor.

Finnán stepped between them. "By Ceffyl Dŵr, belay there. I, Druid Finnán Cadeyrn, counselor to the Alrakis Potentate, Dylan MacAskill, do vouchsafe this man a friend."

"Spare me your ephemera, Druid, I know who you are." The speech was muddled by burbles, the consonants sharp splashes of water. "The ancestors quake that he avails himself to mysteries suited only for initiates. You call upon my master, the Winged Steed, and opine the unbeliever a friend. Be it on your head if ill comes of this."

A column of water descended upon them and sucked them into a conduit.

They were dumped into a room of sandstone walls.

"Bout time I had a bath," Finnán quipped. Their clothes dried instantly, undines fleeing from around them like lemmings.

One wall of the chamber was a vortex. The whole wall, spinning relentlessly, a constant slurping whirlpool on its side, defying gravity. The other three walls were the native metamorphic sandstone, two of them shimmering, insubstantial.

Finnán kept looking at the whirlpool on its side, the constant slurping sound a distraction.

"Fascinating, isn't it?"

"Mesmerizing. What in Tír na nÓg is it?"

"Never seen its like? Nor have I."

"Wish I had one made of brew."

Chuckling, Culann tore his gaze from the whorl. On the adjacent wall, their shapes were replicated in vague outline. Opposite that was the rune wall, the indecipherable runes that deciphered themselves as he looked at them. The anomaly that was there, wasn't there when he looked away.

"This wall," Culann said, turning to the fourth wall.

Plain sandstone stared back at him.

"What about it, Cull?"

"I know it does something," he replied. "Nann warned me about it when we were down here, a warning she doesn't remember giving me."

"Eh?" the big Druid said. "Doesn't remember? As though some invocation ..." Finnán turned his gaze slowly toward Culann. "The High Druidess herself, possessed."

"No, but similar to responses at all four henges. It had the quality of some spirit speaking through her."

"What'd she say?"

" 'No, Cull, not yet.' And then she swore she hadn't said a thing."

The wall stared back at them, plain sandstone, rough and uneven as though from weathering.

Finnán stepped to the fourth enigmatic wall and spread his arms. His hands wide and an inch away from rock, he slid them down the surface, as though to feel for any emanations.

Culann didn't see magic in the wall.

"Completely inert, not a hint of magic to it."

"Shall I try?"

Finnán stepped aside with a gesture.

Professor of Astral Physics, Culann Penrose, stepped up to the fourth wall of the chamber beneath Göbekli Tepe, a henge in operation nearly fifteen hundred years, built by Proto-Gaels from technology beyond the ken of their descendants, but replicated partially in A-warp driven interstellar vessels.

The wall shimmered and a mist appeared, a thick cold mist that spilt into the chamber, soaking Culann's sodhoppers instantly, as though he'd walked miles through dew-saturated grasses. He stood in dew-saturated grasses, hints of blue sky above him, not a single wall around him.

"Now you've done it, Cull," the Druid said behind him.

"That I have, Laddie," he replied. "But what exactly have I done?"

The mist was impenetrable, not a hint of shape around them except the open sky above and the soaked grasses at their feet.

Somewhere, a stream gurgled. When he listened with half his attention, it almost sounded like speech, but in a language he didn't know. He saw Finnán was looking that direction as well.

A few steps brought him to the brook, and beside it was a young woman, weeping.

She looked up as he approached, her face fair and streaked with tears. "Fair sir, I beg you, help me across, for though the stream looks shallow, it is deep as eternity." She wore a short, fetching green dress the color of the grass around them, below its hem a pair of legs as perfect as those a goddess might have.

"What is thy name, Damsel?" Finnán asked, a step behind Culann.

She looked at the big man. "What business is that of yours, Devil?!" Gone were the fair looks. Cloven hooves and hairy shanks replaced the comely legs, a pair of horns sprouting from the brow. The half-goat, half-woman leapt across the stream and fled into the mist.

"Maighdean Uaine, herself," Culann remarked.

"And just as likely to slit your throat." Finnán looked either way along the stream, then at the stream itself. "That's odd."

The water rippling in the brook gave no hint as to which way it flowed, seeming to flow both ways at once. There wasn't a hint of inclination to the landscape. "No upstream, nor down," Culann said, exchanging a glance with Finnán.

"Looks to be Tír na nÓg itself."

"Then why's it so blasted cold?" He pulled his tunic tight, a light jacket meant for warmer climes.

"Never heard it promised that the supernatural realm of everlasting youth would be warm as well," Finnán said with a chuckle.

"Think a spell for warmth would be all right, old man?"

"Just don't summon a giant salamander, eh?"

He muttered a quick incantation, and a tiny salamander ran up and down his body. He relaxed a little in the warmth. "Any direction as good as another, look like. This way, Finn." He chose the right, following the stream which seemed to flow both ways and neither.

To their left, across the stream, a copse of alder manifested from the mist, reaching into the blue sky. The dew-soaked grass beside the stream changed little, evincing no sign of trampling, no evidence of trail.

"Cull, the grass behind us straightens and obscures our passing."

"So if Captain Lozac'h came this way, we wouldn't know it."

"Nor will any who seek to find us."

The two men exchanged a worried glance. He wondered at the near-featureless landscape, and how far it extended. Walking along at a goodly pace, Culann suddenly stopped, sensing danger. Finnán bumped into him.

Ahead, the grass ended at a precipice. They might have walked over it, had they been distracted. The stream and grass both clung to the vertical surface, seeming immune to the vertigo.

"Puzzled me, too," said a voice. Across the stream stood a uniformed woman, her flaming red hair tied tightly back in a bun.

"Where'd you come from?"

"Alrakis, in the Gamma Draconis system, Gael Federation. By the looks of you, you're Druid, one of you at least. Captain Niamh Lozac'h, at your service."

"Thank Idris, you're safe, Captain," Culann said, relieved. "Professor Culann Penrose."

"And you, you're Druid Cadeyrn, aren't you, Laddie?"

"Well met, Captain Lozac'h. Glad we found you."

She looked askance at him. "Found me? Tisn't me that's lost, is it?"

Culann had been about to leap the stream, but stopped, Finnán preparing to leap as well.

"Finn, no!"

One leg in the air, the big Druid stopped.

"Undine steal, essence reveal," Culann said.

Hairy legs and cloven hooves replaced the woman's legs, and horns grew through the carrot locks. "Deviltry again!" and Maighdean dropped to all fours and galloped off into the mist.

Finnán traced a knot on his breast. "She almost had us, eh, Cull?"

"Almost." There's too much that's too familiar about all this, he thought, wondering why the entire environs seemed to seep into his subconscious.

Then he knew. "We're not here, Finn."

"Eh? What do you mean? Of course, we're here. Where else would we be?"

"In the chamber."

And they were, three walls of rock and one of water enclosing them, the floor and ceiling of solid sandstone.

"Deviltry is right!" Finnán looked none too pleased. "Let's get out of here before it grants our every wish. Seems to be the work of Shayṭān, the Eltanin evil manifest."

"I agree we should go," Culann said, backing away from the wall.

"Look out!" Finnán grabbed him by the lapels.

The whirlpool wall had already latched its tendrils to him, and the giant whorl strained to pull him into it. Culann grasped the other man's arms, and Finnán slowly hauled him back from the abyss.

Gasping, the Druid and Culann collapsed to the floor, both of them soaking wet, as though they'd physically fought the whirlpool. "Between Scylla and Charybdis, we are! Ceffyl Dŵr, hear me! Place us at the gate, I plead!"

He and Finnán tumbled from between the stele, the night complete, the dusk long gone.

"Thank Arawn. I swear, Cull, I'm never going anywhere with you again," the big man said, getting to his feet.

"No? Why's that, Finn? Bewildered by that completely." He grinned at the other man and got to his feet. "Time for that brew you've been wanting, eh?"

"After that, I'll be needing a malt or two!"

#

A single malt in front of each, Culann looked across the table at his two companions.

Druidess Sionann Lìosach had arrived just as they'd come down from Göbekli Tepe. "Twrch Trwyth has been at you, looks like," she'd said upon seeing them. The ravaging boar had terrorized the ancients, killing people and livestock alike. They'd told Sionann their tale over their first pint.

"First the south wall, then the north?" she said to them now, knocking back her scotch in one gulp. She saw their looks. "Don't worry, Captain Bébe will be flying us out of here, not me."

"Us?" the Druid asked.

"You and Cull can bunk together in the guest cabin," she replied.

"After what just happened? Not on your life!" Then Finnán grinned. "Well, maybe on yours, but certainly not on mine."

"We need you, Finn," Sionann said soberly.

"Eh? Whatever for? I'm a washed up old Druid, fit only to be put out to pasture. You young ones go and save the universe. I've long since lost that starry-eyed ambition."

"Nonsense, Finn," Culann said.

"Washed up, and washed out, too, after that escapade. I don't think so, Cull."

"What is it, man?" He didn't like the look in the older man's eyes.

"I'm tired, Cull. Quite the fright that gave me, the wall sucking you in like that. And the mist. You should have seen it, Nann. One moment in the chamber, the next surrounded by mist. Maighdean Uaine twice, once in the guise of Captain Niamh Lozac'h, manifested right out of our heads, she was. Not a conjurer known who could've done it better. We're up against the unknown in all its terrible wonder, and it's all too much for me."

Culann looked at the big Druid deeply. Enervated from their tribulations himself, the Professor could certainly understand the other man's fatigue.

But it was more than that. Finnán's face was thinner than Culann remembered, the skin of his cheeks hanging lank. Deep, dark circles rimmed the orbital sockets. The other man seemed defeated, as though beaten into submission. His aura was the indigo of ennui, sapped of its vibrancy and luminance.

"It's not you, Finn," Culann said.

"Eh? Of course, it's me. I'm tired, Cull, much too tired."

"The whorl wasn't just water."

They both looked at him. "Eh? What are you talking about?"

"I'm tired, too, Finn, and not just out of exertion. The whirlpool sapped our strength, literally. It siphoned off our energy. I think it's meant to do that."

The bewilderment on both their faces deepened.

"The equations we saw at Las Cogotas, Nann, and the one at Stonehenge, I took them to a colleague, Professor of Particle Physics, Clíodhna Ròsach. She'd done an induction of its torsion foliation to its infinitesimal extreme, and then reversed the induction."

"Isn't a reverse induction just a deduction?" Finnán asked.

"Hear me out. The reverse induction didn't match the initial induction, and the equations from Las Cogotas clearly delineated a displacement of exotic matter in excess proportion to its infusion between foliations."

Finnán snorted. "You've lost me, Laddie."

"The whorl was designed to compensate for the excess proportion of exotic matter."

"What's he talking about?" Finnán asked Sionann.

"I think he's cracked the gate technology."

"He's cracked, all right."

"Hush for a moment, old man." Sionann hadn't taken her eyes off the Professor. "So what you're saying is that the A-warp used in Gael Gate operation relies on a variation in hypersurface foliation that causes excess exotic matter displacement, and the whorl was built to absorb that excess?"

"You understand that stuff?" Finnán asked her in an aside.

"I was an engineering major before I entered the Druidry," she told him.

"And," Culann added, "I'm betting we find a similar excess exotic matter absorption mechanism at each of the gates."

"I need another drink," Sionann said, her eyes wide.

"I second that emotion," Finnán replied.

#

In the galley aboard the gremlin, Sionann stared at him through bleary eyes. She and Finnán had continued to drink for several hours in what had seemed an unspoken competition to see who could drink whom under the table.

Culann had watched, sipping from his single malt, musing he'd be hard pressed to find better company. Finnán was still sleeping it off, snoring mightily in the bunk below Culann's. The Professor had lain awake most the night, contemplating the mysteries haunting them.

"Why'd you come find us?" he asked her over morning tea. "I got the impression when you loaned me the Meave that you couldn't be quit of me fast enough."

She peered at him and groaned. Her breath smelled of hairy dog, and her hair was a tousled shag. She wore a bathrobe and slippers, a hot tea in front of her practically untouched. "Ceannaire's orders," she said bluntly.

He chuckled at her misery, commiserating. Not that he'd never been inebriated as they'd been last night, but that it had only taken once. "Aye, and I'll be betting she's itching to get the gates open, too."

Sionann waved a hand miserably in his direction. "The other thing she wanted me to tell you. She's opening them again in two days, results or not."

"Eh? Why's that?"

"The Ministry of Druidry sent a delegation."

"They weren't happy, no doubt."

"They threatened to open the gates themselves."

Culann pondered that, wondering if Druid Lubri at Las Cogotas had abided by the order in the first place, El Caciquismo relying on their gate access to facilitate their contraband distribution, drug sales funding their patronage network. "So she negotiated for a delay."

Sionann nodded and winced. "Ouch, I shouldn't do that."

"What does Lady Ceri expect we can do in just two days?"

"What can anyone do? It was either that, or lose their loyalty."

And the last time that'd happened, it had toppled the Ceannaire, Gwilym's predecessor, lesser schisms in the administration known to cause similar havoc.

Culann considered what would happen if they started using the gates before the malfunction and disappearances had been resolved.

Hundreds of passages per day at each installation, thousands at the larger ones, such as Stonehenge and Göbekli Tepe.

And what about Montefortino di Arcevia? he wondered. A time-space vacuum now occupied the physical space where the Henge had been, the nine posts vanished Arawn knew where. Would they try to use other gates on Tucana Prime? Would the time-space vacuum warp interfere with their operation?

Culann brought himself back to the galley. Not like me to be swept away by my anxieties, he thought. He could protest he needed more time, but all it might avail him was less, since it was time wasted, air expelled for naught. Any objection would rile the Druidry to louder rebuttal, perhaps even retaliation.

There were those in the Druidry who remembered his denouncing the order.

They'd nearly hanged him for it—and would have had the Ceannaire not intervened.

He looked at Sionann. "Is there a com I can use?"

She emerged momentarily from her misery. "Private, eh? In my stateroom. I'll sit with Captain Bébe for awhile."

"Thank you. Oh, uh, Nann, another favor, if I might ask?"

She looked at him through bloodshot, miserable eyes.

"That Meave you loaned me? Would it be all right if I borrowed it for a little longer?"

She nodded wearily and stumbled from the galley toward the cockpit.

She had a small, separate work area in her stateroom. He sat at the desk and accessed his and Professor Ròsach's research, pulling up the induction, its reversal, and the transcribed runes from Las Cogotas.

Two days wasn't enough time. He had to have some way of testing his hypothesis beyond the confines of a Gael Gate chamber! Articulating the extended

A-warp to some mechanism outside the Gael Gates seemed an impossible task. And now he had two days to get it done.

"Com to Cathasach Bolloré, Nerolade Interstellar, please."

An A-warp engineer in R&D at Nerolade, Cathasach was probably his best hope. It helped that she had as much noggin power as her sister, or more.

"This is Satch." Only the audio, no video.

Might be midnight on her planet, Culann reminded himself. "Satch, this is Cull. If I've caught you at a bad time, tell me to leap into a singularity."

"Cull! Never a bad time for you, Love. Besides, wouldn't want to hurt that poor black hole. What have you got, this time? Driving the Druidry to distraction, last I heard."

"Doing my best, Satch. Listen, I've got an impossible deadline to meet and I need your help, if you've got a day or so."

The blank screen filled in. The wild-haired woman on the other end looked as if she might have pranced out of a whirling dervish—or had just given birth to one. "Pardon the looks, Cull."

"Beautiful as ever, Satch."

"Liar, but bless you for it," she said, grinning. "What are those equations? Looks like A-warp, but extra."

Culann had made them visible on the com. "Exactly. Transcribed that third set from an obelisco on Las Cogotas, and the first two are Clio's work. Sends her regards, by the way."

"How's Sis? As prim and proper as always?"

"Worse."

"I was afraid of that, got all our parents' propriety, left me without a shred of it. So, looks like an extension of a hypersurface foliation, but … " She put her hand to her wild locks, peering into her viewscreen. "Is that what I think it is?"

"Let me tell you what I want, and then I'll send this to you. I'm thinking you already know."

"Aye, Cull. I wasn't thinking you wanted an A-warp core replaced."

"And fill some teacup with your intellectual fire hose? No, Satch, what I want is an A-warp prototype reconfigured with these hypersurface foliation extensions."

She ran the tip of a finger across the screen. "But, Cull, this will produce an excess displacement of exo-matter. I can't build that!"

"Afraid you'll make the universe pucker up?"

She tossed back her curls and laughed. "A glance at me will do that! All I have to do is look it in the eye. And you want this in a day? Great stars, man, it'd be difficult in a decade."

"See what you can do, would you? There's a Meave arriving about now at the Durouḭ̄ernon spaceport on autopilot. Feel free to install this foliation extension into the Meave. Lady Gwilym's given me only two days to finish my investigation."

"Impudent wench, who does she think she is, the Ceannaire herself?" Cathasach grinned. "All right, I'll give it my best. And Cull?"

He heard a note of concern in her voice. "What, Lass?"

"Careful around those gates, eh?"

"Certainly, Satch, thanks."

Culann stared at the screen long after it went blank, reminiscing. He and Cathasach had been married briefly, their divorce as torrid as their marriage. Somehow they'd managed to stay friends.

Chapter 13

"What do you mean, it's off limits?"

"Perdón, Profesor," Belenos Ontonio said, looking across the dusty counter. "La Condestábela has ordered that no one go near the excavation site. And she's placed it under twenty-four hour guard to enforce the order."

Culann stood in the reception area of the University office once occupied by Archeologist Ríoghan Tanguy. Piles of boxes lining one wall and desks stacked atop one another indicated a move in progress. Sionann and Finnán waited outside, the three of them having arrived at Santiago de Compostela just a few hours ago. Neither had quite recovered from their night of debauchery.

"Perhaps we'll just go up to the obeliscos, then." He reached for the door.

Belenos blanched. "If El Profesor so wishes."

"You wouldn't recommend it, Dom Ontonio?"

"It would not be advisable, Profesor." Belenos looked down and away, organizing a stack that needed no organizing.

"Perdón, Dom Ontonio, please help me understand. With El Druido Lubri in jail, who would object to our taking a look around?"

Belenos shrugged and checked the wrapping on a well-wrapped box.

The customs in Galicia of indirectness, deference, and respect were beginning to annoy Culann. Patience, he counseled himself. "Dom Ontonio, this must be difficult for you. Losing Profesor Tanguy, losing your job, having to close your office." Culann gestured at the move in progress around him. "And bearing the scorn of El Druido Lubri simply because you worked for the archeologist. A difficult position to be in. But I sense something else, Dom Ontonio. Has El Caciquismo perhaps made themselves known?"

The other man looked around quickly, as if they weren't alone in the office, sweat breaking on his brow. "Profesor, do not mention os demos! You will summon them as surely as you do as sílfides, the sylphs. No, it is not them. El Druido Lubri is no longer in jail. A lot has changed in just a few days, Profesor."

"Ah, not in jail anymore, I see. Why didn't you say so?" Culann knew perfectly well why he hadn't said. "But no matter. And La Condestábela's placing guards at the excavation site was suggested by El Druido Lubri, sí?"

Belenos met his gaze. "I do not know, Profesor."

Culann took that as assent. "Very well, Dom Ontonio, grazas. You have been gracious with your assistance. Perdón my intrusion. Adeus, Dom Ontonio." He bowed to the other man and stepped out the door.

"Let's go," he told the other two, and set off toward the quay, a good thousand feet below them, down a winding road that hugged the steep descent.

"Eh? Where are we going?" Finnán asked.

"Where *are* we going, Cull?" Sionann said. "The excavation site is this way. And why isn't Dom Ontonio going with us?"

He passed three buildings, their red-tile eaves hanging over the sidewalk, the flagstone streets smooth under their feet.

Then he turned to the south and walked a block.

"What's the deal, Cull?"

"Lubri's out of jail and the excavation site is off limits by order of La Condestábela, but we're going there anyway."

"About to piss off the Galician El Caciquismo some more, eh, Cull?" Finnán said. "Go easy, Lad. I'd like to enjoy my retirement."

The brisk breeze blowing up the incline carried brine and pine. The sun was straight overhead, beating back the chill of morning. Culann might've liked to live in such a place as this, the sight of the ocean below, the hills above, the ancient architecture, the quaint streets. But on those quaint streets went passersby, throwing looks at Los Brancos, the white people.

"Listen, the both of you," Culann said. He told them about the flitter incident on Alcyone, as he and Pryderi had walked along Boulevard De Nantes near City Hall.

"Eh? El Caciquismo may already want you dead? Quick work, Cull." Finnán snorted, looking around as if for assailants. "I'll just cancel my retirement, since they're sure to retire me before then anyway."

"For Arawn's sake, Cull, why didn't you tell us before we got here!?" Sionann looked furious.

"Sorry, I should have." He didn't blame her. It seemed so long ago, already. "Pryderi thinks Druid Lubri has been working for them all along."

" 'Working' for them?" Finnán asked.

"Using the Gates on their behalf," he added.

The big Druid recoiled as though struck. "El Cabrón! Precisely the kind of illicit behavior you so eloquently denounced at your matriculation, Cull. Twas a mistake we never granted you membership. For this, I'll be happy to come along to the excavation site."

Sionann too looked up and down the street. "We stand out too much, Cull. Let's go, eh?"

#

"What are we supposed to do? Tell 'em to let us past, by order of the Ceannaire herself?" Finnán glanced at Sionann with a shrug.

"Ceri might object to that," she replied, crouched beside Cull, the three of them hiding behind a large pyracantha.

"She wants her answers, doesn't she?"

Culann hushed them both, peering at the three soldiers between them and the excavation site. Behind the soldiers, the tor glowed with ethereal brilliance, sylphs flittering around the blocky pillar like bees around a hive. He glanced at his companions. "Look at all the sylphs."

"Must be millions of them," Sionann said.

"Finn, any affinity for sylphs?" He marveled at the other two, at how pleased he felt to have them beside him.

"I've never met an Elemental I didn't like. Quite a few apostates, though."

I should have expected that, Culann thought, the pleasure fleeting. "Care to see if you can get their cooperation?"

Finnán gave him the famous Finn grin and then turned to look toward the tor. "Sylph of mine, hear my call, give these guards el sesta, a nap."

Culann saw a luminescent cloud of sylphs swirl around the three guards, and in moments, they were all snoring audibly, asleep on their feet.

Sionann led the way to the tor, stepping past the soldiers on her tiptoes, Culann right behind her. Finnán stopped to tie their bootlaces together, grinning madly.

Culann stepped up to the base of the tor, the wind-worn rock towering above him. Where the granite rock met the ground was a perfect right angle. Perfect circles and angles don't occur in nature, he thought, detecting traces of an old invocation. He glanced at the two Druids with him.

They both nodded their readiness.

"Sylphs of tor, take us into your chamber," he murmured.

A cyclone leaped from the top, swept down upon them, and whipped them into the air. The breath sucked from his lungs, Culann couldn't even gasp. Then they hurled the trio at the tableau atop the pillar of rock. The tableau collapsed just before impact, and they fell into the triangular chamber.

"I swear, Cull, you'll be the death of me yet!" Finnán whispered, panting.

Sionann lifted herself to her elbows. "If I'm not the death of him first, Finn."

"Swear you'll let me help, eh? Where the hell are we, Cull?" The Druid looked around, saw the obeliscos, and drew his brows together. "Inside?"

Culann pushed himself to his feet, his breathing ragged, wondering how to get the walls to replay the scene of the anthropologist's disappearance. He tried to distinguish one wall from another. They all looked to be the same blank, weather-worn granite as the tor. Extending his senses, he turned to the wall having the most resonance, its aura somewhat brighter than the other two. "This wall, Finn," he said, glancing up.

Eighty-one feet above him, a triangle of cloudy sky peered down upon them.

Wasn't it sunny when we arrived at the tor? Culann wondered, trying to remember.

The walls melted away, becoming diaphanous, as though ephemeral, and around the tribelisco circled the villagers, Druid Arturo Lubri leading them with dance and ululation.

"We're in for it now, Cull," Finnán said.

"They don't see us, Finn," Sionann told him.

The big man looked at the villagers surrounding them, and saw that, indeed, in spite of all the people looking their direction, not a one evinced any indication that they saw the trio of Anglos.

"Watch Druid Lubri, Finn."

The Galician Druid pointed to the archeologist. "We have an infidel in our midst! She who mocks the sylphs and desecrates our sacred sites!" He launched an arm in her direction. "Seize her!"

Multiple villagers converged on the archeologist.

"Bring her here," Druid Lubri commanded. "A rope!" The villagers tied her between two obeliscos. Lubri stuck his face into hers. "You'll desecrate no more, Infidel! You'll meet the sylphs face to face, and then you'll believe!"

Scents of lemon, cinnamon, and spices wafted around Culann.

"What are you doing, Cabrón?!" she spat, struggling against the ropes.

He backhanded her, and her head flew to the side. "Perra pequeña! Cona! Back in position, everyone! Let's send this succubus to moura encantada!" He backed away and resumed his chants and gyrations.

Culann glanced at the Druid beside him.

His brow furrowing, Finnán concentrated on the motions of El Druido.

Then he untied his cape, dropped his hands to the ground, and whisked the cape upward. Granite rock replaced the scene to a clap of thunder.

"There's no gate at those coordinates!" the big man said, his eyes wide with shock. "Not that I've ever known."

"Can you duplicate them?" Sionann asked.

"Eh? And send us into oblivion, too?"

"Can you or can't you?" she demanded.

"Aye, Lass, but I won't!"

She sighed and looked at Culann.

"Listen, my friend," he said, putting his hand on the big man's shoulder and leaning close, "we've got about thirty-six hours before Lady Gwilym reactivates the gates, and those six missing people are depending on us to rescue them. You know what will happen if the gates go back into operation before we've retrieved them from whatever limbo they've been sent to?"

"Much less chance of bringing them back, that's true." Finnán peered at him with a bloodshot eye-ball and sighed heavily. The esters of metabolized ethanol washed over Culann like a hot sirocco. "All right, Cull. For them, and especially for Captain Niamh Lozac'h. For her, I'd do anything."

"Thanks, Finn."

"Stand back in case I slip up, you two."

Culann retreated toward the far obelisco across from the mirror stone, an outline of the big Druid dominating the wall.

Finnán launched into the same wild gyrations as the Druid Lubri.

Between the obeliscos, the grasslands vista appeared.

The one Cull had tried to enter, only to strike the stone wall.

Sionann stepped up behind Finnán. "You did it, Lad. Come on."

He looked over his shoulder at Culann. "Give an inch, eh?"

Grinning, he shrugged at the larger man. "For them, Finn." And he stepped around the Druid and crossed the threshold.

#

"Where do you suppose we are?"

Culann had been wondering the same. Unlike the illusion at Göbekli Tepe, in which they'd been surrounded by fog, here the distant horizons were visible, rolling grasslands dotted by copses of tree spreading in all directions, a steep escarpment of mountains looming to the west. To the south was what looked to be a thicker line of tree, perhaps a river. The grass was a bright emerald green, the sky an aqua azure.

Near the threshold was a tree, leaning against it a sharpened stick, a mat woven from the three-foot grasses hanging over a branch. The ground at their feet was matted, as though trampled or flattened by someone sleeping on it. Tracks of trampled grass led away from the site.

"It's gone!"

Culann turned to look.

The portal they'd come through had vanished.

"Do we kill him now, Nann, or wait until we're out of this fix?"

"I suspect we ought to wait, Finn." Sionann threw a murderous look at him. "But it's tempting, isn't it? I swear to the Green Goddess of all creation and even to that evil Ether you profess is causing all this havoc, I'll take you apart limb by limb and beat you to death with each limb as I remove them." Then she heaved a huge sigh, her voice eerily calm. "Why do we let this pagan apostate persuade us, Finn?"

"I don't know, Lass, bewilders me, too. Let's get on with it. What are we doing here, Cull?"

The calm resignation in their voices led him to believe they might be serious. Not the first time a Druid had ever wished him dead. "Trying to find the

Archeologist, Professor Ríoghan Tanguy, and hopefully, your fellow Alrakian, Captain Niamh Lozac'h. Any heat-detection spells in your repertoire, Nann?"

"Salamander, grant me favor, show me footprints made most recently."

A little lizard shot from under her robe.

"I was wondering where you kept the little fireballs," Finnán quipped.

"Hottest place this side of Alcyone," she retorted.

The salamander ran around them in ever-widening circles, leaving bright spots in the shape of human footprints on the trails. The set of footprints heading to the south glowed the brightest.

"South, little salamander," Sionann said. "Follow the warmth."

The Elemental headed along the line of trampled grass at a fair clip.

The three humans followed, having to walk at a brisk pace to keep up. They dropped into a dell, a stream coursing along the divide, and then ascended the other side toward a copse of tree. The thicket of alder showed evidence of occupation as well. The hide of a small mammal hung from a bough, and a small lean-to of woven branches sat at the base of one tree.

"Looks as if she went back to the gate quite often," Finnán said.

The salamander led them to one tree in the copse, around its base, then to another tree. From there, it headed south again, out of the copse.

Down the hill on the other side, a few miles to the south of them where the land leveled out, a wide, glittering arc of water snaked from east to west, glimpses visible between patches of forest.

"How old are these footprints?" Culann asked.

Sionann gestured in the salamander's direction, and it paused, glanced at her over its shoulder, and then resumed following the trail. "Just a few hours, it says."

Culann let the others get ahead while he followed more slowly and tuned in the landscape. Several species of birds were evident, a few raptors high in the sky, flocks of smaller birds just above the treetops. A few rodents, leporids, and canids poked their heads up from the grasses to espy this strange trio passing nearby. Culann sensed little or no magic, at least no appreciable concentrations of such, just the usual background radiance that imbued all matter.

And all exotic matter, too, he reminded himself, a full eighty-five percent of the universe hovering beyond the ability of his senses.

What Culann didn't see, and had been his most pressing concern, was the presence of large predators. A small canid stood atop a nearby knoll, watching them without fear, an excellent sign that nothing larger might stalk these environs. He hurried to catch up with the others, assured they had no fear of being preyed upon, at least not by the indigenous fauna.

They reached the base of a long descent. The meadows spreading before them abutted a stand of tree some five hundred yards away, the canopy thick and alive with bird calls.

A figure appeared at the forest edge, leaning on a staff. Bent and old, the person peered at them from beneath a shock of tangled white hair, the robes clearly those of a Druid.

Finnán peered back, shielding his eyes with a hand to his brow. "Druidess Gwrtheyrn Jézéquel, if mine eyes don't deceive me."

One of the missing Druids from Montefortino di Arcevia.

"Wouldn't we be fortunate if they're all in the same place, eh?"

"Certainly would," Culann echoed the sentiment, having dreaded going back to Montefortino di Arcevia on Tucana, the prospect of retrieving the Fanum from oblivion weighing on him heavily.

They saw her look over her shoulder, and then hobble toward them across the meadow.

Sionann gestured, and the salamander skittered back under her robe.

The old woman moved with surprising alacrity across the uneven meadow.

"Druidess Jézéquel!" Finnán called.

"Never thought I'd be glad to see your hairy hide," she croaked, meeting them halfway.

At woods' edge appeared three other individuals, one of them in plain, dun-brown digs. The other two wore Druid robes, one in red and the other in white.

"Who else is with you, Druidess?" Sionann asked.

"A gaggle of us, tis sure, six all told." Gwrtheyrn glanced over her shoulder. "It'll be such a relief to get home. Never thought I'd miss a hot bath so much."

Culann saw two more figures emerge from the wood, one wearing a uniform. "Are they all here, Dame Druidess? Apprentice Llewellyn Gutraidh, Captain Niamh Lozac'h, Professor Ríoghan Tanguy, Druids Armel Gallou and Óengus Tàillear?"

"All present and accounted for. I know that face, Apostate. Have ye come to besmirch us with all your lies, Professor?" she sneered, her gnarled hands wringing the staff.

"Much rather do so with the truth, Druidess," he said affably. "Culann Penrose, Astral Physicist and Lead Forensic Investigator in the Gael Gate disappearances, at your service."

"Eh? Well, then, do us the service of disappearing yourself."

"Didn't you hear, Dame Jézéquel?" Sionann asked. "Lead Investigator, appointed by Lady Ceannaire Ceridwen Gwilym, herself."

"May she rot in everlasting Ether alongside this curmudgeon."

Culann suspected she'd not come away unscathed when he'd denounced the Druidry some twenty years before, Ceri regarded as much the villain after she'd used his denouncement as pretext to sweep the old guard from the Ministry of Druidry.

"Well, wherever they rot, Druidess, we wouldn't have found you in this life without them."

Jézéquel threw a doubtful eye in Finnán's direction. "Well, maybe unbelievers have their merits."

The others were now approaching, exchanging greetings with the newly arrived trio.

Culann listened to the banter with half an ear, divining that the first four had arrived all about the same time, but at places far apart from each other. They'd found each other through happenstance, all drawn to the river winding through the woodland basin. They'd continued to monitor their arrival points, in case the portals opened again, and thus had quickly found the two late arrivals from the Sanctuary on Tucana Prime.

Concerned about the portal closing behind them, he glanced back the way they'd come.

"Aye, Cull, what about it? Think I'll be able to open the portal again?"

Silence fell, and Culann looked at the Chief Druid from Göbekli Tepe, aware all eyes were on him.

#

Druid Finnán Cadeyrn stood at the confluence of matted grasses and launched into the wild gyrations that had opened the portal on Las Cogotas. The big Druid thrust his palms at the ground, and then threw them over his head, the final gesture.

Culann sighed when nothing happened. "Druidess Jézéquel, what were you doing at the time you were transported here?"

"Eh? What difference does it make? Give you more of our secrets for you to damn us with?"

On the trek back to their arrival point, he'd spoken with each of the four initial arrivals. Three of them hadn't been invoking magic at the time they'd been drawn into a gate.

Procter Gwrtheyrn Jézéquel had rebuffed his initial inquiries, and seemed no more amenable now to giving him information.

The red-robed Armel Gallou, the Golaseccan Druid, stepped up beside his colleague and spoke with her in low tones, a passel of salamanders peering from beneath his robe.

The three Druids from Montefortino di Arcevia had been colluding on a project to fuse Elementals—to combine the essences of gnomes, undines, sylphs, and salamanders across Elemental. It was one thing to summon two elementals to work together, but it was quite another to engineer a change to their fundamental structure.

Culann remembered what Scathach Ogham, Druidess of the Exalted Martyrology, had told him about Procter Gwrtheyrn Jézéquel, calling her "bent," an odd way to describe a colleague.

Sionann stepped up beside him and faced away from the group, as though to say something in confidence. "These three conspired to fuse Elementals and will certainly face censure from the Ministry when we return." As Druidess to the Ceannaire Ceridwen Gwilym, Sionann Lìosach was titular head of the Ministry of Druidry, and it was she, newly appointed at the ripe young age of twenty-three, who'd carried out the Ceannaire's purge.

"Their cooperation here will certainly help to mitigate the censure, wouldn't it?"

She frowned at him. "I suppose."

"I'd appreciate your being more convinced of that. It'd help us all, eh?" He smiled at her.

"You take all the fun out of things, more so because you're right."

Culann turned to the bent, ancient Druidess. "Dame Jézéquel, I don't expect you to trust me. In fact, I'd rather you didn't. But here we are, stuck, and I'd really appreciate your cooperation." He gestured to indicate the landscape around them. "Same boat, all that."

"I didn't put us on this sinking garbage scow, infidel."

"No, you didn't, and I still need to know what you were doing at the time." He shrugged at her.

The white-robed Óengus Tàillear, the Cisalpine Druid, stepped to his colleague's other shoulder and said something in a low voice to her. A single fuarander peered at Culann from the synched white sash.

Culann didn't like the schism developing in their group.

"Arawn bless," Captain Lozac'h said, her uniform soiled from travel, "just tell the professor. We've been here three weeks, and I'm terribly tired of rabbit stew."

She and the other non-Druid, Archeologist Ríoghan Tanguy, had naturally gravitated to Culann's side on the way to the portal site. As pilot, Captain, and starship commander, Niamh Lozac'h was quite conversant with A-warp and had peppered Culann with questions about the torsion foliations and excess exotic matter displacement.

"What was I doing?" the old Druidess asked. "And give you the means to put Druidry itself to death?"

"That serious, eh?" Sionann asked. "Listen, Dame Jézéquel, as Minister of Druidry for Ceannaire Gwilym, I can sway the course of events upon our return."

"I've said too much already, wench."

"And stand convicted by what you've said, already, witch." Sionann smiled. "And now you have an opportunity to redeem yourself. Professor Penrose is the lead investigator and can certainly attest to your complete cooperation in getting everyone back to safety, as can I. What of it, Druiess? Dig in your heels and remain on this backwater for the rest of your days, or cooperate, help us all return home, and mitigate the censure you'll surely face?"

"Daft, every one of you. You're all daft, I say. Maighdean Uaine take you, Meretrix, and all those pagans burrowing up your skirts!" She brushed her open hand across her forehead and shook it out above the grass, as though to wipe the thought of them from her mind. Then she turned and walked back the way they'd come, the other two Druids in tow.

"That went well," Finnán said.

"Sorry, Cull. Not very diplomatic, was I?"

"What do we do?" Apprentice Gutraidh asked, standing between the other two non-initiates. As apprentice, he'd not yet matriculated nor taken his Druidic Oaths.

"Six of us, three of them. We could coerce them," Finnán suggested, the grin on his face indicating he'd like nothing better.

"Fat lot of good that'll do," Professor Tanguy said.

"We do what we intended to do," Culann said. "And we take them with us even if we don't have their cooperation."

"What's that?"

"We find a way to get back home."

#

Druid Finnán Cadeyrn finished his frenetic dance by thrusting his arms toward the sky, sweat flinging from his brow in spite of the chill.

Nothing happened.

They stood at the base of a rocky ridge in the foothills of the mountains they'd seen looming to the west. The valley in the distance was broken by slivers of river, barely visible. The sun had set, and cold had crept into their bones, a cold held at bay by the exertion of their climb. It'd taken them most the afternoon to get here, traveling up increasingly rugged terrain.

"You sure this is where you appeared, Lad?" Finnán asked the apprentice, panting heavily.

Llewellyn nodded, looking around again as if to verify his landmarks. "Certainly is, Sir."

The dim light of evening wasn't all that dim, Culann realized.

Above them, stars scintillated with the brilliance of a treasure chest. Blazing suns of orange, red, blue, white, and yellow. Purple novas and maroon nebulae. Vibrant pulsars and spectacular spectra.

"A sky like that means we're mighty close to the galactic core," Captain Lozac'h said. "Not even the Jewel Box at Kappa Crucis is anywhere near as dazzling as this."

"What now, Cull?" Sionann asked.

"Captain, how far to the place you appeared?"

Niamh Lozac'h threw a glance at Druid Cadeyrn, her fellow Anatolian. "Same distance as whence we came." She gestured to the southeast. "Druidess Jézéquel and her scurvy minions appeared due east of us."

He looked the way she pointed. North, west, south, east, Culann thought. The cardinal directions. Four points equidistant. What was he missing?

The fifth direction.

Culann recalled that in some cultures, the number of ordinal points on a compass were five. North, west, south, east—and here. But where was "here," at least on this grasslands planet somewhere near the galactic core? A fifth direction and a fifth Elemental, comprising eighty-five percent of the universe. It couldn't be a coincidence, Culann thought.

"I don't like that look in your eyes, Cull," Sionann said.

"Got every appearance of thinking, doesn't he?" Finnán asked.

"And when he does that, we all end up places we wished we hadn't gone."

Culann grinned at them both. "Such confidence you have in me. I'll add your sterling recommendations to my CVs."

Finnán looked at them all. "It's too late now to get to Captain Lozac'h's point of arrival. Not something I want to try in the dark."

"So we camp here for the night, try the other two points in the morning?" Sionann asked. "What's the purpose in that, Cull?"

He looked at her, feeling the attention of the others. "We've an Elemental at work here, Nann, whom we know nothing about. Mayhap one of those Dark Disciples might, but I never got the chance to find one. I suspect we'll need to summon all our resources in our efforts to find our way back."

"'Dark Disciples'?" Llewellyn said. "Disciples of what?"

"Ether," Culann replied.

Chapter 14

At mid-morning, they approached the copse where Captain Lozac'h had appeared. Culann had spent a chilly night under a jutting ledge of rock, the cold relieved slightly by a salamander spell. Dinner had been a gristly affair, a stringy leporid so scant of meat it'd seemed all sinew, tendon, and bone.

"This is it," Niamh said. Two trees stood across a narrow trickle from each other, the quiet gurgle barely audible under the breeze and the birds. The way the trees stood made a natural gate. The other two sites hadn't had similar features.

Culann saw immediately that the others had come to the site, the essences of three Druids easily visible.

"Looks as if they've been here and tried," Sionann said.

"What? Copied my incantation?" Finnán shook his head. "Thieves! Unwilling to help us but perfectly willing to steal our invocations."

Culann wondered how that would affect their effort. "Finn, go ahead, try to summon a gate here, please."

"Why? If they've tried and failed, the three of them, what good would it do for me to give it a go, eh?"

"Trust me," he replied. "Not that I'd expect you to, given what we've been through." He grinned, knowing what the big man was thinking.

Finnán threw him a doubtful glance. "In for a farthing, in for a pound." Druid Cadeyrn sighed and straddled the trickle. A female undine splashed at his feet, not six inches tall, glancing upward and twittering. "Little succubus," Finnán muttered. He positioned himself and launched into Druid Lubri's wild dance. When he hurled his arms into the air, as at the other two sites, nothing happened.

No change in the ambient aura, not even a residual glow.

"Well, let's get on with it then, off to the east," Culann said. "Let's complete the circuit."

The others exchanged glances.

"You've lost your mind, Laddie," Finnán said.

"Feeling discouraged, Finn? Right that you should. We all are. But I'll not stop at half-measures. What'd you say just minutes ago? 'In for a farthing, in for a pound.' Did you stop at a shilling? Well, I'm not stopping, by Arawn, and if it means dragging your carcass halfway across creation, then that's what I'll do." He looked among them all. "Coming with me, or roasting rabbit for the rest of your lives?"

He turned and set off to the northeast, not caring whether they followed.

"It'd be easier this way, Cull," Niamh said from downhill.

He saw the others were going that way, and he joined them.

"I guess we deserved that rebuke," she said, looking quite bedraggled in her unwashed uniform.

"Brave Captain, Hero of the Eltanin War, losing hope in the face of adversity?"

"It's not the kind of war I know how to fight, Cull."

"I wish I knew, too, Nia." He sighed, shaking his head. "But it doesn't stop me from fighting."

#

Apprentice Llewellyn Gutraidh led them to the eastern-most site, where first Procter Gwrtheyrn Jézéquel and then Druids Armel Gallou and Óengus Tàillear had appeared. As their group of six sojourners approached, they'd seen no evidence that the three Cisalpine Druids were anywhere nearby.

"We found her after we'd been here a week," Llewellyn was saying. "She hadn't eaten and looked delirious. Another day or two, and she wouldn't have made it. The other two Druids arrived the next day. The rest of us had long since pooled our resources and talents and had established a camp equidistant from our three arrival points, checking each daily."

Culann looked at the portal.

Two oblong boulders standing on end framed a defile, making a natural portal. The rocks evinced no trace of aura other than the natural ambience.

"They haven't been back here, Cull," Sionann said.

"You can tell?" Professor Tanguy asked. She'd been preternaturally quiet throughout their travel, almost withdrawn.

Culann had been wondering if she'd been traumatized by her arrival. "The use of magic nearly always leaves traces," he told her.

"You mentioned a fifth magic, in addition to the four Elementals. What's Ether?"

"Ether was thought by the ancients to be the medium between stars that light moved through, which did not exist on terrestrial planes in any appreciable amount, our world composed of the other four elements. As our understanding grew, Ether was assigned the name for dark matter, which comprises some eighty-five percent of the universe, also known in particle physics as exotic matter. And we know it exists throughout the universe, even inside you and me, beyond the range of our senses, but there, nonetheless."

"I'm eighty-five percent Ether, and I don't even know it?"

Culann nodded, grinning. "And the manipulation of exotic matter is how we travel between planets. A-warp inverts the torsion forces between foliated hypersurfaces, displacing exotic matter and forcing conventional matter across space at greater-than-light speeds."

"That's the simple version, Professor," Niamh said.

"I suspect the full version isn't any easier to understand," the archeologist replied.

Culann grinned at them both.

"What are you doing here?!"

The red-robed Druid, Armel Gallou, stared at them balefully from the edge of the clearing. Behind him was the white-robed Druid, Óengus Tàillear.

"Same thing you are, Druid," Culann said. Their lockstep conformity here was quite at odds with their constant bickering when he'd first met them on Tucana Prime.

"Get away from that gate, by Gwitihn!" Gwitihn were welsh fairies petrified in iron and steel, hated humans, and whenever possible, led them to swamps to drown.

Captain Lozac'h stepped up to him. "You've no more a say in what we do here as the assistance you've given—none! Help us or begone, Druid, you and your scurvy crew!"

Gallou gesticulated with both hands, starting an invocation.

Sionann opened her palm at him, and blew him backward into his companion. They fell in a heap to the ground. Standing over them, the baleful Druidess smiled pitilessly. "Didn't you hear, or are you deaf as well as stupid? Begone!"

"Wait," Culann said, stepping to her side. "Where's Procter Jézéquel?"

Tàillear glanced behind him, his robe still the purest of white in spite of his inability to wash or change clothes.

A dirt-repulsion spell, Culann thought. "Go get her," Culann ordered. "Finn, go ahead, give the invocation a try."

"Eh? You're serious about taking these reprobates with us, aren't you?"

"Of course, I am. We've a lot to gain by taking them, much more to lose if we don't," Culann said. He looked among them all. "We're here to rescue everyone, by Arawn, not just those who agree with us." His voice was scathing.

The others looked abashed, all except Captain Lozac'h. "We can try them at tribunal later, once we're safe."

"And let you fry us as witches?" Gallou asked.

"Parboiled," Finnán quipped. "More tender."

Culann shot him a glance to shut him up, seeing Druid Tàillear approach with the elderly Druidess.

"Listen up, everyone!" he said, using his lecture-hall voice, the one that reached into every distant corner, whose command could not be mistaken. "We stick together, whatever our differences. If necessary, I'll invoke emergency military protocol, and not cooperating will be dereliction of duty and court-martialed accordingly. All of you are needed to get us back home. Cooperation is required, even if we disagree. Do you understand?"

He got silent nods from them all, except Procter Gwrtheyrn Jézéquel. "Dame Druidess?"

The defeat in her gaze was crushing. "They rejected us, Cull."

"Eh? What was that?"

"Rejected us out of hand, all four Elementals," she continued, not seeing him, seeing someplace else. "Big ones, five times their usual size, chased us into the woods, screaming like banshees, sniping at our heels." She raised her gaze to him, and a tear trickled from one all-seeing eye. "I've never been rejected before."

Culann looked at Druid Tàillear.

"We went to the Archeologist's arrival site yesterday and tried to summon a gate to Las Cogotas," the white-robed Druid said, his shoulders slumped. "They came out of nowhere."

"That must have been difficult," Culann said to her.

Druidess Jézéquel leaned against her staff and wept.

Sionann stepped to her side to comfort her.

A lifetime of constant Elemental companionship, only to be rejected now, when one most needed them, he thought. And five times their usual size? he wondered. He'd never seen an Elemental taller than six inches, other than the undine opposing him and Finnán at Göbekli Tepe. Are the ones who reside in these environs close to the galactic core more advanced? he wondered. Do magic creatures undergo evolution?

He stepped back to Finnán's side. "What do you think?" he asked quietly.

The older Druid shrugged. "She tried to morph the Elementals on Tucana Prime, didn't she? Retaliation? Maybe we need to find out exactly what she did before we proceed."

"What about the size?"

"The mythical giants who once occupied the length and breadth of the Gael Federation?" Finnán asked. "Doesn't seem likely."

Culann nodded. "Captain Lozac'h," he called.

The red-haired woman stepped toward him. "Sir?"

"We'll set up camp for now. It'll be an hour or so before we can try to summon a gate."

"Yes, Sir, I'll make sure everyone's busy." Niamh winked at him.

He stepped over to Procter Jézéquel, nodding to Sionann. "Walk with me for a moment, Dame Druidess."

The old woman took his arm and held tightly, as though to steady herself. The terrain here was slightly sloped and somewhat rocky. She glanced up at him occasionally between steps. "You want to know what I was doing at Montefortino di Arcevia, don't you, Cull?"

"If you'd be willing to tell me."

"Scathe probably told you the three of us were dabbling in other Elementals."

"Something to that effect."

She threw him a glance with a knowing glint. "She didn't know the half of it. We'd begun to fuse Elementals, to blend their essences. Think what a gnome and an undine could do together, Earth and Water combined! She demanded we cease, but of course, we continued in secret. The three of us managed to fuse Elementals into five combinations, but never could get Fire and Water to bind. No mystery there, eh? But we tried."

They stepped around a tree to the edge of hillside, the valley spread below them.

"On the night I was sucked into the gate, we were—"

"They were with you?"

"All three of us, yes, and you're surprised they didn't say anything? We were sworn to secrecy, Professor."

"Call me Cull. But still, you were gone!"

"Secrecy no matter what," Gwrtheyrn said. "Call me Gwerth, Cull. No, they were sworn, as was I, no matter what the result. None of us wanted to risk our membership in the Druidry. On the night I was sucked into the gate, we were trying to fuse three Elementals."

He raised his eyebrows at her.

"Yes, Cull, three—Earth, Air, and Fire. I fear we took it too far. As adherents of salamander and fuarander, we eschewed the pitfalls of dilution inculcated into us all. You know the ideology, Cull."

"I do, Gwerth," he said.

"'Tis a necessary fundamental of the craft, to be sure, meant to protect us all, but ultimately a proscription that limits our capacity."

"But you neglected something."

"Aye, we did, Cull. I heard you telling the Archeologist about Ether." The old woman shook her head. "Ever wonder why there are no adherents?"

"But I understand that there are, the Dark Disciples."

"No, Cull, there aren't any, haven't been for over a thousand years. Well, that night, as the three of us began a long incantation to bring the three Elementals into the Ring, the megaliths were aglow with quintessence, as though they channeled all the ambient magic for us. We had one Elemental in each triangle, one nurtured by each of us to its full manifestation, each as large as the four who chased us yesterday, of a size I'd not seen before. And just as we brought them together, chaos struck."

Culann waited, the woman looking down on the valley with sightless eyes.

"Armel and Óengus had the good sense to desist and retreat." Again, she was silent, as though enduring once more the maelstrom that must have whisked her away, a typhoon of three Elementals, all battling each other for a chance to beset this human interloper.

"It wasn't pleasant, Cull. For a time, I didn't think I'd make it." She gestured at the group behind them. "Without them, I wouldn't have survived."

"Was Ether amidst the chaos?"

She nodded. "It was, Cull. Oh, it tried to disguise itself as the others, but I could tell. I've dabbled in the Elementals far too long to be deceived. I'm not sure how or why the Ether rose up to smite us. So you see, Cull, the reason I wouldn't cooperate wasn't that I didn't trust you. I thought for certain you were here to bring me to justice, to call me to account for causing all their disappearances." Again, she gestured at the group behind them. "But now, it's worse. The Elementals rejected me outright yesterday. I've no hope even if I return to Montefortino di Arcevia of ever summoning an invocation again."

"Oh, I don't know about that, Gwerth. I've a hunch it wasn't you at all."

"Eh? Of course it was me. Twasn't your exotic matter that chased us yesterday, screaming like banshees."

"Not entirely, perhaps. Here's what I think happened." And Professor Penrose explained the torsion foliation and excess exotic matter displacement—and the whorl built into the chamber wall at Göbekli Tepe to absorb that excess.

"Eh? You're sure about all that? You make it sound like some science experiment."

Culann smiled. "What I suspect, now, is that the excess absorption unit at the Montefortino Fanum somehow malfunctioned."

Procter Gwrtheyrn Jézéquel peered at him. "Causing an overload in exotic matter, and making it spill over into the firmament?"

He smiled. "Manifesting as Ether, or for that matter, as outsized Elementals. And certainly enough in excess dark matter to cause the spontaneous displacement of anyone near the gate. Further, I suspect the backlash activated the other three gates as well, maybe more."

"More gates? Did you hear about them? I thought none but us four disappeared."

"Perhaps there was no one else near enough to the gates to get displaced, Gwerth."

"But didn't you say the Montefortino Fanum is now in some hypersurface limbo?"

"It certainly isn't in this universe. Did I tell you I walked the edge of the Milky Way?"

"Star walker, they'll call you," she said, grinning. "'Twas a mistake to deny you the Druidry, Cull, a mistake we may yet remedy."

#

Druid Finnán Cadeyrn glanced over his shoulder to Culann as if to get his permission.

He nodded, everyone in position.

In anticipation of something going awry, as it had for the three Druids from Tucana the day before, Culann had arranged the members of their company in a defensive line behind Finnán, a line of four Druids—Sionann, Gwrtheyrn, Armel, and Óengus—protecting the four civilians at the rear.

They'd invited Culann to line himself up with the Druids, but the ancient proscriptions had been abused far too frequently of late, so he'd elected to stay back with the laity, beside Ríoghan, Niamh, and Llewellyn.

Despite the near-absence of response at the other three sites where Finnán had tried to invoke a gate, their group had not an inkling what would happen here. If indeed a malfunction at Montefortino had caused an overload of exotic matter and reverberations at other gates, then they had no way of anticipating the result here and now.

This was all an experiment, here on the other end of where the overload had dumped Procter Gwrtheyrn Jézéquel.

The big Druid with the long beard called upon his magic and launched into the gyrations he'd tried at the other three points of arrival.

Ready for anything, Culann watched, following Finnán well enough now he was sure he could duplicate the dance.

Finnán dropped to a knee to put his hands on the ground, and then launched his arms into the sky.

Nothing happened.

They waited, five, ten, fifteen seconds.

"Is fhearr fheuchainn na bhith san duil," Sionann said with a heavy sigh.

It is better to try than to hope, Culann translated from the ancient Gaelic.

"What's that?" Ríoghan asked.

He saw she was looking toward the valley behind them.

A raveled mist swirled in the valley around a depression. Above the hole, a small cyclone formed. A brisk wind struck him in the back, and the ground rumbled beneath his feet.

A giant pit opened.

"Everyone down!" He crouched, in case the rumble grew.

The swirling funnel above the pit reached into the sky, an inverted tornado, and lightning leaped from the pit, thunder rumbling across to them soon after. And then the cyclone dissipated. The earth stopped rumbling, and the wind ceased.

Slowly, Culann stood.

A vortex had replaced the valley floor, from this vantage looking like a perfect cone.

"Now we've done it, Cull," Finnán said.

"But what have we done?" Sionann asked.

"Well, I guess we'd better go find out, hadn't we?"

#

They stood on the rim of the cone at high noon, the sun directly overhead. A mile across at its rim, it sloped at over seventy degrees toward a center easily three miles below the surrounding terrain.

"Why doesn't everything slide to the bottom?"

Indeed, the sloped surface was covered with forest, and even the river appeared to flow through the cone at its usual rate, following the contours of the warped geography.

Of course! he thought. "A-warp," Culann said.

"Eh? More of your Astral Physics, Professor?" Ríoghan asked. "This certainly defies conventional physics."

"It's a wormhole, of sorts," said Captain Niamh Lozac'h.

"That's a mighty large worm," Finnán said. "We could catch a mighty large fish with it, too."

Culann stared in wonder, his mind trying to apprehend the forces necessary to morph the landscape to such an extreme.

"What's that at the bottom?"

Culann didn't see anything, except a slight curvature to the forest canopy indicating a spout at the bottom of the funnel. "Looks as if it continues on into the earth, doesn't it?"

"Can't quite tell from here, Cull," Sionann said. "We'd have to go down there."

As far down as it was, he didn't see how they'd do that, except to fly.

"Here, Lew, lower me over the edge with this," Niamh told Llewellyn, dragging a downed limb from the underbrush.

Armel and Óengus pitched in, all three holding onto one end while Niamh backed over the edge and crept down the seventy-degree slope.

Suddenly, she let go and stood straight up, holding her arms over her head. "Look! No hands!"

Culann looked down at her, her body twenty or so degrees from horizontal.

"Here, let me see if I can step back up." She took a step toward the rim, and then put one foot over it. The three men near her offered her a hand, but she waved them away. Slowly, she righted, easing herself gradually to terra firma. "Now, that's disconcerting."

It looked disconcerting, Culann's senses unable to grasp any but a fully up-and-down existence. Seeing wasn't believing.

"Go on, give it a go," she told him.

"I'll spot you, Laddie," Finnán said, extending his arm.

It didn't occur to Culann to be afraid. He grabbed the other man's arm and edged over the rim. His equilibrium shifted and he started, feeling as if he were falling—toward the big druid. Both feet firmly over the rim and in the funnel, Culann stood.

All the others in their group stood in a sideways forest.

He grinned at them, the sky in front of him a thousand times larger now that there wasn't a horizon. "Well, what are you waiting for?" He looked among them.

"Oh, dear Green Goddess, what are we in for now?" Sionann said. "I don't suppose threats of death will deter you much, will they, Cull?"

"I suspect not, Nann."

"Rumors of his murder have been prematurely exaggerated," Finnán told her.

Then Culann turned to look toward the funnel.

The forest overhead was daunting, arching from both sides and meeting nearly straight over him. The river meandered in from the west, coursed across the ceiling above the spout, and then exited to the south, its flow undeterred by the cone.

"A bit unnerving, wouldn't you say?" Sionann said, coming up beside him, her eyes roving the bizarre landscape before and above them.

He smiled, nodding.

"We travel in trios for safety, everyone," Captain Lozac'h told the group. "Arms linked at all times. If any of us gets pulled into a gravitational anomaly, the others can help pull us out. Got it?"

Culann linked arms with Finnán on one side, Sionann on the other. The three Druids from Montefortino di Arcevia linked themselves, Procter Jézéquel in the middle. Taking up the rear were the three laity, the Archeologist between the Captain and the Apprentice.

They moved into the cone, the forest around them as alive with wildlife as that outside the cone.

"There isn't a concomitant distortion to the landscape, Cull," Ríoghan said from the rear. "And yet, somehow it's contiguous."

"What do you mean?" Procter Jézéquel asked over her shoulder, her eyes never leaving the overhead forest.

"If you punch a flat surface with a conical object, the surface either stretches or tears around the conical shape. And I don't think I've ever seen a landscape stretch."

"Nann, any permutations in particle physics that you know of to account for this?"

She shook her head. "Not a one, Cull."

Culann stepped around a fern, its long, lush leaves still moist from morning dew. The sun shone from an angle indicating late afternoon, despite their having arrived at the rim at high noon. The entire phenomenon baffled the senses and defied understanding.

A mile into the funnel, Culann began to feel the sky encroaching. The meandering river was nearly directly overhead, a half-mile away, burbling happily and placidly over rocks held disconcertingly in place by gravity that somehow had no effect on them here.

"Localized gravity? Any hunches, Captain?" Culann called over his shoulder.

"We've antigrav," she said from behind him, "but that just creates small fields absent of gravitational forces. This is way beyond the ken."

"About as frightening as those outsize Elementals we conjured," Óengus said from the middle row.

They kept to their formation as they moved deeper into the forest cone despite the obstacles. The forest appeared no more or less dense than at the rim, even as the cone narrowed.

Cull caught increasingly clearer glimpses of the spout at the bottom of the funnel, although "bottom" didn't adequately describe it. This three-dimensional cone no longer abided by three-dimensional rules.

The spout appeared to be a tunnel some fifty feet across, trees clotting the entrance, the forest canopy ranging from twenty-five to thirty feet above them. Did the forest extend all the way through the tunnel? Culann wondered, trying to wrap his mind around the warp. Wrap my mind around the warp, or warp my mind around the wrap? he wondered sardonically.

The gloom increased gradually, the sunlight more and more eclipsed by the narrowing cone. Culann wondered whether the spout had any light whatsoever.

"Cull, I'm concerned," Sionann said, stopping.

The cone loomed around them, the forest canopy above them not a hundred feet away, the tunnel entrance an equivalent distance ahead.

"I don't see any ambient aura," she added, her gaze wandering across the landscape that now nearly surrounded them. "Not a trace of magic."

Culann too was having a difficult time keeping his attention on the tunnel, the arch of forest overhead pressing down on them like some giant wall. He couldn't dismiss the feeling that it was about to fall in on them. His brain couldn't override his senses. Impending doom screamed at him.

Culann hadn't noticed the absence of magic, so fascinated by the terrain. There wasn't a vestige.

"What's it mean, Cull?" Gwrtheyrn asked.

"Can you see magic too, Proctor?"

"Aye, Lad, and this place is as absent as any I've seen."

He tried to think through what type of permutation in the firmament might lead to the absence of magic.

One name for Ether, a name other than exotic matter sometimes used by physicists, was "anti-matter," the opposite of matter. Another term was "dark matter," hence the corresponding Druidry term of "Dark Disciple."

Matter and anti-matter were fundamental opposites, unable to occupy the same place at the same time. Internecine, mutually destructive of each other. One mystery in the scientific debate on exotic matter was its comprising eighty-five percent of the universe. If indeed matter and anti-matter were fundamental opposites, wouldn't they then be present in equal proportion? Light, and anti-light. Gravity, and anti-gravity. Matter, and anti-matter. Magic, and anti-magic? The existence of one presumed that of its opposite. Culann smiled at the irony.

Science re-wrote the rules of magic every few hundred years. And now, magic was re-writing the rules of science.

"You're going in there, aren't you, Cull?"

"I don't see why not. Maybe they've a good pub in there, Finn."

"I'm still looking for that whirlpool in a pint, Laddie." The big Druid looked across at Sionann. "What about you, young lady? Any concerns about following this daft fool in there?"

"Just that I'm becoming daft, too, Finn." She shook her head.

Culann half-turned to look over his shoulder. "Anyone want to turn back? Perfectly all right to do so. We're about to walk into a phenomenon not known to human kind, one that can't possibly exist by any laws of physics we know."

"If it's not possible within the laws of physics," Procter Gwrtheyrn Jézéquel said, "then it must have been manifested through magic." She looked eager to proceed.

"Río, Nia, Lew? You've no stake here, no Druidic reputation to uphold. Not that I do either, but I'm lead investigator. And Lew, there's no consequence to staying behind, Lad." He wondered what the young man would do, Llewellyn under tremendous pressure to be as brave as these fool Druids whom he aspired to join.

"I'm in, Cull," Apprentice Gutraidh said without hesitation.

"Can't rightly stop me, Cull," Captain Lozac'h of Alrakis, hero of the Eltanin war, said promptly.

"If it'll get me back to digging faster, I'm all in, Cull," Archeologist Tanguy said.

"Well, all right, then!" Culann said, gratified at the response. "'Tis an honor to have you at my back!"

He turned back around to face the tunnel mouth, wondering what they would find.

#

"There's ice underfoot," Sionann said.

Culann had wondered what the crunching was. The farther they'd gone, the colder the temperature had grown. A wind blew steadily past them, toward the tunnel mouth behind them, nipping at their ears, faces, hands, and ankles.

The darkness was now complete, the thick foliage in the tunnel behind them occluding any sunlight. A light spell lit their way, floating ten feet in front of their party, a floating salamander casting its glow upon a dwindling forest inside. At some point, they'd noticed that the trees weren't quite so robust, the grasses not so tall, the undergrowth not so hardy. The first half-mile into the tunnel had looked no different from the forest surrounding the cone, but absent its avian life. No other animals had been spotted, either. Now, the terrain was mostly grasslands, an occasional bush breaking the monotony.

The adventurous Captain had experimented by walking up the side of the tunnel, over the top, and then back down the other side, the entire company watching. Culann had gaped in wonder, marveling that she didn't fall head-first on top of them.

"Can't say I've had this much fun since I was a lass," she'd said.

Culann was concerned about the increasing cold. A warmth spell would only do so much to shield them from the chill, and a sustained period of intense cold could easily leave them hypothermic, none of them dressed for cold weather.

The Captain and Archeologist seemed to be suffering most, neither able to invoke salamanders to warm themselves with. He summoned a spell for each.

A white flake floated past him. And another.

Culann frowned, walking into a small flurry of snowflakes.

"Can't say I came dressed for the occasion," Finnán said. "I neglected to bring my skis."

"Nann, send a light ahead, could you?" Culann asked, stopping and wondering what lay ahead. He canceled his light invocation.

The Druidess muttered an incantation and hurled a ball of light straight down the tunnel.

The flare lit the sides as it traveled down the tunnel. Ahead, the snow thickened and the grass grew sparse. Deeper and deeper the light went, growing gradually smaller, until it was all but a pinprick. And then it extinguished.

Sionann had a bewildered look on her face. "I didn't do that."

"Aye, you didn't, Lass," Gwrtheyrn said. "Something put out the light. Twasn't but a flash of something I saw, but it was there, unmistakably."

Culann extended his senses, trying to detect the faintest hint of magic. Nothing at all registered.

"You, either?" Sionann asked him.

He shook his head. "Finn, Armel, Óengus, do any of you detect anything ahead?" He didn't know if they had any ability to detect the ethereal essences, but he knew some Druids to be sensitive to particular Elementals.

"Not a thing, Lad," Finnán said.

Armel and Óengus both shook their heads at him.

Flakes continued to float past them, sticking to their hair and clothes. Salamanders ran up and down their bodies, beating back the cold. I suspect we'll be getting a lot colder, Culann thought. "Let's go, eh? Stick close together, for safety and warmth. The exertion will help keep us warm, too." He cast his light spell ahead again, the small flare lighting the tunnel ahead like a large halo.

They set out, face first into the wind, the cutting cold causing their eyes to tear up.

Head down, Culann pushed onward, a Druid against him on either side, synchronizing their strides with his. Finnán put his arm across Culann's shoulder, and Culann across Sionann's. Huddled, they pushed into the blistering wind, slogging through snow drifts that seemed to grow increasingly deep by the moment.

"Salamander King, bring us your warmth!" Armel called.

A smidgen of warmth touched Culann's cheek, but was soon swept away.

Shafts of ice spiked through his heels up his legs. He couldn't feel his fingers, imagining their tips darkening with frostbite. He didn't want to think about his toes. His feet seemed miles away.

"Cull, I don't think we can make it," Óengus said behind him.

He glanced over his shoulder. The white-robed Druid indicated the Proctor. Gwrtheyrn's lips were blue, and her gaze was empty, an icicle hanging from her nose.

Something triggered his awareness, the way the Druid had said it, reminding him of the chamber wall at Göbekli Tepe, the mist wall.

"Spirit of Ether, dwell thee deep, banish this cold, warm us keep."

The cold dissipated and so did the snow drifts, disappearing in a flash.

"Twas all magic," Lew said.

But the tunnel remained. Or was it created by magic as well, magic too powerful to penetrate? Culann didn't have a way to tell, his senses blinded to the forces at work here. He reminded himself that they had all probed the area for any traces of magic, had found none, and yet they'd all been bedazzled by the magical illusion of snow.

Ahead, the tunnel expanded.

"It's another cone."

The light he'd cast ahead entered a space far larger, one whose sides expanded outward.

Into darkness.

#

"We've explored it all, Cull, and not a sign of egress. How are we to get out?"

They'd entered what appeared to be a cone nearly equal in size and shape to the warped forest floor they'd entered some hours before. This time, the open end of the funnel was a blank, black wall, instead of a sky filled with the stars near the galactic core.

Upon entering the cone, Culann had sent two people each direction to explore the bounds of the space, the ground a smooth surface having the solid hardness of rock but without the texture of ... anything. The two exploratory pairs had met overhead, encountering nothing underfoot but the same solid surface.

Capping the cone was a blank, black wall. Culann put his hand against it. It wasn't even a wall. It simply stopped his hand, but without sideways resistance, as if frictionless. Casting a light spell, he held the illumination near the wall and saw none of the light reflected.

He struck it with the flat of his hand. His hand stopped, but without a corresponding slap.

"It doesn't even reflect sound," Finnán said, his voice reaching Culann without hint of echo.

"What now, dauntless leader?"

He grinned at Sionann. "I'm about as blank as the wall, Lass. Any suggestions?"

"It's a gate," Lew said. "A gate that hasn't opened anywhere."

Of course it was a gate.

His mind tumbled through the reasoning, making the distinction between a closed gate and one not open to a destination—two very different occurrences. Reason reached its tentacles deep into the human psyche, attempting to find structure and meaning from any and every phenomenon. It didn't surprise Culann that someone would propose the idea. What he found curious was his own utter bewilderment, so severe as to blunt his reason. His perceptions and the eons of evolution that had served to inculcate reality into his genes had come up against a physical realm that refuted those evolutionary eons. He couldn't comprehend, and therefore, he'd stopped trying. Of course it was a gate.

"So how do we open it?"

"Might as well do El Druido Lubri's dazzling dance one last time, eh, Finn?"

The big man looked at him with an I-can't-believe-you're-asking-me-that look. "This gate is nothing like any we've ever seen, and you're wanting me to open it willy-nilly, a mile-wide hole in the universe? Hear me out, Cull." He held up a fleshy paw. "If it behaves in similar ways to the other gates, where the malfunctions brought these six people to a planet somewhere near the galactic core, far beyond the range of conventional gate technology, reason would indicate we'll all be sucked into a void where nothing is remotely familiar.

"I'm not finished, fool," he said when Culann opened his mouth. "And given the size of this gate, an aperture a full mile in diameter, the likelihood is far greater that it will suck more than our nine condemned souls into that remote void, perhaps the planet in its entire, the primary it orbits, the constellation it sits in, and mayhap, the entire Milky Way Galaxy."

Cull smiled at the Druid, his erstwhile mentor, a glowing salamander lighting him from above, the faint light throwing stark, ghostly shadows across his features. "All true, my friend, every bit of it." And he said no more, letting the silence say it for him.

After a minute or two, Gwrtheyrn said, "But you don't agree."

"Actually, Gwerth, I do agree." Again, he didn't elaborate.

"Cagey, ain't he?" Sionann said to Niamh, throwing a smile Culann's direction.

"Sure is. And you followed this nefarious reprobate all this way?"

"More the fool I be, the farther I follow him." She shook her head. "And somehow, given similar circumstances, I'd have made the same choices." Sionann gestured at the blank, black wall. "But not here, not now."

"Blighted fools, the lot of us," Finnán added. "Out with it, Cull. What are you thinking?"

"Me? Thinking?" He put a dramatic hand to his chest. "Why, nothing, Finn, nothing at all. Tis clear you're decided, and I respect that. It'd be against my nature to try to dissuade you out of a stance made from your deepest convictions. You're perfectly within your rights to have concerns, all of them valid and well-reasoned. Further, from the perspective of Astral Physics, this is probably what you describe, an aperture of a magnitude beyond our ken, as likely to take us back home as to punch a hole in the galaxy. Opening this gate has extreme risks, ones I wouldn't ask you to take. Especially not my dear friend, Druid Finnán Cadeyrn." Culann smiled at the Druid, and looked among the others. "And certainly not any of you."

"He wants us to leave so he can open the gate when we're gone," Professor Ríoghan Tanguy said. The others in their company turned to look at her, and then returned their gazes to Culann.

He didn't deny it.

"And there's no persuading him otherwise," Sionann said.

"Now's the time, Nann," Finnán said. "If we're to murder him, now's the time."

"We could just tie him up," Lew said, "discretion being the better part of valor."

"Dissection is the better part of valor," the big Druid retorted. "Let's cut him up and be done with it."

Culann remained as silent as a cowardly lieutenant on the battlefield pretending to be dead in front of his king. He looked among their faces, many of them glancing at the solid black wall behind him, anxiety clear in their gazes.

Gwrtheyrn glanced at the group itself and then to Culann, her spider-web hair casting a chiaroscuro across her face. "Well, I'm not convinced, Cull."

She was the last person he expected support from. "What was that, Gwerth?"

"It may be everything that you say, but I'm not convinced it'll swallow the galaxy—nor even us, for that matter."

"Oh?" The big Druid asked. "And how, if I may ask, did you arrive at that conclusion?"

"The gate would have done so already, Finn, if it's as redoubtable as you say. What'd you call the Ether, Cull? Eighty-five percent of the universe? What prevents the Ether from gobbling the remaining fifteen percent? Nothing. And yet it hasn't, at least not for the last fifteen billion years. Further, if your Astral

Physics is any indication, it sits there in stasis with that other fifteen percent, symbiotic, it seems, in peaceful coexistence since the beginning of time. Nay, Finn, all that you say being true, I don't agree it'll do any of that." Then she looked among them all. "And I'm longing for home, myself. Finn, if you won't summon the gate, I surely will. Better that a bona fide Druid do it, than some scurrilous apostate like Cull."

"Thank you, Gwerth. Another glowing recommendation to add to my CVs," Cull said, turning to look at the others. "Anyone else care to join us?"

They looked uncomfortably amongst themselves.

In an aside to the ancient Druidess, Culann asked about her fusing the Elementals.

"I do believe it was three at once that overwhelmed us," she said.

"The other five combinations seemed relatively stable?"

"In a magical sense, yes, but astralphysical sense? Who knows? That's your realm."

"I don't believe they're as separate as it's often purported, Gwerth. Frankly, I don't believe there's any separation between Science and Magic at all."

She threw him a glance full of ancient wisdom. "Just different ways of articulating the same principles?"

"That's my thought, Gwerth." He watched the other seven people, huddled in an intense haggle.

"Seems reasonable, Lad, the only hurdle being magic itself, which we both know repudiates reason."

"Seems to, Druidess, seems to," he corrected gently.

She cackled at him, a wicked gleam in her eye. "Not a mystery why they call you apostate, is it?"

"All right, Cull, you win again," Sionann said, turning along with the others toward him.

" 'Win,' Nann? Not a fight we're in, to my knowledge. And ultimately, no one loses. In fact, all humanity wins by our attempting to open this gate."

She stepped up close to him, her eyes inches from him. "I pray you're right, Cull. And whatever happens, it's … been an honor and a pleasure to know you." She blinked rapidly and stepped back with a sigh.

Culann felt a loss at what might have been. How was he just now seeing what she felt for him? Odd how we blind ourselves to something so precious and valuable right in front of us, he thought, wondering how he'd missed it. "Ready to give it a go, Finn?"

"Aye, Lad, I am." He too looked closely at Culann. "And damn it all, boy, I've liked knowin' you too."

Grinning, Culann hugged him, dismayed at the strain apparent in Finnán's face. Over the last few days, he'd seen the dark circles around his eyes get darker, and the skin sag from his cheeks all the more. I'll have to ask him about that when we get home, Culann thought.

He cleared the immediate area in front of the Druid, placing the other four Druids just behind the big man, and putting himself and the other three laity in the rear.

"Nann, get a light high above us, would you? A bright one."

"Where at, Finn?"

"Half-way to the top, bright enough for us to see the whole cone, eh?"

"All right." Sionann spread her arms wide. "Escalla and your hellhound Cinders, conjure for me a light so bright that we shall see the universe revealed before us!" And she brought her hands together.

At the loud pop, a ball of fire leaped from her hands and sailed upward, floating to a position a half-mile high, beside the impenetrable, unreflective barrier, lighting the cone all around.

"The Princess of the Fey has returned from her self-imposed exile," Gwrtheyrn said, throwing an impressed glance at the younger woman.

"Tis the love of Cinders for its mistress," Sionann said.

"Thank you, Nann. Ready, all?" Finnán looked among them, nodded, and then turned to the black, blank portal. The fireball lighting the chamber around them gave no hint to the composition or permeability of the barrier in front of them.

As though it exists out of time, Culann thought idly.

The big Druid began the invocation, launching into the gesticulations and gyrations that Culann had seen from him five times before.

He dropped his hands to the floor, lifted his head, and then hurled his arms in the air.

The fireball vanished, and then the chamber did too.

And everyone around Culann was gone.

Chapter 15

Absence.

He didn't know how else to describe it.

Complete absence.

I'm still here, aren't I? he wondered, trying to distinguish his body from his surroundings.

A great black other.

If the wall inside the cone had seemed to be a void, with its featureless, unreflective, frictionless surface, this was worse.

This was nothing.

Further, he couldn't tell where he ended, where he began. The demarcations separating his body from his surroundings no longer existed. He felt for his face, and didn't find it. He groped for his leg with his hand, same result. He shouted just for the joy of hearing his own voice, and heard not a word.

If a tree falls in the forest … he thought inanely.

Nothing under his feet, nothing against his hands, no light streaming into his eyes, no air against his cheek, no temperature at contrast to his skin, no feel of anything against his body, not even the clothes he'd been wearing.

I think, therefore I am, his mind insisted.

And he chuckled at that inanity, there being no proof to his existence whatsoever. It was that existential argument all over again. I am nothing without an environment around me, he thought. If I'm nowhere, then I'm nothing.

Did time even exist, with nothing around to mark its passing?

Of course not, his mind told him.

Of course it does, his mind told him.

Two completely opposite states. Either time was passing, or it wasn't. Mutually exclusive conclusions, both true at the same ...time.

He roared with laughter at the conundrum.

He thought about the others, about Sionann. A beautiful woman a few years younger than he, tremendously talented, smart as he was, politically astute with a tough hide, a sight tougher than he was. And then Finnán, a friend for life, as close to him and as alike in his perceptions that they might have been brothers, more outspoken than Culann and more likely to make those views known, but nearly the same views.

Where were they, his companions?

And the three Druids from Montefortino di Arcevia?

And the other three abductees, the Druid Apprentice, the Starship Captain, the Archeologist?

What oblivion have I consigned them to? Culann wondered.

And for the first time on this expedition, he felt remorse for the tribulations he'd put his friends through, the danger he'd placed them in.

Especially Sionann.

He'd seen the beginnings of deep affection in her eyes before he'd relegated them all to obliteration. And now he'd never know the promise in her gaze. Culann had been married twice before, had loved both his wives deeply, and had known joy in their embraces. And now to have lost the possibility of similar joy in the arms of a person of Sionann's caliber, a woman of stunning beauty, a person of high integrity, a Druid practically snatched from the matriculation podium by the Ceannaire herself, Lady Ceridwen Gwilym, President of the Gael Federation. Gone.

If he'd had breath or eyes or tears, he'd have wept.

Sadness seemed to be his existence. It was all around him. It was what separated him from the void. The inanimacy of his surroundings was incapable of feeling, and the fact that he felt such a deep penetrating sadness gave him definition in that indefinite void.

How long he wept, he wasn't sure. If he wept at all.

He guessed he slept, but that too wasn't a certainty. He dreamt of the grasslands planet, an idyllic, bucolic life with a companion as committed to his wellbeing as she was. And it was only its ephemeral quality that alerted him it might be something other than reality. His attempt to count the number of times he'd slept ran afoul of what counted as sleep, his changes in awareness marked by nothing other than the absence of anything around him or the ethereal information funneled into his sensory pathways by a brain overwhelmed by the absence of input.

Distinguishing himself from the void wasn't a struggle. It wasn't possible to do.

It would be so easy to cast myself adrift within the wild blue event of my mental horizons, he thought. If I just had some routine, even one as mundane as emptying my bladder, he thought, I'd at least have some way of marking time!

Comparisons to canines came to mind, and he drifted among the permutations of urination, trees, and the difficulties of establishing boundaries in a place that was no place, a time beyond the measure of time.

So it was that his first awareness of "other" came when a pair of eyes manifested out of nowhere and nowhen.

He'd not been expecting it, and he was certain it was either a dream or a hallucination.

They're Sionann's eyes, he first thought. The eyes that had stared into his soul with a deep affection, the ones so full of promise, and he hoped, yearning.

Eyes he hoped might still reflect his own yearning, should he look into them just once more.

The eyes in front of him contained no affection, no yearning, no pity.

Eyes with bewilderment in them, tinged with bemusement.

Deep liquid pupils inside irises striated outward to a slightly discolored juncta, inside a sclera white as the purest driven snow.

Startled, Culann jerked, as though his incorporeal body had some means to shrink from the overwhelming soul behind the eyes in front of him. He was terrified, he realized.

There was no hiding.

They were eyes that saw in all directions, knew all knowledge. Eyes everywhere at once, and nowhere at any time.

And in his terror, Culann finally knew relief. The other, that which distinguished him from his surroundings, some demarcation between himself and the universe.

But the universe was him, and he was the universe, and the eyes were his, and he was the eyes. Confusion and terror bloomed anew in Culann, and had he lungs and air to fill them, he would have screamed.

The eyes widened with something akin to surprise.

And his terror abated slightly. If it feels something different, he thought, then I am separate.

The eyes remained his and he remained the eyes and somehow the emotion in them wasn't what he felt and all he was left with was his confusion, his terror slowly subsiding.

And somewhere in his confusion, he realized what he knew had become superfluous, and least in the here and now, which was nowhere and nowhen. The mutually agreed-upon reality that he'd shared with Sionann and Finnán and fifty trillion other human beings strewn across the Milky Way didn't exist any longer, if indeed it had ever existed, time in its permeability and fluidity not a river any longer, but the very plasma of space itself, inchoate and chaotic.

The eyes continued to stare, as though fixed to him in everlasting wonder. Still, they contained no affection, no yearning, no pity.

But at least they don't contain indifference, he thought. If God had ears, what would I say? Culann wondered, staring into those eyes.

"What are you?" he asked. The words didn't issue from a mouth through a larynx mounted atop a set of lungs. He didn't have any flesh to generate words.

"Ether."

The word came to him not through vibrations in air hitting an eardrum, but as vibrations in his mind. The vibrations suffused him, surrounded him, became him, and left him shaking. The voice was deeper than the oscillation of continental plates rubbing together. The sound was louder than the explosion of a nebula. It was so deep that, if it had come to him through air, he wouldn't have heard it. He would have *been* it.

Questions cascaded through him so quickly that none had the chance to form themselves fully before the subsequent question spilled out on top of it. The avalanche of thought eroded his ability to think.

"What do I call you?" Culann finally asked, his thoughts congealing somewhat.

"You may call me Balor."

King of the supernatural beings who had occupied the Gaels' ancestral lands on Earth, often described in legend with a third, gargantuan eye on his forehead. When opened, it wrought destruction, drought, and blight.

"Where am I?" he asked.

"You are everywhere, and nowhere."

He should have expected that. In fact, he'd already known that. Think! he told himself, and he took a deep breath into lungs he didn't have. Beyond who I am and where I am, he thought, lies a race of bipeds who face a great mystery, who yearn for the return of some normalcy, who pine for nine of their own who've gone missing.

"What happened at Montefortino di Arcevia?" He projected with his question an image of the Henge being taken into some other dimension, the backlash of its disappearance inflicting heavy damage upon the sanctuary.

"You have awakened me to ask me this?"

Culann might have voided all over himself, if he'd possessed a digestive tract. His heart might have hammered, and he surely would have been drenched in sweat. What did a being as omnipotent and omniscient as Balor care for a stand of megaliths that no longer occupied a space in real-time? "Forgive me. My concerns are petty, tis true," he said. "I seek to solve the mystery of the Gael Gates."

"Petty, indeed." And the reverberations faded away, the eyes becoming unfocused.

I no longer occupy Balor's attention, Culann thought with relief. The baleful glare had nearly caused his non-existent heart to explode. "How are we even talking?" he asked the all-knowing eyes.

"Since you do not have the senses to perceive me in my actual incarnation, I have manifested what you see to make myself known to you. I exist beyond the universe you occupy."

Since I no longer have eyes, Culann thought idly, I'm now free to see beyond the narrow spectrum of visible light. Given I no longer have neurons, he wondered, am I now free to think beyond the narrow calcium channels of my brain? "Are you outside my universe?" he asked, thinking about that separation from other, how self was defined by where it ended, the place where other began.

"There are three answers. No, yes, and—"

The word reverberating through Culann's awareness held no equivalent in the language that limited his awareness. He had no basis for comprehending that third word. It wasn't, it was, and a third concept that included both but meant more than that. In the realm of human comprehension, "no" was one point on a segment, "yes" was the point at the opposite end of that segment, and the concept reverberating through his mind in Balor's voice were all the shades of meaning in between. Further, Culann saw that the segment didn't stop at "no" or "yes," but continued beyond these simple concepts ad infinitum. Conceptualizing the chiaroscuro blew his mind beyond his brain.

"Your universe is a single cell among the infinite number in my body. Your universe is in disease. It is turgid with time, and exotic matter exceeds its allotted measure, creating imbalance. A rent has appeared in the surface, and excess exotic matter pours out through the rift."

Turgid, distended, attenuated. Strained to the point of splitting.

"The Proto-Druids corrected for that. These ancestors built absorbers into the Gael Gates to compensate for the excess proportion of exotic matter."

"Where did that excess proportion come from?"

Culann didn't know.

"You move matter by displacing Ether from outside the membrane."

Of course. How could he have missed that? How could he have known that? The conundrum was like an oxymoron of two mutually-exclusive states existing in perfect harmony together at the same time and in the same space.

He did know.

Further, he knew how to correct it. The inversion of torsion forces between foliations of space-like hypersurfaces drew on exotic matter from random locations, some of them inevitably beyond the existing universe. All I need to do, he thought, is limit that exotic matter draw to the here-and-now, and direct its displacement to the there-and-when in equal proportion to the physical matter that it displaces.

It seemed so simple that he wondered why he hadn't come up with it before.

"All isn't so simple, human."

And Cull was hurled from between two obeliscos onto his backside.

Chapter 16

"There's the apostate! Agarre esta lula abortada!"

"Vai cagar ostias becerro do carallo!" shouted Belenos Ontonio, lunging past Druid Lubri.

Culann wasn't about to find out what they were saying. "Queen Paralda, make me thin as air!" And he rolled to his feet, helped by Belenos.

Several villagers converged on Culann and tackled him to the ground.

"Halt! By order of the Ceannaire herself!"

The ground exploded to their left and their right, and all activity ceased.

Captain Bébinn Nankivell and a contingent of Federation soldiers surrounded the obeliscos, the bright green-and-purple uniforms commanding respect even in this lawless province. She stood at the ring edge, her lazgun aimed at Druid Lubri.

Culann extracted himself from the villagers' grasp, wondering why his spell hadn't worked. "Captain Bébe, how timely."

"Professor Penrose, nice to see you, Sir."

"Arrest Druid Lubri, Captain, and place Dom Ontonio under Federation protection," he said, indicating the man who'd opposed the Druid's command.

"Certainly, Professor," Bébinn said. "Where's Dame Lìosach?"

He shook his head. "I don't know, Captain." While she made arrangements for the prisoner, Druid Arturo Lubri, Culann looked among the villagers beyond the ring of Federation soldiers.

A man of similar build and coloration to the thesis student he'd met on Alcyone was hurrying toward an alley.

"Captain, seize that man! That's Breno Feijóo, who works for Los Caciques!"

"You and you, get him!" The Captain poked a finger at two soldiers, who took off after the fleeing man.

"Druid Lubri has been selling gate transits to the bosses through Feijóo."

"Even while they were closed?"

Culann nodded. "Have the gates been opened yet?"

Bébinn shook her head. "Her Ladyship was waiting for the return of Dame Liosach."

The Professor breathed a sigh, doubting that Druid Lubri had obeyed the order. He examined the gate he'd just come through. Traces of multiple transits in the past few days still lingered between obeliscos. He wondered whether those transits would prevent him from finding the others. "Do you have a com, Captain?"

"Here you go, Professor."

Culann stepped to one side and commed his ex-wife, Cathasach Bolloré, the Nerolead Interstellar Engineer.

"Satch here." Her face came instantly on-screen. "Cull! And you don't look well!"

"How long since I left those A-warp equations with you?"

"A week, Cull. I was wondering what happened to you."

"I need that ship quick, Satch. How fast can you be here?"

"By conventional A-warp, it'll take me a day. With that new engine in the Meave, about ten minutes."

"They work?"

She grinned at him, her bright, red hair a wild penumbra around her head. "I'm headed to the spaceport now, Cull. Out!" The screen went blank.

He looked up at the gate that he'd come through, the one Druid Lubri had used to banish the Archeologist, Professor Ríoghan Tanguy, wondering how to get back to the grasslands planet. He stepped toward the trio of Federation soldiers guarding Belenos. "Dom Ontonio, has La Profesora come through here?"

His eyes widened. "She's alive? I haven't seen her since she disappeared, Profesor, but you have?"

Culann nodded and smiled. "Sí, Dom Ontonio, and in good health, but if you haven't seen her, I fear she's not safe. We were separated, all of us."

"You found the others too, Professor?" Captain Nankivell asked.

"For a few days, anyway. All nine of us. I don't know what happened to everyone else, but I've got to try to find them."

Bébinn nodded vigorously.

A roar filled the sky, a ship streaking suddenly overhead. Culann looked up between the obeliscos towering over Las Cogotas.

The Meave rocketed to the square behind him, just outside the ring, peasants scattering.

Culann remained transfixed, the runes on the obeliscos making sense to him now, his mind translating every symbol into meaning, as though he'd studied the Proto-Gaelic all his life.

And he saw where to correct the flaw.

"Cull, sorry I'm late." Cathasach Bolloré in her glorious halo of flaming red hair stood behind two Federation soldiers, who were blocking her way. "Tell these Fed bugs I'm with you."

Culann nodded to the two soldiers, who let her pass. He gestured at the obelisco behind him. "Glad you got here so fast, Satch. Can you read those runes?"

"Looks like gibberish to me, Cull. What is it?"

"The equations you put into the Meave."

Her carrot eyebrows climbed her forehead. "I was wondering where you'd got them, but how did you ...?"

He could see the conclusions tumbling through her mind.

"Haven't those runes always been indecipherable? And if you can decipher them ..." She was grinning hugely. An engineer, she knew exactly what that meant.

"How quickly can you make adjustments?" he asked.

Her gaze narrowed. "On the fly? Not too fast, Cull. I just figured out how to calibrate the interface."

"How long to install it in another ship?"

She recoiled as if struck. "Great green mother, Cull, I'm an engineer, not a Druid!"

"Captain Nankivell," Culann called, "is there a tractor beam on that Gremlin?"

She looked over from a Sergeant, two bright purple stripes on the soldier's green sleeve. "Certainly is, Professor."

He raised an eyebrow at Cathasach. "Faster to do that or install the equations into a different ship? I got eight people to fish out of oblivion, and I need something larger than the Meave. Can you make the adjustments?"

"You don't ask much, Cull. Ought to raise your expectations a bit, man! And a Gremlin? Ugly as a sinning saint! How much time do I have?"

Bragging by way of complaint, he realized. "As soon as you can get it done, Satch."

"Two hours, and that's tying two black holes in a knot."

"Thanks, Satch."

Bébinn had come over, her cap at jaunty angle.

"Captain, this is Cathasach Bolloré, engineer extraordinaire. Satch, this is Druidess Lìosach's personal pilot, Captain Bébinn Nankivell. Satch is going to install an A-warp upgrade in the Gremlin, the same upgrade that got her here from Alcyone in ten minutes in that Meave."

"Helluvan upgrade!" Bébinn said. "Come this way, Satch. I can tell we're going to be great friends."

Culann grinned after them, the com still in his hand. "Lady Ceridwen Gwilym, please."

After a few exchanges, a few bureaucrats, and about twenty minutes of waiting, the Ceannaire herself came on the line. "Cull, what have you done with my Druidess?"

"I was afraid you'd ask me that, Lady. I'm afraid it's not good news. She and the other seven are in some limbo, one I'm not sure how to get to."

"Seven? When you started, there were only three! And now I suppose Finn is trapped there too, eh?"

"Well, yes, Lady, afraid so," he said, having forgot she knew Finnán, too, although relations were probably somewhat strained between them, the Ceannaire having swept the Druid from the Ministry some twenty years ago. "But the good news is, I found out what caused the malfunction, and people won't disappear into the gates again."

"I knew you'd find it. Always come through, you do. But what about Nann, eh? Bring my girl back to me, Cull. Bring them all back."

"Yes, Lady, you can count on that," he said, without telling her why, without knowing how. "You can count on that."

#

He stood above the pit where the Henge at Montefortino di Arcevia had stood, the rim of flagstone hanging above a maw where Ether had taken a bite

174

out of space. Fuaranders slithered up his legs like snakes, the cold seeping easily through his thin clothing.

"You sure about this, Cull?"

He looked over at Captain Nankivell, his breath fogging. "I've never felt as uneasy about anything, Bébe," he said, glancing past her at Cathasach. "But the basic question still stands. Will the Gremlin fit?"

"In there?" Bébinn pointed at the maw, shivering. "Looks to be big enough. Who's going to fly the ship?"

Because I'm certainly not, she hadn't said—and didn't need to.

"I will, of course. No reason for you and Satch to risk your lives."

The Captain looked at the Engineer. "And you were married to him? Not much question why you divorced him."

"As stupid as he is brave, isn't he?" Cathasach shook her head.

It'd taken Cull just ten minutes to get to Tucana aboard the Meave, while Bébinn and Cathasach had followed in the Gremlin. After landing on Tucana, it'd taken the engineer just an hour to finish installing the modified A-warp.

The squat, powerful ship sat in a snowy clearing not far away, the wreckage of the Fanum looking forlorn and forsaken nearby, half-crushed by the shock wave created by the disappearing Henge.

"At least take her for a short jaunt, Cull, so you'll feel somewhat confident at the controls."

He nodded. They were right, he realized. He was being stupid.

And his headlong rush to resolve the mystery and find the six victims had led to the three of them stepping through a gate without a means of returning, a rash decision in hindsight.

If he were smart, he'd have Scathach Ogham, Druidess of the Exalted Martyrology, open the gate to the grasslands planet for him, instead of willy-nilly plunging the Gremlin full speed into the aperture.

"Professor Penrose?" called a voice, the sound nearly snatched away by the wind. A cowled figure emerged from the swirling snow.

He peered through the wind to see who was approaching.

"It's Scathe," she said, throwing back the hood. Fuaranders scattered at her approach.

Culann immediately felt warmer. "What are you doing out here?"

"I heard your ship land, wondered who could possibly be here. My cabin's just over yonder."

He introduced the other two women to the tall Druidess.

"That fool Cull is going to drive this ship into that hole, Dame Ogham!" Cathasach told Scathach.

"Like your name, by the way. Call me Scathe."

"Love yours, too, Scathe. Call me Satch."

"Seems we have a duty to detain him for his own good, don't you think, Captain?"

"I think so, Scathe. Just Bébe, please. Well, there might be one exception to our having to detain him, I think."

"You aren't suggesting we go with him, are you, Satch?"

"It's about the only way to stop him."

In an aside, Bébinn leaned over and whispered loudly to Scathach, "And she knows, 'cause she married him!"

"Now, Satch, that was a pretty fool thing to do in the first place, wasn't it?"

"In hindsight, I suppose it was, Scathe, but I enjoyed it while it lasted. Anyway, doesn't matter what we say or do, we can't stop him." She turned to look at him. "Can we, Cull?"

He grinned at her.

"I didn't think so." She turned to the other two. "See? Stubborn as a goat."

"Well, then, we don't have a choice, do we?"

They all three turned to look at him, and said in unison, "We're going with you, Cull!"

#

Culann sat at the controls, Captain Nankivell taking the copilot's seat, Scathach and Cathasach just behind them.

From above, the pit where the Henge had been looked like a wormhole. Subtle scintillations raveled the edges where the time-space anomaly met with normal fabric. The interior drew the eye with its warped view of the Milky Way.

Culann remembered walking along the galaxy edge inside the pit, at the time feeling a curious detachment from reality, a moment of epiphany at the wonder of striding like an ancient giant through the cosmos.

"What makes you think it's a portal?" Scathach had asked him.

Reason and logic had failed him. He hadn't been able to say, knowing only that he was convinced it was the way to rescue the other eight people.

To rescue Sionann.

He'd told Druidess Ogham about his conversation with Procter Gwrtheyrn Jézéquel. "Apparently, she and the twin Druids tried to combine three Elementals, Fire, Earth, and Air. And that's when they rebelled, snatching her through a portal to some planet near the galactic core."

"But you said you thought it was an excess of exotic matter displacement, or a failure of the henge's absorption unit."

"Yes, I think it was, one of those multi-planar phenomena, Scathe."

"You mean to say it was both?"

He'd frowned at her, then grinned. "Yes, that's what I mean to say."

"A scientific and a magical explanation?"

"Indeed, each mutually inclusive of the other, a fundamental concept in Astral Physics. There isn't and has never been a separation between science and magic. They're different only in their articulation."

"Scorned by scientists and reviled by the Druidry."

"Managing to make everyone angry in the process."

"Certainly excelled in something, now, haven't you?" his ex-wife had said.

He'd shrugged at her, grinning.

The portal below them was flush with the planet surface, startlingly clear. The storm had exhausted itself not long after Druidess Ogham's arrival, the fuaranders scattering en mass. On screen in the Gremlin, the pit swirled lazily, and the A-warp interface showed the permutations in time-space through its navigation projections. The gate's destination, if indeed the whorl below them were actually a gate, remained a mystery. Between the modifications he'd filched from the obelisco at Las Cogotas and the flaw he'd later seen, Culann wondered whether the untested technology that he'd had Cathasach install in the Gremlin would get them through to the grasslands planet intact.

And even then, Culann wasn't really sure how to access the void where he'd come eye-to-eye with Ether.

Behind him, Cathasach sat at a console where she could monitor the A-warp drive functions. One fail-safe she'd rigged had tapped the exotic matter displacement monitors; if too great an imbalance occurred, the A-warp engine would shut down. Another she had rigged was a manual kill-switch, in case something went awry.

He suspected that any attempt to use the manual switch would come too late, their translations across time and space taking no time at all.

He wondered whether they would have any chance to solve the mysterious disappearance of the Proto-Gaels.

"What's the background aura like, Satch?"

"Satch, Scathe, I'd get confused if you weren't both right in front of me," Bébinn said.

"So would I," Scathach retorted.

"I'm reading an increased density of plasma toward the interior, Cull. The closer you get us to the bull's-eye, the better off we'll be."

"Promise you won't wreck my baby, Cull."

"I promise, Captain Nankivell," he said. "I'll be using a trilithium pulse-jump and an A-warp compression fold back-up in case our gate turns out to be illusory."

"A gate behind the gate," Scathach said.

The course programmed in, and the engines at high idle, Culann counted down to zero. "Engage," he told the ship.

They plunged toward the planet surface, the terrain becoming blurred streaks on the vids as the Gremlin plummeted.

If he'd had the sense to blink, he would have. The ship struck the portal and reality morphed around him, the cabin elongating, the distance to his hands stretching at least a mile, the Captain's face in his peripheral vision developing the nose of an inveterate liar.

Everything snapped back into place and blackness surrounded them.

"Where are we?" Cathasach asked.

"Coordinates!" Captain Nankivell demanded of the ship's computer.

"Calculating, one moment, please," the ship's soft contralto voice said.

A Gremlin at least ought to growl, Culann thought idly.

A full minute passed, the blackness outside unchanging.

"Calculating, one moment, please," the ship's soft contralto voice said.

"Buckets of urine, the damn thing doesn't know!"

Another minute passed, the tense silence between them difficult to listen to.

"Calculating, one moment, please," the ship's soft contralto voice said.

"Prompt off, continue to calculate," the Captain said, swearing softly.

"I believe that means we've arrived," Culann said, grinning uncertainly.

"Where, though?"

"Precisely," he replied. "Nowhere. For that matter, nowhen. Exactly where we're supposed to be."

"Cull, I'm getting readings, concentrations of quintessence clustered off starboard, six, seven, eight of them!"

"That's them, girls. I'm going to try to modulate the A-warp field to adjust our position."

"Doesn't he know we're women?" one asked the other.

"He used to know *I'm* a woman," Cathasach said, "Not sure what happened to him in the meantime."

"Here we go, women," Culann said, compressing space in front of them.

The dots moved closer. He was somewhat surprised the A-warp worked in pure Ether, its principles meant to work only in normal space-time. He compressed the space in between with short bursts, until they were finally alongside.

The eight dots on Cathasach's display looked to be only yards apart from each other. The ship's forward display was still blank, as if they didn't exist and weren't right in front of them.

"Where are they?" Bébinn asked.

"It's the nature of A-warp," Cathasach said. "They look close, but there's infinite space between us and them. It's the equivalent of that metaphysical question in Christian parlance about the number of angels on the head of a pin."

"A single point in space occupies all points in space." Cull looked at his ex-wife. "Satch, can you adjust our position so we occupy the same space as one of our lost companions?"

"And hope they just appear inside the Gremlin?"

"I don't know another way to get them aboard. Any other ideas?"

"All points in space occupy a single point in space, Cull. By the nature of universal field theory, we should be there already."

"Let me try," Scathach said. "You told us Ether manifested itself to you. If true, Ether can certainly manifest them to us, right?"

"We just have to ask," Culann said, nodding for the Druidess of the Exalted Martyrology to go ahead.

"Who first, Cull?"

"Sionann," he and Bébinn said at the same time.

Scathach brought her hands together, then extended them toward the ceiling. "Balor, hear and grant me favor. Bring our companion Sionann Lìosach to us, please."

Nothing happened, and from the galley issued a cry.

Culann was out of the pilot's seat and into the corridor, Bébinn right behind him.

Sionann came barreling out into his arms. "What in creation was that, Cull? Bébe, where've you been? I've been calling for …" And she looked between them, one on each side, both holding her tightly. Her eyes lost focus and softly, she began to weep.

"You're safe, Nann," Culann whispered. "You're safe."

#

It'd taken all his strength to pull away and return to the cockpit. He kept telling himself that Bébinn was in a far better position to comfort her, and that seven other people still required his assistance. Even so, he'd found it among the most difficult things he'd ever had to do.

"What about the others?" Sionann had asked, looking from him to Bébinn, an arm around both of them.

"Still in limbo," he'd told her.

"Please, Cull, I'll be all right, go on," she'd told him, nudging him toward the cockpit. In her eyes was the promise he'd hoped for.

Cathasach had gone to prepare the stateroom, the others likely to be in as bad a shape, or worse. Only he and Scathach remained in the cockpit. "Who's next, Cull?" she asked.

"The three laity, Ríoghan, Niamh, and Llewellyn."

Druidess Ogham did an incantation for each as Culann named them off. As each appeared aboard the Gremlin, Cathasach herded each into the stateroom and attended to his or her basic needs. The Archeologist was in the worst shape, weeping incoherently. Captain Lozac'h came aboard composed, evinced a slight surprise, and immediately stepped in to help Ríoghan. Apprentice Gutraidh appeared in the corridor, blinked at the low level chaos around him, and kept groping his own body, as if disbelieving his reincorporation.

"Now your three colleagues, Scathe," Culann said.

Scathach brought the old Procter, Gwrtheyrn Jézéquel, out of limbo first.

She blinked at the both of them from beneath spider web hair. "I've seen the face of Arawn, Scathe, so I think I'm ready to retire."

A stunned Armel Gallou stepped from the void in his red robe with a mystified look on his face, but immediately emerged from his lethargy when his colleague, the white-robed Druid, Óengus Tàillear, made his appearance a moment later. The two men embraced, weeping with joy at seeing each other.

"And now Finn."

Druidess Ogham grinned at him. "Oh, great father of Ether, Balor, bring back our brother Finnán Cadeyrn and restore him to our company." She cast her hands at the last remaining chair.

The barrel-chested man with the long gray beard fell into the chaise, looked around and nodded to Cull. "Knew you'd come to find us, Laddie. Gads that place was boring, with only my thoughts to entertain me. Spare me Tír na nÓg, if it's anything like that at all. Everyone accounted for, Cull?"

Culann sighed and nodded. "I swear, I'll never ask you to follow me through another portal, Finn."

"Never make a promise you're not absolutely sure of keeping. You got us out, that's what counts. You got us … " His voice trailed off at the black viewscreen. "You did get us back, didn't you?"

He grinned at his erstwhile mentor. "Let's do that now, Finn. Satch, where are you?" he called over the din, all the doors open throughout the ship and all the rooms full.

His ex-wife made her way forward. "Want to go home or something, Cull?" She glanced over the A-warp monitors. "It all looks good. Indicators at full capacity."

"Thank you, Satch. Scathe, give us the invocation for the Montefortino di Arcevia gate, please."

"Certainly, Cull." The tall Druidess gestured elaborately while Culann powered up the engines.

The binary at Alpha Tucanae appeared in the viewscreen, and Cull breathed a sigh of relief.

"Coordinates!" Captain Nankivell demanded of the ship's computer from the doorway, Sionann looking on from over her shoulder.

"Alpha Tucanae, point-five parsecs from Tucana Prime."

Everyone cheered and Finnán pounded Culann on the back.

"Way to go, Laddie, way to go. Dame Scathe, any brew on that ice ball of yours? For some reason, I'm terribly thirsty."

Culann set a course for Tucana Prime on trilithium power only, breathing easy for the first time in a month.

Chapter 17

"All right, Cull, you've got us all here. What's going on?" Sionann asked.

Before him were seated five of the seven most powerful Druids in the Gael Federation, the Chief Druids at the major henges in the six constellations of the Gael Federation: Pleiades, Ophiuchus, Puppis, Gamma Doradus, Tucana, and Draco constellations. Only Proctor Druid Medraut Bhodhsa, Chief of the Gael Gates in the Pleiades Constellation, had not been able to attend the meeting. And with them was the most powerful Druid of them all, Minister of the Druidry, Sionann Lìosach.

Before the meeting, Finnán had pulled Culann aside. "She'd make you a formidable wife, eh, Cull?"

He'd snorted in disbelief, bemused. Then he'd looked closely at his long-time friend and mentor. Finnán's deep-set eyes looked even deeper, the black rings around them giving him the aspect of a raccoon; his facial skin hung in scaly sheets from cheekbones far too prominent. The big man's threadbare robe hung off a frame whose girth was substantially diminished. It's almost over, Culann had thought. Finnán just needs rest.

The Ministry building stood across from the Presidential Palace on the wide esplanade. One street over was Canterbury Cathedral, its toll on the hour just fading from the air.

Culann looked around the room. With the exception of Scathach, Finnán, and Sionann, he'd not worked in any significant way with the others. Four blank-faced Druids glowered at him, a certainty in their eyes.

All of them certain that he, Professor Culann Penrose, Apostate extraordinaire, was the singular cause of the gates remaining frozen by order of the Ceannaire, Lady Ceridwen Gwilym.

"We never should have allowed politicians or scientists to interfere with our sovereignty over the gates in the first place," Fáelán Trevelyan, Chief Druid at Ophiuchus, snarled at Sionann. "How can you sit there and ask this unbeliever anything about the gates?"

"I wouldn't, Lane, if I hadn't been with him nearly the whole time," she replied, her voice nonchalant.

Finnán's glance floated from one to the other.

Culann, watching him, knew him to be doing the same as he, assessing each for their receptivity. "Dames and Lords, I don't expect you to believe anything I tell you. I expect you to weigh it against all you know and the new information I provide you. This isn't about the Druidry. It's about restoring integrity to the universe."

Three Chiefs scoffed openly, only Fáelán keeping his silence.

"Fifteen hundred years ago, the Proto-Gaels vanished inexplicably, leaving behind Henges in six constellations along the Orion Spur. Your predecessors retained enough knowledge to operate the gates, but little else. Your order has safeguarded that knowledge for hundreds of generations, providing a foundation for the Gael Federation to flourish. We don't know how or why the Proto-Gaels vanished. We don't know how or why the Gates continue to operate. What we've suspected for a long time that the gates operate on a variant of A-warp, but one that has eluded our mastery.

"About a month ago, three individuals disappeared within moments of each other into three separate gates, and the Ceannaire, Lady Gwilym, ordered their closure pending an investigation. Oddly, these disappearances occurred at gates governed by each of three Elementals. A visit to a gate of the fourth Elemental turned up another disappearance, one which occurred at the same time as the others but went unreported to the Druidry.

"At this fourth gate, an attempt was being made to blend three Elementals into one, to merge their properties and essences. This attempt going awry was what caused an overload in the exotic matter absorption unit, whose ripple effects initiated a series of malfunctions across all the gates. Only three other individuals were within range of the gates at the time, causing their disappearance."

"It could have been worse, then, eh?" Caoimh Baragwanath, Chief Druid at Puppis, asked. The heavy, dark brow and deeply-recessed eyes gave him the aspect of a throwback to some previous evolutionary epoch.

Culann knew him to be among the smartest. "Much worse, Lord, considering how many gates there are at each major Henge, and all the subsidiary gates in each constellation."

"The overload was my fault," Scathach Ogham, Druidess of the Exalted Martyrology, said. "I tried to put a stop to Procter Gwrtheyrn Jézéquel's experiments but never insured she wasn't continuing them in secret."

"What the hell's an exotic matter absorption unit?" Méabh Abgrall, Chief Druidess at the Southern Triangle, asked. Druid Arturo Lubri on Galicia was under her jurisdiction, Gamma Doradus one of many star systems in the Southern Triangle constellation.

"When the Ancient Gaels built the gates," Cull said, "they relied on a version of A-warp that allowed instantaneous transmission between portals through the torsion of hypersurface foliations, generating excess exotic matter to hold open wormholes, and they compensated for the excess exotic matter by building absorption units at each henge."

Fáelán Trevelyan turned to Sionann. "What the bloody hell is he talking about?"

"Hear him out, Lane. There's more."

"What they didn't anticipate was that the source of the excess matter was outside our own universe, and that the absorption units displaced that excess matter to another location within our universe."

"Leading to an imbalance inside our universe, eh?" Caoimh Baragwanath asked.

"Exactly. And the overload at Montefortino di Arcevia was the first overt indication of that imbalance. All the individuals who disappeared were found on a grasslands planet just a few parsecs from the galactic core, a spontaneous relocation."

"They could have ended up anywhere," Finnán said.

"Further, when Dame Lìosach and I attempted to investigate the henge at Montefortino, the instability in its exotic matter absorption unit caused a rift or a puncture in the universe membrane, creating the hole where the henge used to be."

"Hogwash," Méabh Abgrall said, looking among her colleagues, "The apostate destroyed it out of spite!"

Culann regarded her, she whose jurisdiction included Druid Lubri and the obeliscos at Las Cogotas. She probably wasn't happy he'd been arrested for aiding and abetting El Caciquismo, the bosses. "If that were true, Dame Abgrall, Montefortino di Arcevia wouldn't have been my choice of henges. El Druido Lubri's arrest must have been upsetting. The periods of illicit portal use at Las Cogotas appears to have coincided with his periods of freedom. Illicit use that stopped only when he was incarcerated. A clear abuse of privilege that should be anyone's concern."

"What happens at my gates is none of your concern!"

"But it is mine, Dame Abgrall," Sionann said, smiling, "which we'll address in good time. And when Professor Penrose restores the Fanum at Montefortino di Arcevia, we'll know at that time that indeed he didn't, as you accuse, destroy it."

Culann knew he wouldn't convince Druidess Abgrall. "Let me point out that the rift or puncture created by the overload in the exotic matter absorption unit acts as a release valve to the build-up in this universe. It would be unwise to restore the Fanum until fundamental gate operation has been modified to pull exotic matter from within the universe."

"I've never heard such a load of dreck!" Méabh Abgrall said, fuming.

"The entire system will need revamping before the gates can resume operation."

#

"Could you find some other way of inciting people to anger, please?"

Culann stared at Sionann, flustered at the whole circumstance. He strode along beside her toward the Ceannaire's office, wondering how he could have possibly presented the information differently. It wasn't as if he personally had mis-engineered the excess exotic matter absorption units. Or that he wanted the gates to remain idle.

But he could certainly see how they might have thought so.

He sighed. "My apologies, Nann. Maybe it wasn't the right time."

The fifteen-foot corridors, thirty-foot ceilings and carved relief arabesques reminded him of an ancient time, a distant place. The ceilings actually increased in height and the corridors widened as they approached the office door, the subtle expansion meant to diminish the egos of any particular supplicant.

Culann didn't need any help feeling diminished.

"All well and good, Lad," the Ceannaire Lady Ceridwen Gwilym said later, after they'd eaten. And then she fell silent.

She, Sionann, and Culann sat at one end of the long dining table in the Presidential Suite, the remains of their repast in front of them. She'd not kept him and Sionann waiting at all, but instead had ushered them directly in, then had forbidden any but the most inconsequential of converse until the meal was done.

Culann had just finished recounting the disastrous meeting with the Gael Gate Chiefs.

"I think I understand," President Gwilym said. "If we continue to use the gates, the puncture at Montefortino di Arcevia may widen, or other punctures may appear. What do you need to correct the technology, Cull?"

"Everything that has to be done is beyond my expertise," he said. "However, a Druid, a physicist, and an engineer together can fix every gate, provided they have access to the physical sites."

Ceridwen looked at Sionann. "Méabh won't bloody likely let us, will she?"

"Nor Fáelán or Caoimh. Together, the three of them control more than half the henges, not including those on Tucana Prime. And if we try to force them, Ceri, we risk the Federation coming apart."

President Gwilym nodded. "It frays at the edges as we speak. Cull, if the gates at Gamma Draconis and in the Pleiades are repaired, can the henge at Montefortino di Arcevia be safely retrieved from the void?"

Culann shook his head. "I don't know enough to say. Would it reduce the risk of re-rupture? Certainly. But there's no guarantee, Lady President. Further, we don't know whether there are other weak places in the firmament—or perhaps other punctures."

"Is it worth the try?"

"Absolutely, Lady."

#

Culann, Sionann, Finnán, Cathasach, and Clíodhna stood in the chamber beneath Göbekli Tepe. The sandstone walls around them were blank, and a high, domed ceiling arched above them.

"Clio, show us those modified equations, please," Culann said. He'd taken his idea to her, his mathematical acumen inadequate to formulate the complex sequence necessary to limit the range of the exotic matter displacement.

Clíodhna Ròsach, Professor of Particle Physics at the University of Cardiff, set a holojector on the rough stone floor. "Here's the current set of torsion foliation equations." A multi-layer projection of equations appeared in blue against one wall. "And here are the modified equations." A second set superimposed themselves atop the first set, these in green. "You'll notice a slight variation in the lower left quadrant, where the torsion interface creates the micro-rifts necessary to pull exotic matter into local space-time. These two variations simply tell the A-warp engine where to pull the exotic matter from.

"Since the imbalance of exotic to normal matter is what created the overload at Montefortino di Arcevia, all we have to do is insure that the absorption unit returns the exotic matter to the place it was drawn from."

"You make it sound so simple," Finnán said.

"She's got the easy job," Cathasach retorted.

Culann looked between the sisters, having heard numerous stories about their childhood, Clíodhna dreaming up fantastical machines, Cathasach building them. "How will you get the equations in, Satch?"

"Pipe wrench to the gear case." She looked at him deadpan.

"I prefer a two-by-four," Finnán said. "Much more effective."

"You always did strike me as somewhat blunt," Sionann said, taking a step closer to Culann.

"Now, Nann—"

"Hold the banter, please," Culann said, raising an irate eyebrow at them both.

"On the Meave and the Gremlin, I had to rebuild the A-warp actuator module, but here ..." Cathasach shrugged. "Where's the engine?"

"Over here, Satch," Finnán said, stepping to the northeast corner, where a pillar jutted into the room, its proportions identical to the stele somewhere above them. "It's actually inside this pillar. After you showed me the absorption unit at Stonehenge, I started looking around this chamber." Finnán pointed to the opposite corner. "The mirror wall or actuator interface is along the south wall, the interpretive unit inside the southwest pillar." He pointed to the southeast corner. "And the absorption unit is housed inside that pillar, the absorption screen on the east wall."

"Well, let's crack it open, then," Cathasach said, stepping up beside him.

Finnán turned to the pillar and bowed elaborately, his long beard brushing the floor. "King Niksa, hear my plea, open thy pillars for us to see."

A gnome appeared beside the pillar, looking too small to do anything. The six-inch figure put its shoulder to the pillar and leaned against it. Grating rock cemented in place for centuries groaned open, the chamber itself shaking, a skein of dust drifting down from the ceiling.

"You sure this is safe?"

"No guarantees of anything, Nann," Culann said.

She threw him a glance and shifted closer to him. "You've managed not to kill us thus far."

Finnán began counting on his fingers. "Trapped on a grasslands planet, suspended in an indefinite void. Third time's a charm, right, Cull?"

"You're such an optimist. Go ahead, Satch, pay no attention to my usual detractors."

"Detractors? I've never known anyone to say a bad word about you. Anyone give me a light?"

A salamander ran up Finnán's back and perched atop his head, flaring brightly.

The inner workings of the A-warp engine looked like a jumble of parts to Culann. He wouldn't have been able to distinguish it from a jigsaw puzzle.

Cathasach put her hand on a small box at the confluence of numerous conduits. "You're sure the gate is off, Finn?"

"Aye, Lass, I'm sure."

She yanked it from its socket.

The chamber didn't shake, and the planet didn't crumble.

Culann breathed a sigh of relief.

"All right, my dearie," Cathasach said to the component, "let's update your core." She stepped over to her satchel and extracted a cubic device. "A circuit burner." A small screen atop the device came to life, and an image coalesced. "Got those equations handy, Sis?"

Clíodhna pulled a module from her holojector, the image collapsing, and stepped to her sister's side. "Here you go."

"Thanks." She shoved the module into one side of the cubic device, the A-warp core into the other side.

A bright red warning flashed on the screen and a beep emitted from the device. "Incompatible code," the warning said.

"I didn't get this from A-warp cores in the Meave or Gremlin, but then, it's a different sequence, too. Clio, no anomalies in the simulations you ran, right?"

"Not a one, Satch." Clíodhna shook her head. "Incompatibilities in the hypersurface foliations?"

"I don't think so, Clio. It's in the exotic matter draw and absorption mechanism."

"Here, let me see." Clíodhna knelt beside her sister.

If they'd had similar hair, they'd have been twins, their features and motions identical.

"The draw and release locations have to be the same," Culann reminded them.

"You got it, Chief," Cathasach said.

Clíodhna looked up at him. "They're not aligning, Cull. Remember how the reverse induction didn't correspond with the induction?"

"That's what alerted us to the accumulation of exotic matter."

"Isn't that what keeps the gate open?" Sionann asked.

The sisters exchanged a glance.

Sharper than a Druid should be, Culann told himself.

"It's the dispersal that isn't uniform. There's no physical mechanism to insure where it goes."

"Hardware?" Finnán asked. "You need hardware? Where's my two-by-four?"

"That's it!" Cathasach said. "Pipe wrench!" She reached in her satchel and pulled out—

"Oh, no, you don't! Not to my gate!"

"Finn, wait. Satch, what are you proposing?"

"I need a morph spell, Cull. About this shape, but only a quarter-inch long. We run the exotic matter displacement beam through a magnetic field to focus and elongate its torsion, causing an increase in density lines—"

"And an increase in displacement distance," Sionann finished.

Again, the sisters exchanged a glance.

"As long as the distance is sufficient, the displacement results in a net reduction in exotic matter, and therefore a decrease in universal pressure. Finn, can you give Satch a morph spell?"

"Be happy to, Lad. Just don't whack my pipes with that wrench, Wench."

"Watch who you're callin' names, Rogue. Here." She tossed him the wrench.

"I didna mean nothing by it, Lass, but it was fun to say." He held up the pipe wrench and gestured at it with the other hand. "Ghob, King of Gnomes, twonk this wrench to a wee bit smaller." With a flourish, he handed it back, holding it between two fingers.

"Perfect," Cathasach said. She fished a roll of tape from her bag, secured the tiny wrench to the A-warp core, and produced two wires. "Just attach these leads and see how it does," she said. Finished, she stuck it back into her machine. The screen cleared of its warning. Cathasach took the core over to the A-warp engine. "Ready, everyone?" And didn't wait for acknowledgement, shoving the core back into its socket.

Nothing happened.

"I suppose I should turn it on, or something," Finnán said.

"Or something."

He stepped to the center of the chamber and raised his hands in the air. "Niksa, Queen of the undines, activate this gate." And he brought both hands down.

Somewhere, a whine increased to a hum. The portal wall warped, bowed, yawed, and then snapped back into place. The mirror wall began to shimmer and then formed multiple shapes, reflecting the people in the chamber. The absorption wall developed a whirlpool, the sloshing water spinning toward the center, against the pull of gravity, as if funneling the water toward a singularity.

Cathasach peered into the A-warp engine. "Looks good, everyone. I think we did it."

A cheer went up.

"Great teamwork, all of you. We're half there, Stonehenge next," Culann said, exchanging a glance with Sionann.

#

The largest henge behind them, their team headed to Stonehenge in the enhanced Gremlin. The team had opened the subsidiary gates at Nevalı Çori, Derinkuyu, Ashikli Hüyük, Çayönü, and Çatal Hüyük. Traffic was slowly resuming on Alrakis.

Proctor Druid Medraut Bhodhsa, Chief at Stonehenge, had not been able to attend the meeting with the other Chiefs. Neither Culann nor Sionann knew what his response would be to their intended task.

"His having proctored me won't help us much, I'm afraid," Sionann had told him when they'd secured a moment alone in the galley.

"I know he can be a bit intransigent, but is there something else?"

"She handles like a dream," Captain Nankivell said, barging in before Sionann responded. "We're there already. Landing in five minutes." Bébe glanced between them. "Sorry for the interruption."

Sionann blushed and smiled. "Not to worry, my friend."

Culann glanced between them, mystified. "Wish I knew what was being interrupted. But let's go, eh?"

She gave his hand a squeeze, smiling.

Druid Proctor Medraut Bhodhsa met them as they disembarked, apprentice Llewellyn Gutraidh behind him. "What's this, Dame Lìosach?"

"We need your help, Proctor Bhodhsa. Montefortino still lies in limbo, a hole in the universe where the henge used to be."

"Just because that apostate brought everyone back, he thinks he can traipse in here and take anything he wants?"

Culann had deliberately debarked last, behind Sionann, Finnán, Cathasach, and Clíodhna.

"He's a miscreant, Mede, I'll give you that," Finnán said, "but he's saved our tails more than once, and he's putting the gates back in operation as we speak."

"How do you know that, Finn?"

"Göbekli Tepe and all the gates in Draco are purring along."

Proctor Bhodhsa looked at the sisters. "What's the purpose in these twins, Nann? Are they apostates, too?"

"Clíodhna Ròsach, Professor of Particle Physics, University of Cardiff," Sionann said.

"Call me Clio," she said, bowing.

"And her sister, Cathasach Bolloré, Engineer at Nerolead Interstellar."

"Satch, please, Lord Proctor," she said, nodding.

"Academics and rocket scientists, unbelievers all. Nann, these pagans have corroded your soul beyond redemption. I told you what'd happen if you threw your lot in with that Gwilym snake. You'll—"

"Come with me, Mede." Finnán stepped around Sionann and took the other man by the arm toward the Ring.

Culann stepped up beside the Druidess.

She watched the two Druids for a few moments, and then turned to him. "I was afraid of that," she said.

"What happened between you?"

"I was seeing his son, and he didn't take it well after I broke off the relationship and left for Durouĺ̄ernon. He insisted Ceri corrupted me."

"Still thinks so, apparently."

She nodded. "Am I corrupted, Cull?"

"Pure as the driven snow, my friend."

She smiled and put her head briefly to his shoulder. "Thanks, I needed to hear that."

"You're welcome."

"What'll we do if he doesn't let us into the engine chamber?" Cathasach asked.

Culann shrugged. "Fix all the gates in Tucana and try to restore the henge at Montefortino."

"And if we can't even gain the cooperation of the Pleiades Chief, it's unlikely we'll gain the other Chiefs' trust, much less their cooperation."

"And the Gael Federation comes apart."

#

"What'd you say to him, Finn?"

"Eh?" The big Druid looked over at Culann. "Irrelevant, Cull," he said, shrugging but grinning.

They stood in the subchamber beneath Stonehenge, sarsen megaliths lining the chamber in divine proportion, nine to a side. And at each corner, a megalith intruded into the room.

Druid Proctor Medraut Bhodhsa had stayed above ground, muttering something about remaining ignorant of desecration.

At Finnán's invocation, a gnome appeared and opened the A-warp actuator stone, the grate of ancient rock rumbling through the floor. Cathasach manufactured a magnetic field to focus and elongate the exotic matter beam to increase its displacement distance, Clíodhna watching from over her sister's shoulder in case anything when awry.

Cathasach pushed the A-warp core back into its socket. "We should be here when the gates are activated." She looked between the two Druids.

"Let's go topside and step outside of the ring before we ask Proctor Bhodhsa to activate the gates," Culann said.

"We don't have to do that, Cull. They're the Federation's gates."

"They are, Lass," Finnán said, "but Mede won't be happy if he isn't the one to restart them."

Sionann nodded. "You're right, Finn."

The big Druid summoned a spell to take them up.

Proctor Medraut Bhodhsa was waiting a few feet from the main gate, his jaw rippling. "Well?" Apprentice Gutraidh stood behind him.

"Give her a go, Mede," Finnán said. "We'll wait over here while you do."

Their group stepped down the hill and across the Ring while the Proctor watched them, his brow furrowed.

They stopped just beyond the perimeter, beside the slaughter stone at the southern-most point on the ring.

"What if it doesn't work?" Clíodhna asked.

Culann and Sionann exchanged a glance. The Federation was likely to come apart, he knew, and he saw the same on her face. He shifted closer to her and took her hand, turning his attention uphill.

Between two megaliths, a capstone high above his head, Proctor Bhodhsa knelt before the gate, gesturing in a circle with his right hand. Soon, his left joined in, making another circle in the opposite direction. A ring of gnomes materialized under each hand, marching in unison in tight ranks. The Druid then cast both hands toward the gate, and the gnomes leaped to the sarsen stones, scrambled to the top, and vanished in a flash of light.

The air inside the trilithon began to shimmer and a distant rumbling sound shook the ground beneath their feet.

Then all went quiescent.

Proctor Bhodhsa turned to look their direction. "And what about the other Pleiades gates?" he called.

"Should be good to activate, Mede," Finnán shouted back.

The Druid in the middle of the henge produced a com from under his robes. His voice was too faint to make out what he was saying. A moment later he put it away and gestured the Apprentice to step forward. Llewellyn did so, and the Proctor produced a series of gestures.

The gate shimmered, and Llewellyn took a step forward and disappeared into it.

A moment later, the gate shimmered again, and the Apprentice stepped from the portal.

Proctor Bhodhsa smiled and started down the hill toward them. "Looks to be working fine, Finn. Thank you."

"Glad to see it, Mede," Finnán said. "But it's Cull who made it all happen."

The Proctor looked at Culann as he stepped across the ring. "Thank you, Professor. Forgive me for doubting you. You're a fine man for an apostate."

"You're welcome, Lord Proctor," Culann said with a nod.

Chapter 18

"No change here, Scathe?" Culann asked, pulling his parka tight against the cold. He and the others had just stepped off the Gremlin, arriving at the Fanum within minutes of their departure from Stonehenge. Professor Ròsach had stayed on Alcyone, ready to board the modified Meave and come to Tucana Prime if something should go awry with the modifications.

Assuming we can resurrect the Fanum from the void, Culann thought.

Scathach Ogham, Druidess of the Exalted Martyrology, grinned at the quartet, her parka wreathing her head. "Welcome, travelers," she said. Behind her stood the three Druids they'd rescued from the Ether, Procter Gwrtheyrn Jézéquel with a gleam in her eye, and the other two right behind her, Armel Gallou and Óengus Tàillear, standing shoulder to shoulder.

Behind them, the Scriptorium was ringed with a scaffold. Nearby was a small portable office on pylons.

Culann sensed no division or dissent between the red- and white-robed Druids. He wondered whether they'd resolved their doctrinal differences. There was something else, he saw, a closeness between them, an affiliation that reached deeper than words.

"So you're going to bring back our Fanum, eh, Lad?" Gwrtheyrn asked.

"I've come to help you with that, Gwerth. I don't think it's something I'm able to do by myself, frankly."

They stepped up to the maw where the henge had been.

Dull, unreflective emptiness stared back at them, like some giant eye having only a pupil, lacking any iris.

Even eyes have retinas, Culann reminded himself. "Nann, if you could, bring to mind those moments right before the henge vanished."

"It was hideous, a huge mass of raw ... " She shook her head. "What do you think it was, Cull?"

"Ether," he said. "Ether manifested from out of the shadows." He looked at Cathasach. "Somehow, Satch, the Ether knew this was a weak point in the universe, perhaps made so by a little experimentation, and its excess gathered here, as if awaiting release."

"Like any pressurized gas seeking to escape its vessel," Cathasach the Engineer added.

"I suspect when we approached, Nann and I, that our combined essences created just enough additional pressure to cause the rupture."

"So how do we repair it?" Scathach the Druidess asked.

Procter Jézéquel looked guiltily toward Druids Gallou and Tàillear.

"Didn't you say, Cull, that a fusing of Elementals had been attempted?" Sionann asked.

"The experimentation that I referred to, yes," he replied, "which weakened the exotic matter absorption unit."

"Fusing?" Cathasach asked. "How do you fuse two elementals?"

Gwrtheyrn cleared her throat, her white, withered hands wrapping her staff. Exposed to the extreme cold, they looked to be suffering not at all from it. "Call me Gwerth, please. When two Elementals are fused, they each give up their properties to contribute to the precipitated compound. Earth and Water become mud, for example. But it's more than that. Gnomes govern the space between molecules, while undines govern fluidity."

"Fusing them results in compression and fluidity?" Cathasach looked impressed. "Call me Satch, by the way."

"Call me Mel," Armel said.

"Call me Gus," Óengus said.

"Gus, Mel," Cathasach said, nodding to both, looking bemused.

"They helped me fuse three elementals," Gwrtheyrn said. "That was when the Gate sucked me away."

"Which three?"

"Earth, Fire, and Air."

"How did you keep Fire from consuming Air?"

"Not easily, Finn, not easily."

"I suspect that our undoing that fuse will help to defuse the situation, pardon the pun," Culann said. He looked over the knee-high rock wall, its surface covered with snow. Watching the gentle fall of snowflakes, he noticed that none of them fell into the maw, as though somehow repelled. The puncture held the same textural qualities as the inside of the portal they'd encountered on the grasslands planet, just before Culann had launched them all into the void.

Again, some visceral entity began to amass within the puncture, too insubstantial for his five basal senses and nearly invisible to his magic receptivity.

Ether, he knew. Unlike on the previous occasion, he felt no menace from it.

"What would happen if you fused all four Elementals?" Cathasach asked.

"Like a pagan to suggest the ultimate blasphemy, wouldn't you say?" Sionann smiled. "Probably something far worse than the disaster here, Satch."

And perhaps not, Culann thought. Why wouldn't the fusion of the four Elementals result in the fifth Elemental, Ether? he wondered. No time to experiment now. "Gwerth, Mel, and Gus, if you could step this way, please?"

The three of them shuffled forward, the red- and white-robed Druids on either side of the Proctor.

"Scathe, Nann, and Finn, right behind them, please?"

The three Druids from off-planet did so, Finn in the middle, his bulk and height nearly overshadowing the tiny, frail old woman right in front of him.

"Well," Gwrtheyrn said, "if I get blown backward, Finn is sure to catch me."

The big man chuckled. "Light as a feather, you are. Should be easy, eh?"

"Satch, stand back here with me. I can be ready to back everyone up, but you each know your magic far better than I do. Gwerth, whenever you're ready."

She threw him a grin and turned back to face the Ring.

And her arms went up.

"Earth, Fire, Air. Gnome, Salamander, Sylph. Ghob, Djinn, Paralda. We beg of thee thy forgiveness for the essence we three took from each of you. Appear before us, Oh mighty Sovereigns, and accept from us our remorse. Look upon us as we release you from the bindings we did mistakenly place."

Gwrtheyrn brought down her arms.

Three wraiths appeared just inside the ring across the knee-high wall from the trio of Druids, the salamander in the middle. Instead of its usual reptilian form, it stood upright, easily topping the short, old Druidess. Flames licked around its head in halo. To one side stood a similarly sized gnome, its face a worm-rich loam, its bright green cap of hair made from grass, its build squat and thick like rock. To the other stood the sylph, a storm swirling above her head, her eyes made of rain and her hair made of wind.

"Gwerth, Mel, and Gus," said the salamander.

"You persecute us," said the gnome.

"And then beg for mercy and forgiveness," said the sylph.

The speech went from one to the other without break, as if they read from some unseen script.

"Fuse us, will you?"

"For that, we banished Gwerth."

"But here she is, unbanished—"

"By the power of an apostate?"

"Lo, what blasphemy is this—"

"That an apostate reverses our curse—"

"And undoes our consequence?"

"We who rule the fundaments—"

"And separate the sky from the earth—"

"And the water from the fire."

"We who give succor—"

"To humanity and support—"

"To those who call upon us—"

"For favor and help."

"Those whose lives—"

"Would be lived in limbo—"

"If not for the firmaments—"

"That we give to their universe."

"Please, Ghob, Djinn, Paralda," Gwrtheyrn pleaded, dropping to a knee. "It was wrong. We were wrong to bind you together, to fuse your essences. My companions and I release you henceforth from this abominable fusion."

"Yes, you have suffered," salamander began.

"Banishment, all three," gnome added.

"But it isn't enough," sylph continued.

"Brought back by apostasy—"

"By one spewing blasphemy—"

"You seek the return—"

"Of your sacred Fanum—"

"The Montefortino henge."

"You must sacrifice—"

"To gain what you seek."

"And the sacrifice we demand—"

"Is he who violates—"

"The dictates of consequence."

Culann felt the cold travel up his spine. A shiver shook him from neck to tailbone. He knew that to oppose these sovereign Elementals was to doom the Gael Gates, the Federation, and perhaps even the Druidry itself to oblivion. This wasn't just a trio of magics telling them what needed to happen. This was the King of Salamanders, the Queen of Sylphs, the King of Gnomes.

"Here I am," he said, stepping forward between the Druids.

"Lad, you can't," Finnán said.

"I must, my friend," he said over his shoulder. He inserted himself between Gwrtheyrn and Óengus. "King Ghob, Queen Paralda, King Djinn, I am here. Twas I who brought back Gwerth, Mel, and Gus from banishment. Twas I who rescued them from the void."

"Cull, no!" Sionann cried, her hands on his shoulders. "You mustn't!"

The warmth of her hands and breath on his neck were enough to beat back any cold. Love filled the empty places in his heart. He turned his head, and his breath mixed with hers.

"Cull!?"

He didn't have to tell her he had no choice. By the look in her eyes, he knew she knew. He had to sacrifice himself to the Elemental Sovereigns. "I love you, Nann."

"I love you too, Cull," she whispered. And in her eyes was the silent plea.

He admired her strength. She wanted nothing more than to spend her life with him, and yet she wouldn't ask him not to sacrifice himself, the plea in her eyes as plain as rain. And in those eyes, he knew belonging. Feeling complete, he knew he could meet his end, having lived a life full with all that life had offered.

"Thank you, Nann." He kissed her gently.

A sob escaped her, and a tear froze on her cheek. She nodded and stepped back, never taking her eyes off him.

Professor Culann Penrose, Astral Physicist and Forensic Investigator, turned to face the three Elementals.

"Oh, no, you don't, Laddie," Finnán said, "Take my old carcass instead!" He shoved Culann aside and leaping at the trio of Elementals.

"Finn, no!"

Lightning flashed and thunder rumbled.

Tile tessellated the ground inside the ring, and the nine megaliths of the Montefortino henge stood where the puncture had been. The clouds disappeared, and sunlight bathed the henge.

"Finn?" Culann knelt at the low wall. "Finn?!" He stared at the place where the Elementals had stood, a faint mist of their essence all that remained.

The build-up of Ether was gone as well, the visceral entity nowhere to be found.

And of the Druid Finnán Cadeyrn there was nothing.

"No, Finn, no," he said, his voice soft. He draped himself over the low wall, his face in snow, biting back sobs. The cold of rock stung his cheek. The cold of death stung his heart.

It wasn't supposed to happen like that! he thought. Not like that!

Warm hands pulled him off the wall. They draped him between the two male Druids and dragged him back toward the Gremlin.

Inside, they propped him in a chair, and Sionann knelt in front of him.

"How could he?!" Culann said.

She just nodded, tears running down her face. She gathered him to her.

And Culann wept.

Chapter 19

For a week, Culann searched the Ether, ranging far and wide, searching relentlessly.

No trace of Finnán could be found.

The Ether refused to reveal even a hint of the big Druid's essence.

When Culann returned, Sionann took him to her suite in the palace, not saying a word. First, she fed him and then she put him to bed. Without day or night to alert him to the passage of time, Culann hadn't eaten or slept in the week he'd been gone.

In his absence, Sionann had seen to the remaining Gate upgrades.

At sunset two weeks after the restoration of the Montefortino henge, they held the obsequies for Druid Finnán Cadeyrn atop Göbekli Tepe on Alrakis. Dignitaries from across the Federation came to observe the big Druid's passing. Even the Ceannaire herself, Lady Ceridwen Gwilym, spoke over the empty pyre.

It was all a blur to Culann. They led him to the podium to say a few words, but he didn't remember what he said.

Captain Niamh Lozac'h, whom Finnán had helped rescue from the void, concluded the ceremony. The hero of the Eltanin War spoke of the Druid's resolve, resilience, and defiance in the face of adversity. "And he had one other quality which helped us all through our ordeal: unforgiving humor. With it, he kept our spirits up and helped us to persevere."

It wasn't until the bright flames had dwindled to cinders that Culann turned from the pyre. The two hundred and fifty systems in the Draco Constellation had long since lit the night sky with their torches, bathing Göbekli Tepe with their ethereal light.

Sionann led him down from the hilltop, the snap and crackle of Finnán's memory fading behind them. "Would it help to know he wasn't well?"

"Eh? What?"

"He was diagnosed with a rare disease about six months ago, and he didn't have much longer to live."

Culann remembered the dark rings around sunken eyes, the increasingly gaunt cheeks, the moments of fatigue and hopelessness. He thought of the big Druid's last words: "Take my old carcass instead."

"Most people would have retired when they found out they were dying."

"But not Finn," Culann said.

"No, not Finn." She leaned her head against his shoulder as they strolled toward the last waiting flitter, everyone else having long since departed. "I've received a petition from the other five Chief Druids, Cull."

"Oh? Something to do with me?" He'd made a lot of enemies along the way, and he was convinced they didn't want to grant him some boon. When he'd met with the Chiefs at the Ministry, they'd nearly chased him from the room.

"What would Finn say? 'They're daft, the entire fatuous lot of them!'"

She laughed and nodded. "That he would, wouldn't he?"

"What are they asking?"

"They're asking the college of Druidry to issue a formal apology for denying you membership at your graduation."

"Huh?" Culann remembered Finnán's saying they'd been mistaken to do so.

"And to consider making you a Druid."

Somewhere inside, a dull old scar ached with the last bit of pain that it would ever inflict upon him. Twenty years ago, they'd denied him that honor, and it'd taken him nearly five years to move on with his life.

He was realistic enough to know they wouldn't dare grant him a position of any real influence. They'd have to be daft to do so. "Finn would have wanted to hear that."

Sionann stopped and turned him toward her. "There were six signatures on the petition."

"Eh? There are only five Chiefs, now. Who was the sixth?"

"Finn," she said, smiling.

He stopped, breathless, and turned to look back toward the hilltop, where the stele stood sentinel, silhouetted against the stars, the faint glow of the pyre embers lighting their capstones from beneath.

How Finnán had inveigled such an agreement from that fractious bunch was beyond him.

He silently blessed his friend and wished him well in Tír na nÓg, the realm of everlasting abundance, youth, and beauty. "Thank you, Finn," he whispered. "You know what he'd say about our repairs to the Gates, eh? 'Tis our inglorious end, these A-warp modifications. Removes the mystery entirely.' "

Sionann giggled and did her own imitation of Druid Finnán Cadeyrn. " 'You'll be the death of Druidry, yet, Cull!' "

He nodded, smiling. "Not out of intent."

Sionann glanced at him. "Will you be sorry to see us go?"

"Oh, I think there'll always be a place for Druids and magic, Nann, just not so prominent a place. And you'll always have a prominent place inside my heart."

Sionann smiled, blushed, and leaned into his embrace.

Dear reader,

We hope you enjoyed reading *The Gael Gates*. Please take a moment to leave a review, even if it's a short one. Your opinion is important to us.

Discover more books by Scott Michael Decker at https://www.nextchapter.pub/authors/scott-michael-decker-novelist-sacramento-us.

Want to know when one of our books is free or discounted for Kindle? Join the newsletter at http://eepurl.com/bqqB3H.

Best regards,
Scott Michael Decker and the Next Chapter Team

You might also like:
Legends of Lemuria by Scott Michael Decker

To read the first chapter for free, head to:
https://www.nextchapter.pub/books/legends-of-lemuria

About the Author

Scott Michael Decker, MSW, is an author by avocation and a social worker by trade. He is the author of twenty-plus novels in the Science Fiction and Fantasy genres, dabbling among the sub-genres of space opera, biopunk, spy-fi, and sword and sorcery. His biggest fantasy is wishing he were published. His fifteen years of experience working with high-risk populations is relieved only by his incisive humor. Formerly interested in engineering, he's now tilting at the windmills he once aspired to build. Asked about the MSW after his name, the author is adamant it stands for Masters in Social Work, and not "Municipal Solid Waste," which he spreads pretty thick as well. His favorite quote goes, "Scott is a social work novelist, who never had time for a life" (apologies to Billy Joel). He lives and dreams happily with his wife near Sacramento, California.

Where to Find/How to Contact the Author

Websites:

- http://scotts-writings.site40.net/
- https://www.smashwords.com/profile/view/smdmsw
- http://www.linkedin.com/pub/scott-michael-decker/5b/b68/437
- https://twitter.com/smdmsw
- https://www.facebook.com/AuthorSmdMsw

Lightning Source UK Ltd.
Milton Keynes UK
UKHW040722130121
376872UK00021B/1002/J